the

WARSEC

Interstellar Series

the
WARSEC
Interstellar Series

2

OSCILLATION

2095 - 2097

ASH GAWAIN

ASHGAWAIN.COM

TABLE OF CONTENTS

Map of Earth: 2095

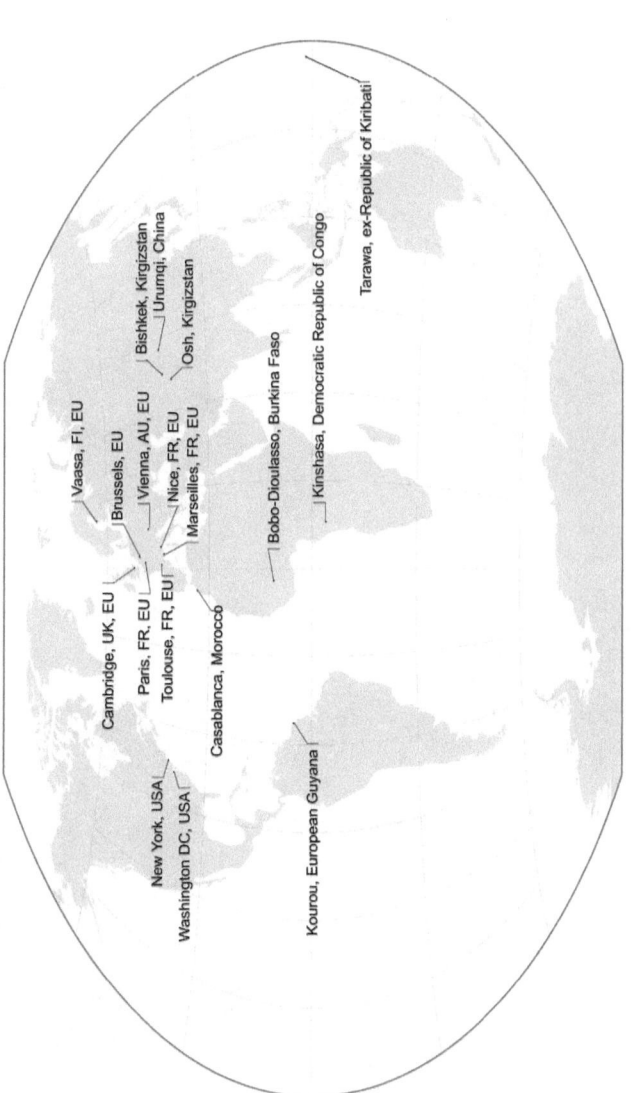

EU = European Union.

INTRODUCTION

In late August 2095, almost one year after the successful testing of faster-than-light travel between Mars and Earth, two opinion pieces, published in two different papers, expressed two distinct views as to the importance of the conquest of space for mankind.

The first Op-Ed, published in the *Wall Street Journal*, had been written by Sophie Couillard, the general manager of V-Space, a subsidiary of Vahlroos Corporation. It was entitled '*Irresistible Space Attraction*'.

Mankind is now irresistibly drawn to space, and let it be so, for there lies prosperity for us all.

The late 2070s saw the deployment of the first space elevator, anchored at Tarawa in the Pacific, making it possible to bring heavy payloads into orbit, including compact fusion reactors manufactured by V-Fusion.

In the late 2080s, national space agencies started to build the new orbital station and deploy lunar installations to mine helium-3 and retrieve hydrogen and oxygen from the Moon's South Pole. V-Space's own aerospace shuttle, the Albaspace, made it possible to bring passengers to the orbital station in only eight hours.

This seemed incredible. At last mankind was back to space 'en force', a welcome change of air after the failure of the Martian colony. But it was nothing compared to the new acceleration space technology would take in the 2090s.

In 2091, Dr. Mutombo, now a V-Space employee, together with Dr. Govorov, eventually succeeded in unifying the general relativity theory with quantum gravity in a single gravity theory. The same year, Dr. Fù accidentally discovered how to generate a so-called green matter with negative energy attributes. This meant that faster-than-light travel became theoretically possible by contracting spacetime in front of a spacecraft and expanding it behind.

The successful testing of the Alcubierre, on 17 September 2094, confirmed that faster-than-light was possible.

What is the implication for mankind? Huge. As our now overpopulated Earth struggles with providing enough resources to all its inhabitants, the mining of celestial bodies may turn out to be just the right thing. Tensions have increased lately between the European Union and Morocco due to the latter's monopoly on phosphate extraction. Extracting phosphate on a celestial body may just decrease the cost of fertilizer production, and, by *extension, food, a must to preserve world peace.*

We at V-Space are currently working on the development of the V-liner, a large warp-equipped spaceship with atmosphere entry capability. The V-liner will enable us to bring extra-terrestrially extracted resources to Earth quickly and cheaply.

The new regulatory frame set by the World's Agency for the Regulation of Space Exploration and Colonization (WARSEC) will initially limit private corporations' reach to within the solar system. However, our star's system is big enough for us to help mankind:

New space technologies will not only contribute to the subsistence of mankind, but also make our lives, as individuals, more comfortable. Another project V-Space is studying is the V-craft. Designed for fast travel within the asteroid belt, this warp-equipped aerospace shuttle will enable passengers to travel from Earth to the Moon or to Mars in less than twenty-minutes.

This new spacecraft will most certainly be much welcomed in the near future, as the orbital station is currently being extended and expects to be opened to tourists within two and a half years.

V-Space's newly founded sister company, Vahlroos Travel, is one of the key stakeholders of the development of the orbital station and further plans to open tourist installations on the Moon and on Mars.

I have to admit V-Space has been heavily questioned for not joining WARSEC and other space corporations in their WARSEC Ventures on the Moon, while at the same time becoming the lead stakeholder of the extension of the orbital station. I shall only say this is part of our long-term strategy.

And while V-Space's position in regard to WARSEC is perhaps oscillating between cooperation and competition, we intend to be a major player in this irresistible space surge.

Sophie Couillard's opinion piece was in phase with the optimistic wind blowing over the world in this late summer 2095, even though plans for the first interstellar journey were still in the very earliest of stages.

Only one dissonant voice was publicly expressed at the time. Esko Punainen, former ambassador of the European Union to the United Nations and currently EU-ambassador to Kirgizstan, had written a slightly discordant Op-Ed, published in *The Guardian*. It was entitled '*Oscillating between dream and reality*':

On 25 August 2095, the Fourth Committee of the United Nations General Assembly ratified three important decisions related to WARSEC (World's Agency for the Regulation of Space Exploration and Colonization).

It first granted WARSEC the permission to build their new headquarters in Vaasa, Finland. In practice, it means that what was born out of a UN coordination bureau will progressively become a true UN space agency. The Fourth Committee then approved the extension of the orbital station in partnership with all the respective national space agencies and leading space corporation, including V-Space and Vahlroos Travel. Most importantly, it gave the right to WARSEC to found WARSEC Ventures, a joint venture between the UN agency and leading space corporations including Boeing, Lockheed, Comac, and Airbus, however with the notable exception of V-Space, not wishing to compete with their own Albaspace.

This WARSEC Ventures will seek to manufacture aerospace shuttles cheaply on the Moon, taking advantage of the free mineral resources there, and most importantly the absence of tax on robot labor in space. The goal seems to be two-fold. This is firstly a way for the UN agency to generate extra income, as the contribution of the member states is quite limited. But this is mainly a way to make travel to space affordable so as to boost space tourism within three to five years. WARSEC has so low a budget that it cannot function if there are no business activities to tax in space.

While many observers now believe that the conquest of space is moving irresistibly forward, with only a slight and healthy wavering between cooperation and competition among players, I believe that we live in a world oscillating between dream and reality.

Yes, the conquest of space is making the headlines, but we should not keep our heads solely in the stars, and keep an eye on Earth too. When WARSEC is talking about making space travel affordable, they think of the 5% wealthiest out of 10.5 billion Earthlings. When V-Space mentions a V-craft able to bring passengers to anywhere in less than twenty minutes, they only have in mind the happy 0.001% of this world.

French writer Victor Hugo once called scientists lost in the dreams of the infinite and forgetting the suffering of their contemporaries as 'despicable'. I shall say the same.

While a majority of people currently seem to look up to space, we should not forget what is happening on this Earth. Economic inequalities have not decreased over the last half century. In Kirgizstan, to which I am currently the European Union ambassador, the situation has worsened between Kirghiz and Uzbek. A political group called Kirghiz Power has decided that all Uzbeks are so-called terrorists, and has started to engage in violent actions against this minority.

I wish sometimes that the international community spent more time on the recent development of the situation in Kirghizstan rather than on the future of mankind in space. It is high time for us to put the conquest of space on hold and focus on the current issues facing the Earth.

01: GEOLOGY IS A REAL SCIENCE (SEPT 2095)

Cambridge was the university town in the United Kingdom of South Britain where every ambitious student wished to study. Especially students attracted to Earth sciences. However, a quick glance around had told this particular student the sad truth. Cambridge students were ugly. A great many were fat, and those who weren't had so little muscle that their bare arms in the summer warmth were jiggling anyway. There were a few handsome young men, but they walked around in fancy clothes, talking a fancy dialect so that they went to 'the loo' instead of going to 'the bathroom' and seemed to consider any female student of lower social status as nothing but a sexual target. That made them uglier.

That did not matter. She was not in Cambridge to mate, but to study. She would have an occasion to meet plenty of doable guys the following summer. She had been selected for the Swiss climbing team for the 2096 Olympics in Riga. This would be her last competition. She was growing tired of it.

She had come 8th in lead climbing and 13th in bouldering at the 2095 World Championship, and the Swiss media had not been nice to her. Did they even know how horrible it was to compete when one was menstruating? These male journalists did not give a damn about it.

She had also, incidentally, broken the hand of the team's doctor, and the coach had been sore about it. She had been in no mood to tell what had really happened.

The doctor had constantly been using any excuse to hug her, pet her and put his hands on her buttocks. Under one medical examination, he had said he wanted to examine her vagina, claiming it needed a massage. Amina Dörflinger was not an expert in medicine, but she had known it was bullshit. She had broken his right hand. After all, she knew how to defend herself. Like most Swiss citizens, she had done her military service.

When remembering the incident, Amina thought she should perhaps have reported him to the police. However, she had no confidence in the law enforcement institution of the most male-supremacist nation on the European continent. Had not Switzerland been the last country to grant women the right to vote? As late as 1991 for one of its cantons! Anyway, she was now out of Switzerland, would still take part in the Riga Summer Olympics as a Swiss athlete next year, and then: '*Uf widerluege*', no more Switzerland.

At least, here in Cambridge, nobody knew her. Climbing

was not the kind of sport normal people were following in the news. Except perhaps here, at the Cambridge climbing gym.

"*Allez, gros lard, grimpe. Du bist wirklich eine kleine aber fette Scheisse,*" she said with an encouraging voice to the overweight boy she was belaying. (French:'Come on fat pig, climb.' German: 'You are really a small but fat shit.').

Amina Dörflinger was a slim and ripped young woman of intermediate height. She wore wide dark brown climbing pants under her harness, and a red sleeveless shirt with the inscription "instructor" in white on her back. Her deep blue eyes contrasted with her black shoulder-length hair and her sun-tanned face and arms. She was pulling the rope up using her self-locking belaying device as the fat kid was slowly progressing upward.

Overall, things were not too bad in Cambridge. The climbing center happened to be located just by the University's geological institution, where she was about to start her studies. She immediately got a part-time job as a climbing instructor. It was not only extra money, but also a free training opportunity.

She had no coach anymore, but she was determined to go as far as possible in the Riga Olympics. After that, she would quit competing, and focus on her studies.

"Next," she said after lowering the overweight kid back down to the ground.

She untied the figure of eight from the fat boy's harness and tied it on the harness of a short and shy black girl.

"Climb," Amina told the little girl.

"Climbing," the little girl said, doing as she was instructed.

She was good and courageous, Amina thought. The little girl made it quickly to the top.

"*Gut gemacht, bien joué*, good work," she said in three languages to the little girl as she landed back on the ground.

It was always like that in a group of young kids trying climbing for the first time. The males would always boast that they were so good and would make it easily to the top, while the young girls remained silent. Then, when it came to actual climbing, young males had a much higher abandon rate than girls.

"You are Amina? Amina Dörflinger? From the Swiss national team?" a black woman asked.

She was standing next to her as she was belaying a thin man of medium height with, likely, South-Asian origins.

"That's me," Amina replied.

"I saw you at the Chamonix competition," the woman went on. "Very well done on that overhang. You finished second on that one."

"Unfortunately, there are eight competitions in total," Amina replied. "Next year, I shall do better at the Olympics."

"What are you doing in Cambridge?"

"I got a scholarship," Amina replied. "I am starting a bachelor's in geology here."

"Hm, with that lunatic of a Dr. Sheldon Cooper. Then perhaps, in nine years, you will become a doctor in geology.

We are only doctor doctors."

"Doctors?"

"I'm Dr. Onwuatuegwu. Just call me Gisèle. I'm a lung doctor. And he, he's Eamon. A psychiatrist. We both work at Addenbrooke's hospital."

Eamon was quite a good climber, Amina noted. Later, that day, Eamon and Gisèle came to her. They both wanted to become better climbers, and they were ready to pay for a good private teacher. All money was good, and Amina accepted.

Amina's first day at university was Tuesday 6 September. It started with a welcome speech by the star of the institution for Earth Sciences, Dr. Sheldon Cooper.

The aula was packed with students, and Amina noted that the young women were in much better shape than the young men. So unfair!

Dr. Cooper was a tall, thin, bald man, wearing a green plaid suit and a red bow tie.

"Geology is real science!" he yelled as he was walking to the reading desk.

There was some cheering in the large lecture room.

"It's also one of the least rewarded sciences," he added when he had reached the microphone. "If you're after a Nobel Prize, you should study economics. And, believe me, economics is not a science. Never. Ever."

The students in geology started laughing. Not far from

Amina was a big, bearded student laughing so loud that Amina could not help laughing at him.

"As an Earth scientist," Dr. Cooper went on, "you can go ahead and prove the continental drift, explain the mechanism behind tides and model the melting of the ice caps, but please never expect to win a Nobel Prize in physics. So, if you're in here for fame, please re-orient yourself."

Amina only assumed that this Sheldon Cooper was bitter for not having received the Nobel Prize himself yet.

"If you are here for a safe job, you should also re-orient yourself. Geology is one of the most dangerous sciences. Every year, geologists get killed on fieldwork. So, when you contemplate the rock structure when standing in front of a cliff, please keep a pair of eyes on your back for the big waves that will come and kill you."

The bearded student next to Amina burst into loud laughter again.

"I hear you laugh, but I'm serious," the geology teacher insisted. "A colleague of mine died that way. Then, of course, you may not want to work with seismology in a country that still has the death penalty and trials by popular jury."

All the students suddenly turned silent.

"In 2081, the US Geological Survey failed to predict the Big Two that hit California. Earthquake prediction will never be 100% accurate. Did it matter to some popular jury in the States? Of course not. Three of the USGS geologists were sentenced to death in Texas, and one was executed, before the federal state intervened."

"I'm from Texas," the teacher added. "I'm not going there anymore. Then, there are the people in it for the money."

A group of students sitting in the right part of the aula cheered. These were the minority of geology students wearing suits.

"Well, that's a good reason," Dr. Cooper reckoned. "However good the circular economy becomes, there will always be a need for an extracting industry. Phosphate for the fertilizers, lithium for the batteries, helium-3 for the fusion reactors. We need that. WARSEC is going to start manufacturing spaceships on the Moon, as you saw in the news last week. There will be a lunar extracting industry, and they will need geologists for that. They will also need construction geologists to expand their Moon base which, as you know, is buried in large tunnel galleries so as to protect astronauts from solar radiation. I'm not sure WARSEC will pay that well, though."

The students in suits laughed, and so did the bearded student next to Amina.

"But mining in space, this is definitely something. However, what is money good for, if mankind perishes? If you have read my book… *Feedback from the Earth*, I don't want to do any advertising, but buy it, it's a good book..."

The bearded student burst again into very loud laughter. Amina should have brought earplugs with her.

"If you have read my book," Dr. Cooper went on, "you will know that the melting of ice caps and the thermal expansions of oceans have been reallocating the mass at the surface of our planet. That's too bad, because it has an impact on the speed of the rotation of the Earth. This, in its turn, increases the magmatic convections within the mantle. This means more frequent earthquakes and volcanic eruptions, as we have all observed. We have hit the planet hard with global warming. Sadly, the planet is punching us back. It will hit us harder than we hit it."

There was a silence. This time, even the bearded student abstained from laughing.

"I know, a lot of geologists across the world are still *sheldono-sceptical*. But what if a massive ice age came as a result of it? Like the Little Ice Age, but more massive. You know what the Little Ice Age is? Also known as L.I.A. for scientists?"

The students kept quiet. Amina knew, but there was no way she would raise her hand.

"It's a period which occurred between 1300 and 1850. Glaciers advanced throughout Europe and Greenland. The Cam river, here in Cambridge, was frozen every winter. The Swedes took advantage of it to invade Denmark by walking on a frozen strait. The French cavalry captured the Dutch fleet by charging over a frozen bay. That was serious. And I suspect that worse is to come. It may take two hundred years, but the coming ice age will be so serious that George R.R Martin's expression *winter is coming* will sound like a mere joke."

The students looked at him uncomprehendingly. What was the professor talking about?

"Nobody knows R.R. Martin? *Game of Thrones*? No? Of course, not... You are too young. Anyway... In the event of a massive ice age, there won't be enough food for 12 billion people. But things could be even worse."

"What could be worse than a massive ice age?" a student asked in the front row.

"I'm glad you asked. But I was going to tell you anyway. If the magmatic convection increases unreasonably, we may be up for super-volcanic eruptions."

Dr. Sheldon Cooper marked a pause and went on.

"65 million years ago, dinosaurs became extinct. Their extinction was caused by a meteorite. But it was the indirect consequences that killed them: a chain eruption of super-volcanoes, darkening the sky with sulfur dioxide and challenging all life."

"We also know for sure that Neanderthal people did not die out because they were slaughtered by our own *Homo sapiens* species, as some unreasonable scientists had tried to make us believe. Their extinction was caused by a super-volcano under the bay of Naples, in Italy. When it erupted, 40,000 years ago, it killed all vegetation over Europe and all European larger mammals starved to death. The Neanderthals died out, but so did all the Homo sapiens present in the area. It was because our species was sufficiently spread out geographically that new individuals were able to come back to Europe to re-populate the continent."

"Of course, the worst is never certain," Dr. Cooper admitted. "But for those of you who would not like to go into the extraction industry or the construction industry, please remember, the world will need good Earth scientists."

Amina had not been impressed by Sheldon Cooper's speech. In fact, she did not fit into any of the categories he had named. She wanted to go into science, for sure. But not because she cared about the future of mankind. Actually, she did not give a damn about it. The only purpose in life was to have fun, and it was exactly why she had chosen geology. She wanted to have a job with the opportunity to do a lot of exciting field work. Imagine! Getting paid to hike on a glacier! That was the dream.

The following day, Amina was given an endless list of literature to read. Scientific articles could be downloaded for free using the university's intranet. But the course books had to be purchased, and they were expensive. If she wanted to eat something other than pasta over the next four months, she'd better give some climbing lessons to Eamon and Gisèle.

Over the next week, she spent all of her non-studying time at the climbing gym, and she started to spot familiar faces. There was this handsome, tall climber, with climbing gears tattooed all over his back. He was always climbing topless. He was kind of hot. But he seemed to be already together with a tall Dutch lady with short messy brown hair. She did not deserve him. She was only a beginner.

By checking on the guy, she eventually realized that he was quite a disappointment: he had no interest in rocks. A climber with no interest in rocks! He did not even know that granite was an igneous rock. He did not know what the difference between igneous rock and metamorphic rock was! How could you be a climber if you did not understand what you were climbing on? Such a stupid guy! The Dutch girl could keep him. Amina eventually got to understand that he was only her "fuckbuddy". Wise of her.

The tall Dutch woman happened to be a '*slavant*' and she was working as a Mathematics tutor in one of Cambridge's high schools. The term '*slavant*', made of the contraction of the words 'slave' and 'servant', was the unofficial denomination used to refer to the young EU citizens doing their mandatory Civil Service after high school. Something Amina had never had to do, as Switzerland was not part of the European Union, but she had done a year of Swiss military service followed by a year of Swiss Civil Service instead.

When Amina was finally introduced to the tall brown-eyed Dutch woman, it was her name that struck Amina.

"Sanne van der Maas? You are the survivor of the Martian Show?"

"Am I still so famous?" Sanne wondered.

"For people of our generation, I'm afraid you are," Amina replied. "Cool to meet a Martian. Do you know Mr. Vroom?" [Vroom pronounced with a long o]

"The entrepreneur who started the Martian Show, declared himself bankrupt, and fled to Switzerland?" Sanne tried.

"Yes, that asshole," Amina confirmed. "Well, when I was doing my Civil Service in Zermatt, I happened to have changed his diapers a number of times. He has very small balls, I mean physically small balls."

Sanne laughed, and Amina started to like Sanne. She understood that Sanne had to do only one year of Civil Service, as she counted as an 'immigrant'. After being born in, and spending her first eighteen years in, the Martian colony, Sanne had finally been evacuated to Earth a year earlier. She had already a Bachelor's in economics from Columbia University and wanted to start a Master's at Cambridge University after her Civil Service had ended.

Over the next few days, Amina met Sanne's climbing buddies. Samir Benyamina was a mid-height, thin young French man with black, curly hair and happened to also be a slavant. He was taking care of senile old people in a retirement home. Emily Chapman was an athletic, red-haired, blue-eyed English girl studying to become a nurse. She was working in the same retiring home as Samir and they were currently 'fuck buddies'.

"Amina," Emily said once as they were all bouldering

together in the gym, "I saw you coach Dr. Windsor and his girlfriend."

"Eamon and Gisèle? They are really good, and making progress," Amina replied. "For the next step, they should consider changing their diet, but they say they don't want to stop drinking alcohol, so I can't really help them."

"Doctors can't be sober anyway," Samir commented.

"Do you know them well?" Emily asked, "Do you know Eamon is the Crown Prince of England?"

"Are you kidding? He does not look like royalty to me," Amina said.

"No, he doesn't," Emily replied, "That's the problem. Our Queen, Queen Lea, she could never marry her boyfriend, because he was Pakistani, and even worse, he had republican ideas. The royal family tried to deny his right to succeed to the throne, especially after her boyfriend had died of the Qatari flu. Because of public opinion, they had to back off. So, there he is. Prince Eamon, heir to the throne of England."

"What are the odds?" Sanne asked. "There are two monarchies left in Europe, one serious monarchy if we exclude Denmark, and we happen to know the Crown Prince."

"His mother has had breast cancer for a while," Emily added. "It seems she will never be cured. If she dies too soon, everybody fears Eamon will refuse to become king."

Samir started to laugh.

"What is it, Samir?" Emily frowned a little.

"Johan Staël was making fun of Sanne for thinking too much about the future of mankind, but thinking about the future of the monarchy is even more ridiculous. Now, let's go back to climbing."

Johan Staël von Trollstein was another 'slavant' living in the same barrack as Samir, and often clashing with both Sanne and Samir.

02: THE SLAVANTS' STORY (SEPT 2095)

About 800 young Europeans were doing their two-year long Civil Service in Cambridge. They were quartered in a dormitory complex made of truck containers arranged in sets of two-story barracks, located between Hauxton Road and the M11 highway.

The main purpose of the European Service was not so much as to dispose of cheap labor for public service missions, ranging from assistance to the elderly and challenged school pupils, to assistance to the homeless and families is social distress. The main purpose of the European Service, as had been explained by Mark Lowcock, the long-haired Irish caretaker of the barracks, was in fact to uproot young Europeans from different nations and social backgrounds so as to favor a true melting pot.

In exchange for their two years of cheap labor, slavants were provided with free housing, free food, free condoms, and, most importantly, given the opportunity to get their driving license for free.

Both Samir Benyamina and Sanne van der Maas had started their Civil service in July earlier that year. Unlike Samir, who had been forced to join the service like any other young European, Sanne had volunteered.

Though, she was technically a Dutch and EU citizen, Sanne had been born on Mars and arrived on Earth less than a year earlier. In the mid-2070s, even before the deployment of the first space elevator in the Pacific, an eccentric Dutch Billionaire, Mr. Vroom (pronounced with a long 'o') had financed the colonization attempt of Mars through his Martian Show Corporation. The goal had been to have a full-time team of researchers on Mars to look for traces of fossilized life on the red planet, as the now cancelled Martian exploration program had failed to find any.

The Martian colonization project had, however, not gone as planned. The seventeen Dutch couples, who had landed at Elysium Planitia in 2076, had failed to dig in the diamond-hard permafrost and had had to content themselves with building their colony on the surface. The consequence had been exposure to solar radiation, even though they had covered their buildings with gravel and ice to protect themselves as best as they could. This initial failure had hindered the Martian Show Corporation from raising additional funding. Instead of evacuating the couples, the corporation had decided to let the couples live on Mars and broadcast their lives on Earth in an attempt to maximize profit.

Except that the solar radiation had taken its toll on the colony, eventually causing the Martian Show Corporation to declare itself bankrupt, as all major broadcasters had started to boycott the show. The sudden bankruptcy had caused an abrupt stop in supplies from Earth, dealing a final and deadly blow to the colony, all the more since no one state wanted to take responsibility and assist with the evacuation of the remaining settlers.

Finally, what was then the United Nations Office for Outer Space Affairs (UNOOSA) had succeeded in arranging a rescue, but there had been only one colonist to save: Sanne van der Maas. UNOOSA had shipped robots to Mars to manufacture a rocket on the red planet. In October 2094, the completed rocket had taken Sanne into Martian orbit, where she had boarded the *Alcubierre*, the first spaceship with faster-than-light travel capability. It had taken them only twenty-five seconds to transit from the Martian orbit to the Earth's orbit.

When she thought about it, Sanne realized how lucky she had been. She had been the first child born on Mars, when they had enough supplies of vitamin D and bone reinforcement medicines. Her parents had been very safety conscious and had forbidden her to go out in daylight, so as not to expose her to solar radiation.

For the first eighteen years of her life, she had not gone out more than a hundred times in daylight, and only ever for a short time. Caution and discipline had saved her from a Martian cancer.

Because of her background, the European Union had not wanted to impose the usual Civil Service duty on her, but she had volunteered and she had gotten what she wanted: to be in Cambridge. Starting with distance courses when still living on Mars, she had obtained a Bachelor's degree in economics from Columbia University in New York, and now wanted to apply for a Master's in the same subject, here in Cambridge.

She happened to know Ralf Åhman, the director of the World's Agency for the Regulation of Space Exploration and Colonization (WARSEC). He had previously been the director of the United Nations Office for Outer Space Affairs (UNOOSA) and had organized her rescue from Mars. She was still in contact with him, and she knew that he had plans to hire 'space economists' in a few years to study the feasibility of interstellar colonization. This would not happen overnight, but she had calculated that she would have obtained her Master's precisely when WARSEC would be starting to look for people with her profile. This was what she wanted, to work at WARSEC as an economist, and hopefully contribute to a better world.

In the meantime, Sanne saw Civil Service as an interesting social experience. She had made her first Earthling friends of her own age. Though she was living in Barrack 12, most of her friends were living in Barrack 5. In corridor 5-C on the second floor lived Samir Benyamina, the young French cook who used to sell cannabis and was from Beaudottes, in the Paris suburbs. He was sharing his room with Magnus Li, a slim Asian-Swede from Hässleholmen raised by his single mom in the difficult suburb of Borås.

Often with them was Carsten Nielsen, a pot-bellied and flat-faced blond Dane, whose father owned a pig farm not far from Haderslev, in Southern Jutland. The poor Carsten lived in corridor 5-A, on the first floor of Barrack 5, and was sharing his room with Johan Staël von Trollstein, a tall, athletic German with slicked-back blond hair, but whom Sanne considered an arrogant prick with a penchant for 'assholeness'.

And as the summer was gradually becoming autumn, things became both better and more complicated for the slavants. The better part was that Sanne, Samir, Carsten and Magnus had all obtained a slot to start driving lessons, though there was no real wonder.

The United Kingdom of South Britain was the only remaining country in Europe driving on the left side of the road. Both Ireland and Scotland had switched to driving on the right thirty years earlier, as the new high-speed boat trips to the continent made it convenient to travel to continental Europe. Eastern African countries had also switched to driving on the right, and so had South Asia, mainly due to commercial pressures from China. Australia, New-Zealand and Japan were the only remaining countries with left side driving, and as a result, the vast majority of the cars driving in the UK had the steering wheel on the left side.

Through a referendum, the British government had asked the South-British nations, five years earlier, whether they wanted to switch to driving on the right. British voters had said no. The government had therefore decided to ignore the will of the people and ask the Parliament, instead. As a result, it had been voted that the United Kingdom of South Britain would switch to driving on the right in a year, on 17 September 2096.

Because of this, many slavants were reluctant to learn how to drive on the left side of the road for only a few months, and most of the driving lessons slots were available. This suited Sanne, Samir, Carsten and Magnus perfectly. If everything went well, they should all get their driving license before Christmas.

However, when it came to social life in the slavants' barracks, things were not as straightforward. On Samir's floor, more or less everybody helped to keep the shared bathrooms and the kitchen clean, except perhaps Giuseppe and Camila, two Italian slavants. Since Samir was obsessed with keeping the kitchen clean, it had an encouraging effect on the other container mates. On Carsten's floor, however, it was a horrific mess.

When four out of the twenty corridor mates not only refused to help with the cleaning but also voluntarily messed the kitchen and bathrooms up, another eight had quit helping, as a form of protest. It had been only a question of time before the remaining eight slavants, including Carsten, gave up.

This was actually an issue, as slavants could be charged fines worth three months of their meagre salaries, should they not keep their corridor tidy.

The first floor of Barrack 5 was now in such a state that Carsten would come up upstairs to use Samir and Magnus's kitchen. Sanne would also join them every time Samir was in a cooking mood.

"It smells like hell in your kitchen," she said to Samir and Magnus, who were setting up one of the two small tables.

By the electric cooker was a chubby blond slavant frying two bugburgers, made of insect paste, and cooking some green beans. It was Ingrid, from Germany.

"Not because of us", she said. "It comes from downstairs. They don't clean, and now they come here to use our kitchen, don't they, Carsten?"

"It's your boyfriend Johan Staël we have to thank for that," Carsten retorted. He was sitting on the small kitchen's sofa, a can of Carlsberg in his hand. "He refuses to clean. He says he does not care if he has to pay a fine. His parents will. They are rich."

"Yes, but your parents won't," Ingrid replied, "So, you'd better keep it clean."

Carsten drank from his can and said: "You're asking me to be the bitch of your boyfriend because he's rich? I don't even want to talk to you."

It was Saturday evening, and Samir had cooked a fillet of beef rolled in goat cheese. He brought it to the table.

"We'd be better spending our meagre salary on food like this than on cleaning fines," he said. "Help yourself."

Sanne, Magnus and Carsten sat down around the small table.

"We also need to save money for the driving test," Sanne added. "And we are entitled to only thirty hours of driving lessons."

"Even Carsten can learn how to drive in thirty hours," Samir said.

"But even then, we will only be allowed to drive non-self-driving cars," Carsten replied.

"It's a paradox," Magnus complained. "To get the right to drive a self-driving car, you need to take an advanced course in robotics systems."

"That's because self-driving cars are not as straightforward as everybody believes," Sanne explained. "Artificial Intelligence has been widely overrated. When I was managing my robots to build the rocket on Mars, I had to monitor them constantly."

"We will only get a regular driving license," Magnus said. "Who would pay ten months of slavant salary to get the extra qualification to get to drive self-driving cars?"

"Very few people," said Carsten. "Most of the cars leased today don't have self-driving capacities."

"It was a bad business idea from the beginning," Samir commented. "Self-driving cars can only be afforded by rich drivers. Rich drivers are just the drivers who like to break the rules and drive over the speed limits, which the AI won't let you do anyway. Rich drivers like big cars, not big intelligence."

"Exactly. Intelligence does not make happiness. Money does."

It was Johan Staël, who had come up to eat dinner with Ingrid.

"Why don't you use your kitchen, instead?" Samir asked him.

"This is Ingrid's kitchen, and you clean it so well." Johan Staël sat down at the other small table, grabbed the remote control and switched the TV on: "*I'm Wolf Welsh. I have served in the EU Marine Parachute Regiment, I have climbed to the top of Everest, I have swum across the melted glacial Arctic Ocean, I have skied across the South Pole's ice cap. I'm going to show you what it takes to survive in the most hostile environments.*"

"Really, you are watching Wolf Welsh?" Sanne said, and she turned to Samir: "Hey Samir, why haven't you invited Emily?"

"We are only FBs, fuckbuddies," Samir replied.

Sanne smiled:

"I think you are already a couple and don't know it." She added, "She is your only FB, and you are her only FB."

"Am I?" Samir seemed surprised.

"She is not seeing anyone else. You can still call her for the movie."

Later that night, they went to the movie theatre to watch *Frozen Lies*, the latest James Bond movie. Emily joined them, and they had to swap seats and Sanne ended up sitting next to Mark Lowcock, the long-haired caretaker who just happened to be there, on his own.

"You earn enough money to come to the movie?" he asked. "President Bonavita is right, we should cut the spending on the Civil Service. Slavants have way too good a time." And he laughed.

Before the movie started, they were shown the following message: *The James Bond movie franchise started in 1962. Back then, the world population was about 3.1 billion. In 2095, the world population is about 10.4 billion.*

Since the middle of the 21st Century, UNESCO had made it compulsory to set the demographic context of each projected movie or franchise in relation to the present time. The purpose was to make the world's population aware of the untenable demographic growth.

The movie started, and it was stupid, funny, and predictable. It was James Bond. It was why they had come in the first place.

As they were walking out of the theatre, Carsten complained:

"In all movies, it's the same thing. The Danish white dude is always first to die. It's so predictable and so *Danophobic*."

"It used to be the black guy to be first to die," Emily replied. "Roles have changed."

The long-haired caretaker seemed to be stalking the group of slavants.

"So, fuckers," he said as they were now on the street, "I'm checking your history knowledge. Who was the first black James Bond? And when?"

"2036. David Jackson," Magnus answered.

"Not bad, for a Swede," Mark replied. "Next question. When did James Bond stop working for MI6 and start working for MIS? It's a trick question."

"The EU became a federation in 2054," Sanne replied. "The European Armed Forces were created at that time, and so was the Military Intelligence Service."

"Yes, but the UK rejoined the EU only in 2063," Emily objected, "And MI6 was dismantled in 2069. So, I would go for 2069."

"Wrong," Mark replied with a large smile. "James Bond continued to work for MI6 until 2078, even though it did not exist any longer. Too many nostalgic people in the franchise."

"I guess it does not matter who he works for, the Queen of England or the EU President," Magnus replied. "It's all about banging and bang, bang."

"Mark," Sanne tried, changing the subject. "I have a more down-to-earth question."

"At this hour?" the caretaker asked.

"Say," Sanne went on, "you lived in a corridor where the rich slavants refused to help with the cleaning. They don't care about having to pay the fine because their parents would pay for it. What would you do?"

"Ah, you are referring to the first floor of Barrack 5…" said the caretaker. "Easy. Punch them."

"I'm sorry?" Carsten said, not sure he had understood correctly.

"Punch those fuckers, beat the shit out of them."

"Are you serious?" Samir asked.

"Of course," Mark replied. "This is what the Civil Service is about. Social integration through bullying. You hit them, you will not go to jail. At worst, you will have to pay a fine, if they make the effort to file a complaint. The fine you get for punching somebody is about the same amount as the fine for not cleaning. But only one has to punch them, and then you can be several to share the fine. Then it becomes cheaper per person to punch them. So, do it."

As the slavants and Emily were biking home to the containers, Samir said: "I like the Irish way of solving problems."

03: NOBEL PRIZES
IN PHYSICS AND CHEMISTRY
(OCT 2095)

On that morning, Sophie Couillard was furious. The tall, athletic general manager of V-space was standing in her office, located on the seventh floor of the main V-Space building, adjacent to the airport of Bobo-Dioulasso, the second city of Burkina Faso.

Even though Vahlroos Corporation was headquartered in New York City, the research & development facilities of its subsidiary V-Space, as well as its factories, were located in Burkina Faso. It was well connected to the sea through Côte d'Ivoire, it was close to the Sahara, above which aerospace shuttles could be safely tested, the workforce there was well educated, and most importantly, there was an absence of earthquakes. Something that mattered most to Michael Vahlroos, the CEO of the Vahlroos Corporation, whose parents had perished in the Big Two in California, in 2081.

It was something else, however, that bothered the general manager of V-Space, on that second week of October 2095. The blond, long-haired business woman in her mid-thirties was wearing jeans and a polo-shirt with the V-Space logo. Sophie Couillard was casting a piercing gaze through the window with her deep blue eyes.

"*Osti d'épais de marde c'te Vladimir*", she swore with her Québécois accent ('What a bloody fucker this Vladimir'). "*Comment pouvait-on lui faire confiance.*" ('How could we trust him?')

Behind her was Brice de Robien, Sophie's V-liner project director. The sun-tanned French engineer was wearing his usual Hawaiian shirt.

"He is just a sex addict," he said. "It's not his fault."

Sophie abruptly turned around, looked her project director in his eyes, and exclaimed:

"Not his fault? My warp propulsion director went to the lady's locker room and taped a spy camera on the ceiling. He is so stupid that he did not wear a mask when turning the camera on. When showering, Ana Luiza spotted it. Ana Luiza, our conventional propulsion director! It took only 10 seconds to see that it was Vladimir who had set it."

"Yes, it could have led to a conflict between the conventional propulsion director and the warp propulsion director," Brice said. "It was right to fire Vladimir Gerasimov."

"What are you talking about?" Sophie exclaimed. "This

Vladimir is a male supremacist! A stupid male supremacist! Male supremacists are not welcome at V-Space. I also hope the Burkinabe police properly takes care of him. I'm happy to see his wife is asking for a divorce."

Sophie walked back to her desk and sat down.

"What worries me most," she added, "is that this Vladimir is obviously incredibly stupid. He keeps saying that a vertical atmosphere entry is feasible, despite the fact that Tintin and Thierry maintain it's not. Tintin is an arrogant jerk, but I trust him more."

"They are still both working on the minority project, the V-craft," Brice said. "I have understood they are making some decent progress."

"Please check on them and tell me when they could present a workable proof of concept for the V-craft. I need a plan B in case the V-liner is a no go."

"I'm confident the V-liner will work," Brice said. "But I can check with the team working on the minority project."

Thierry Diakité and Tintin Mutombo had had a busy summer, in Bobo-Dioulasso. They always worked together, even though the two African engineers had slightly different backgrounds.

Thierry Diakité, a well-built young black man of average height, was from Burkina Faso and had grown up not far from Bobo-Dioulasso. Though he had become an orphan at a young age, his teachers had encouraged him into studying and he had obtained a PhD in robotics at Kigali University, before joining V-Space. As part of his PhD, he had, among other things, developed the robots that had been used by Sanne Van der Maas to build her rocket on Mars.

Tintin Mutombo, a tall, thin young man with a lighter complexion, was a theoretical physicist. He originated from a wealthy family in Congo Kinshasa, but had done his PhD at Moscow University where he had elaborated a new theory unifying relativity theory and quantum gravity. While his supervisor, Anatoli Govorov, had wanted to keep him for a post doc in Russia, the Russians had evicted him when his visa had expired, but Tintin had found employment at V-Space, in Burkina Faso. After all, he was one of the minds behind faster-than-light travel and so called 'warp-technology', or Alcubierre Metric.

A year earlier, Tintin and Thierry, two of the lead engineers at V-Space, had questioned V-Space's initial plan to a build their V-liner, a large cylindrical spaceship equipped with both warp and atmosphere capability. It was supposed to take off vertically, propelled upward like a very thick rocket, and warp out of the atmosphere after reaching a safety altitude. It was large enough to conduct several week-long missions, mostly for mining operations on distant asteroids or on planets within the solar system.

There were two problems with this V-liner project. First of all, as far as Tintin was concerned, it was not adapted to the market needs, as extraterrestrial mining further away than the Moon would probably not be needed before several decades' time. But, most importantly, it was flawed. The V-liner was supposed to come out of warp in the atmosphere vertically, stabilize, and land vertically like the old Space-X rocket's first stage. As far as Thierry was concerned, it was impossible, and even if an algorithm could hypothetically stabilize the V-liner upon re-entry, which he doubted, all the passengers would die of the subsequent extremely high G-Force endured.

As a result, Tintin and Thierry had been tasked with leading a 'minority project' to assess the feasibility of the V-craft. The V-craft was a much smaller cylindrical aerospace shuttle meant for the transportation of passengers only. It would take off like a plane and warp out of the atmosphere by aiming slightly above the horizon. Likewise, it would re-enter the atmosphere by coming out of warp with a low angle entry, deploying wings and then braking by making a series of S-turns like an aerospace shuttle. It was meant to land like an airplane.

The so-called minority project had proved to be an interesting but time-consuming challenge. The deployment upon landing and take-off of the front and rear wings and engines was a huge problem in itself. It caused the center of gravity to displace itself on a body subjected to air turbulence. The front of the ship also had to be protected against Hawking radiation during the warp-journey, and it was easier said than done.

Besides, Tintin had his own ambition. He wanted to find a way to have a spaceship warp through spacetime faster than ten times the speed of light. He was convinced there was no upper limit. Shortly after the Big Bang, spacetime had, after all, expanded infinitely fast. He was certain it would be feasible, within ten to twenty years, to travel at warp 300 instead of warp 10. Since Thierry was better at programming and at modelling, Tintin would constantly ask him for help.

However, the reasons both Thierry and Tintin were devoting so much energy to the minority project was not to be well graded at the next year-end review. Hopefully, by the end of the year, they would both have left V-Space, and taken their findings with them.

They would be employed by WARSEC and working for the United Nations instead. On top of their work, both had been studying for the competitive exam to enter WARSEC's Youth Professional Program. The written exams were scheduled for October.

There were two reasons they wanted so badly out of V-Space to WARSEC. First of all, Ralf Åhman, the Director of the UN agency, had promised them senior positions if they made it through the Professional Program. They would be involved with upcoming interstellar exploration rather than designing spaceships with no other purpose than maximize short-term profit.

The other reason was that neither of them was on good terms

with the senior management at V-Space. Sophie Couillard was a decent general manager, but she was squeezed between Michael Vahlroos, the ideological CEO based in New York, and her own senior management, more interested in short-term incentives on their salary than viable long-term plans.

The only good thing with V-Space was that they had better computers than anything they would get at WARSEC. As a result, they wanted to do as many calculations as possible so that they could take their findings with them to WARSEC.

By the end of September, they had worked out all the problems they needed to in order to build a working V-craft: what material to use, how to balance the ship under the wing deployment, how to safely negotiate the atmosphere entry, but Tintin was not quite satisfied. They had had to compromise on the warp speed. The V-craft would only make it to warp 2, five times less than the *Alcubierre*. He wanted to be able to find a way to reach warp 300. All the time, he was trying new creative approaches, but it seemed it was a dead-end.

The R&D division of V-Space was activity based. This meant that employees had no assigned desks. They kept their keyboards, laptops and notebooks in lockers and every morning had to bring them to the desk they chose to sit at.

In theory, employees would benefit from the setup, working efficiently with just the colleagues they needed on a given day. In practice, this organization had led to a 'congregationist' group dynamic. Employees usually sat close to the colleagues they liked more, and further away from the colleagues they liked least. It was like in the study room in high school.

On this particular Wednesday, Thierry sat next to Tintin in the silent area, a section separated from other, noisier, open sections. They were normally left in peace by the top management. Not that day.

Brice de Robien, the V-liner project director, was paying them a visit.

"What's happening, Thierry?" Everything under control?" Brice asked.

"Everything under control, boss."

"The minority project? When do you think you could present a proof of concept?"

"By Christmas," Thierry replied. "We will have something to present, I'm confident."

Thierry was lying. They would be ready in two weeks, he hoped, but he wanted to have some slack.

"Not bad," Brice replied. "For the atmosphere re-entry of the V-liner, Ana Luisa wanted some help to check an algorithm designed by her team. Have you looked at it yet?"

"With the warping out at 80 km altitude?" Thierry replied. "It seems to be working in 1% of the simulations."

"Make it be 99%, will you; be kind, my dear Thierry," Brice replied.

"Boss," Thierry objected. "It would be simpler to have the

whole V-liner enter the atmosphere from 120 km of altitude, like a normal spaceship."

"Except that current regulation prevents spaceships entering the atmosphere with compact fusion reactors onboard," Brice said.

"Regulations may change," Thierry replied. "A safe vertical landing with the V-liner is never gonna happen. It's impossible."

"Ts ts ts, *impossible n'est pas français*," ('Impossible' is not French') said Brice, before turning around and leaving.

"Neither am I", Thierry whispered, silently showing his middle finger to Brice's back.

On his chat messenger, he received a message from Tintin, who was sitting silently next to him:

> » **Mutombo, Tintin:** *"WARSEC test in six days. Hold on. We are soon out."*
> » **Diakité, Thierry:** *"What an asshole, this Brice."*

Suddenly, Tintin's phone started vibrating on the table. He took it, went to the nearest conference room and closed the door behind him to take the call. Two minutes later, he went back silently to his desk and sat down. Thierry returned to the chat messenger.

> » **Diakité, Thierry:** *"Something has happened?"*
> » **Mutombo, Tintin:** *"2095 Nobel Prize in Physics: Anatoli and me. Oh yeah!"*
> » **Diakité, Thierry:** *"Congratulations! Now, you'll get any*

position in Europe even if you fail the WARSEC test."

» **Mutombo, Tintin:** *"In any case: Fuck Vahlroos!"*

The following day, Thierry was pleased to read who had won the Nobel Prize in Chemistry: It was Alice Fù, for the discovery of the green matter, which made warp travel possible. She was also the first Afro-Chinese person to receive a Nobel Prize.

"To Africa!" he said that night, as they were sipping some *Sobebra* beer in their favorite bar, Sankara.

During the next weekend, Tintin and Thierry relaxed as much as they could before the WARSEC entry test. It took place the following week in Ouagadougou, the Burkinabé capital.

Thierry reflected that it may have been a mistake to study in the comfortably air-conditioned offices of V-space. He had forgotten that Ouagadougou was warmer than Bobo-Dioulosso. There was no AC in the test rooms, and it was much hotter than he was used to.

Sweat was dripping onto his papers, the air was heavy, and the sound of UN officials walking back and forth along the aisles, checking nobody was cheating, was oppressing him.

He hoped, though, that he had managed OK. It was a competitive exam, after all. The goal was not to be perfect. Just better than the other candidates. They would know in the first week of November if they were to be called to the final interview and group exercise.

The wait was untenable for Thierry. Tintin, on the other hand, was confident. Anyway, he would rather talk about the Nobel Prize ceremony. If all of Tintin's Congolese family wanted to attend, they would need to book a charter flight to take them from Kinshasa to Stockholm. Since he was the first Congolese person to win a Nobel Prize in Physics, even the Congolese president would show up. Tintin promised Thierry he would invite him to the banquet in Stockholm. That way, he would have a chance to visit Europe anyway.

The first week of November came, and so did the results. Tintin was called to the final test part in Vienna. Not Thierry. He was devastated. What had gone wrong?

Later on, Thierry received his grades. He had top grades in mathematics, physics, and problem analysis, but he had performed very poorly in ethics and philosophy. This was enough not to go forward in the selection process.

Tintin tried to console him. Shit could always happen. Anyway, Thierry now knew what he had to work on. He could redo the test in one year. Thierry really did not want to waste an extra year of his life at V-Space, though. Tintin convinced him it was the best alternative. As long as he stayed at V-Space, he had a salary, lodging and, most importantly, he could study during working hours without anybody noticing. Thierry resigned himself to the prospect.

04: The European Foreign Legion (Fall 2095)

They had arrived in Castelnaudary, not far from Toulouse, Southern France, on Sunday 7 August 2095. 56 volunteer recruits, among whom there were only seven women. Aisha Barjaoui was one of them. They were about to start Legionnaire School, and the first six weeks were said to be the toughest. She had made it so far, and she was here to stay. So far, the selection process had been easy.

At seventeen, Aisha Barjaoui was an atypical volunteer recruit for the Foreign Legion. On the other hand, she was not the average young woman one would expect any teenage girl to turn into. Though shorter than average, she was incredibly fit and muscular. In another life, and in other circumstances, she had wanted to become a police officer in Morocco, her home country. Except that things had not turned out that way.

Back in Morocco, she had had an affair with a Chinese

expat, which was not unusual for a sixteen-year-old Moroccan girl. He had a nice villa, with a swimming pool where she had learnt how to swim, and punching ball, where she had worked on her fighting skills. He had been a gentleman, and when she had accidentally become pregnant, he had arranged her trip to Ireland, since having an abortion was illegal in Morocco. Her abortion in Ireland had gone well. Unfortunately, she had been denounced to the Moroccan police and could not return to her home country, lest she spend four years in jail. However, in the European Union, she had been nothing else than an undocumented person after her four-week visa expired.

She had wandered from Ireland to Wales to England and, in Cambridge, had met Samir and Sanne. Samir had suggested she joined the Foreign Legion. She was physically fit enough. It was totally safe, as the European Union had not been at war for decades. After three years, she would be granted EU citizenship. The only issue was that she was still underage, but she could still apply provided she had an authorization from her parents. Her father had sent her his written consent.

At the Legion's barracks in London, they had informed her she would have to eat pork when served pork. Everybody ate the same in the Legion. Was it a problem? Of course not, as long as she would not grow fat. They had laughed. Growing fat in the legion was difficult.

There had also been a few physical tests, and she had proven to have the second-best stamina of the London applicants. Only six of them had been sent to the Legion's recruiting center, in Aubagne, close to Marseille, on the Mediterranean Coast.

She had really enjoyed her train journey across the Channel and through France to Marseille

In Aubagne, they had met many other volunteers of all nationalities. They had all been given blue training clothes and had gone through more tests.

One of the NCOs had told her she had quite an impressive IQ, but would not say how high. It had boosted her morale, nonetheless. At the medical check-up, she had been told that she had very good vision (12 out of 10). There had only been one physical test: they had had to run as far as possible under twelve minutes. Aisha had run 3.3 km (2 miles 89 yards) and had been far from being the slowest.

The recruits' personal backgrounds had been scrutinized by the Legion's intelligence. They had to stand individually in underwear in the major's office and answer his questions. Did she have a good relationship with her parents? Yes, obviously, else they would not have sent their parental consent. Had she come solely because of an abortion? Yes. What was her primary motivation? She wanted to become a European citizen to be able to stay. Was it worth five years in the Legion? Yes, it was. Had she tried drugs? No, she hadn't. Had she been violent at any point toward anybody? No, not really. Was she really sure? They would check all the records anyway. She'd better speak the truth! OK, she admitted. Once, there had been this bully who had stolen her shoes twice and had constantly mocked girls in junior high school. No teacher had ever wanted to punish him because he was the son of a senior official. She had had to do justice herself. What had she done? She had kicked him in the head. She had subsequently been suspended for three days, but then the boy had stopped bullying girls. The major had made a note of it, but Aisha had not been sent home.

They had also been asked which regiment they were interested in after basic training. Most of the guys would answer the 2nd REP (*Régiment Étranger de Parachutistes*), the Foreign Parachute Infantry Regiment. She had decided she was better than the men and also wanted to join the 2nd REP.

Finally, Aisha had been one of the 56 recruits to be accepted to Legionnaire School in Castelnaudary. They had all had their heads shaved (women were allowed to let their hair grow back), and received their military clothes and a green beret. Their white *Képis* (legionnaires' headgear) would be given to them after the fifth week of Legionnaire School, should they make it through.

In Castelnaudary they were quartered in an ancient farm, and put through an intense program, with barely any sleep. They had physical training, marching, and running with a 30 kg (66 lbs) rucksack, but also courses in French and English.

They were organized in four-man teams (*quadrinômes*), in which at least one was bilingual in French, and one was bilingual in English. Aisha was paired with a Nigerian, a Chinese person, and a Norwegian. They were to coach each other so that all of them would have a working knowledge of both French and English by the end of Legionnaire School. Aisha did not learn much, as she was already fluent in these both languages.

They also had to learn some legionnaire songs, something Aisha hated as she sang badly. The legionnaire's parade march was also a challenge. They had a very specific pace, much slower than in any other army in the world. Learning it was not easy.

Because of very tight schedules, all the platoon had to shower at the same time. Most men were embarrassed to have seven women showering with them, and everybody was behaving very prudishly, except Aisha's Norwegian quadrinôme who liked to go around showing his manhood to everybody, strumming it, while pretending to play the guitar.

Their drill sergeant, Niina Koskela, did not like it.

"Legionnaire Eriksen," she yelled, "Your penis is not beautiful enough to show off. Fifty push-ups, naked, now!"

Physical training was very tough, and the women were given no special treatment. One of the least popular exercises was the so-called *marche en canard* (duck-like march), where recruits had to walk while squatting, carrying their assault rifles above their heads.

"Bands of pussies, the Donald is gonna come and grab you," Sergeant Koskela screamed after the platoon had failed to run to the top of mound fast enough.

"What Donald?" the Norwegian soldier asked.

"*Donald Duck! Bande de connards. Allez! Marche en canard!*"
('Donald Duck! Band of assholes. Come on! Duck-like march!')

At the end of the first week, four women had quit and only three were left. One of them was a young girl from India, who was only sixteen. Her family had perished in an earthquake, and she had had a rough time with a French humanitarian worker. There was also a Saudi woman who looked very tough. It was rumored that she had beheaded a Saudi prince who had raped her. Aisha never managed to find out if it was true, but her Norwegian *quadrinôme* assured her it was.

"The Legion used to be an outfit for rapists," he laughed. "Now it is an outfit for raped girls."

"What did you say?!" Sergeant Koskela yelled. "Torbjørn Eriksen, you think you are funny? All the men here, fifty push-ups. The women, you keep standing."

Collective punishment was part of everyday life in Castelnaudary and Drill Sergeant Koskela was a Finnish woman committed to putting an end to male supremacism:

"Finnish women were the first to obtain universal voting rights, in 1905. Finnish women were the first to make it through Legionnaire School in 2044. Back then, the Legion was still French. I'm gonna teach you what it costs to mess with a Finnish sergeant like me."

By the end of the second week, all the men in the platoon

feared her, and if there were any male supremacists left in the outfit, they were very good at hiding their game.

At the end of their fifth week, they had to do a two-day and 80 km (50 miles) long march with their full equipment. It was very demanding for a seventeen-year-old girl to carry 30 kg (66 lbs), and by the middle of the second day, her back was hurting so much that she thought she would have to give up. Then, Sergeant Koskela came and asked her teammates to carry her rucksack. The Saudi lady also had trouble and had her rucksack carried by her *quadrinômes* for the last fifteen kilometers. Someone complained that it was unfair that men had to carry extra weight for incompetent women, and Sergeant Koskela asked all the men in the platoon to do twenty push-ups with their rucksacks on. Preshti Ahma, the young Indian girl, was the only woman to finish the march carrying her rucksack.

On the finish line, Torbjørn Eriksen commented:

"It seems that there is something good about child labor in India after all".

Sergeant Koskela heard it: "All the men: twenty push-ups again, with the rucksack on. Thank your comrade Eriksen."

Later that day, under a boring-but-you-had-to-pretend-you-were-moved ceremony, the recruits were given their white *képis*. Aisha felt safe. She could no longer fail. She only had to hold on for five years. She would be a French and, by extension, European, citizen after just three years.

After the *Képi march*, Aisha had suffered from pain in her back.

"Barjaoui," Sergeant Koskela said. "That sucks, but it's common for female soldiers to have back problems. They have specially designed rucksacks for women in the European Army, but you won't get one before your assignment. And it may even take some time. I had to wait two years for mine."

"*Oui, sergent.*"

"However, you have to do something about it. The trick is to strengthen your lower back. I will show you a set of exercises you should do every day."

"*Merci, sergent.*"

Over the following weeks, they practiced different forms of weaponry such as light and heavy machine guns, anti-tank recoilless rifles, and the 51 mm individual mortar. Aisha turned out to be quite gifted with the individual mortar. She and her *quadrinômes* were picked to form a 600 m team, or B team. Their role was to give suppressing fire between 300 m and 600 m ahead of them to give cover to their affiliated A team, or assault team.

During the tenth week, they practiced mountain warfare in the Pyrenean mountains. It was the middle of October, and there was absolutely no snow. Her Norwegian *quadrinôme* was disappointed.

There was a lot of hiking, and a little climbing and abseiling down, and, most importantly, drinking. The 10th week was when bottles of alcohol started to make their way to the legionnaires, and to Aisha's surprise, their NCOs encouraged them to drink.

"You don't like alcohol?" Sergeant Koskela asked Aisha, one evening at dinner. "Try this: *Koskenkorva*. Finnish Vodka. Everybody likes it."

Aisha tried a few sips. It did not taste good, and warmth filled her stomach.

"I know you are not even eighteen," Sergeant Koskela said. "But you are in the legion. Legionnaires drink. Be part of the legion!"

"It's a pity there is no snow," Torbjørn Eriksen complained, "I would have shown you how Norwegians ski."

"Finns ski better than Norwegians," the sergeant replied. "If you like the mountains so much, you should apply to the 2nd REG, the Foreign Engineers."

"I still hope I make it to the paratroopers," Torbjørn replied.

"The Paratroopers?" Sergeant Koskela said. "What is good about the Parachute Regiment?"

"They are the toughest," Torbjørn answered.

"They are the stupidest," the sergeant retorted. "What do you want? Do you want to be *arnhemized*? Or do you perhaps prefer to be *dien-bien-phued*? My advice, always keep away from airborne operations, they always end up badly."

Sergeant Koskela explained that Arnhem was town in Holland where British paratroopers had been slaughtered in 1944, and Dien-Bien-Phu was a town in Vietnam where French Paratroopers had been decimated ten years later.

During Legionnaire School, they were also told a lot about the history and the structure of the legion. The legion had been created in 1831 by a French king to recruit non-French soldiers that could be expendable in the colonial wars to come. Aisha, who was from Morocco, knew that the Legion had distinguished itself with some quite gruesome massacres in Northern Africa in the nineteenth century. This, however, was not taught in the history of the Legion.

Emphasis was laid on how ancient the legion was. It had been at the service of France's last monarchy, the French Second Republic, the Second Empire, the French Third Republic, the Free French under World War II, the Fourth and the Fifth Republic, and, last but not least, under the European Union.

Aisha's Norwegian *quadrinôme* concluded it was like herpes; once you had it, you could not get rid of it (There was some laughter and no push-ups).

The Legion had won many battles but also lost a few, though always with *honor and fidelity*, as was the legion's motto. A battle that had great importance in the culture of the Legion was the battle of Camarón. In 1863, 62 legionnaires sent by Napoleon III to restore the monarchy in Latin America stood against 3,000 Mexican Republicans. Of course, they had lost, but they had fought gallantly against a far superior force until the last bullet and their last strength. Aisha wondered if it was wise to celebrate a defeat, but, judging by the attitudes of the legionnaires, who seemed to worship Camarón, like Catholics the Virgin Mary, she deemed it wise not to question their faith.

Sergeant Koskela summarized the spirit of Camarón as the Finnish *Sisu: "To the last bullet and the last gasp of air we fight!"*

The legion had three Infantry Regiments, one Cavalry Regiment, equipped with light armored vehicles, two Engineer Regiments, and one Parachute Regiment. The recruits would be assigned to their different regiments at the end of Legionnaire School.

On November 20th, their basic training was over, and they went back to Aubagne, to wait for their assignments. Almost everybody, including Aisha, had put the 2nd REP (*2nd Régiment étranger de parachutiste*) in Corsica as their first choice, except Torbjørn Eriksen. Aisha's ex-Norwegian binôme had finally decided to join the 2nd Foreign Engineer Regiment (2nd REG – *Régiment étranger du génie*) to do some skiing and mountaineering.

The 2nd REG was part of the EU Mountain and Arctic Warfare Division, and its legionnaires had the opportunity to progress to becoming mountain guides, something that had recently attracted Torbjørn's attention. Aisha had put the 2nd

REG as her second choice.

An NCO advised Aisha to lower her expectations. Historically, only four women had made it to the Parachute Regiment. If she wanted absolutely to parachute jump, she should have applied to the 1st Foreign Engineer Regiment (*1er Régiment étranger du genie*), who were in fact parachute combat engineers. She would have stood a chance.

On November 25th, they were given the affection results. A fifth woman had now made it to the parachute regiment.

It was Preshti Ahma.

Aisha felt a bit disappointed, but she got her second choice: She would be a mountain engineer. Perhaps she would get an opportunity to learn how to ski. It was not that bad after all.

The only drawback was that she would have to keep working with that idiot Norwegian who liked to show his dick in the shower.

05: One Week In Sweden (Dec 2095)

In the last week of November, Tintin went to Vienna, where he stayed two days. He had not had the time to see anything of the city, he claimed, but the interview had gone rather well – he was, after all, a Nobel Laureate – and the group exercise as well. All he had to do was now wait and enjoy his Nobel week in Sweden. It was great that Thierry could come with him.

At the end of the following week, Thierry Diakité and Tintin Mutombo flew from Ouagadougou to Paris, in France, where they caught a connecting flight to Stockholm, Sweden. At Arlanda airport, the Congolese delegation was waiting for them. This was irritating, but ambassadors liked to show themselves in the presence of brilliant minds. They took them to a Radisson hotel in downtown Stockholm, located just behind the Grand Hotel, where Nobel Laureates were usually accommodated. Dogs were not allowed in the Grand Hotel and Anatoli Govorov, the co-recipient of the Nobel Prize in Physics who would arrive the following evening, had insisted they should all be accommodated in the Radisson, where he could bring his brown kokoni dog.

On Sunday, Tintin and Thierry had the opportunity to do some sightseeing in Stockholm. It was cold and gloomy. The temperature was slightly above zero Celsius (32 °F), and the air was wet. The day felt dark, partly because of the thickness of the clouds, but mostly because the sun was so low over the horizon in this season. Nightfall started at three in the afternoon, and the Christmas light decorations would not cheer them up.

"Damn it," Tintin said, as they were standing in front of the former Royal Palace, "I had forgotten it took so long to get used to the cold. When I did my PhD in Russia, every autumn, it took me four or five weeks before I got used to it."

On Monday, they met Anatoli Govorov, a tall, hefty man in his late twenties, with short brown hair and blue eyes. Anatoli dragged with him both his little brown kokoni dog and the Russian ambassador.

On Tuesday, Thierry, Tintin, Anatoli, and their respective delegations went to Uppsala, the university city north of Stockholm, to hold a conference at the Ångström Laboratory. After the conference, they had the opportunity to do some sightseeing together with a delegation of Swedish students.

Thierry was particularly impressed by Uppsala's castle. It was located above the cathedral, and one of the bastions was oriented toward the cathedral, its cannons trained at it.

"That's how King Vasa made the bishops obeyed him, in the sixteenth century," one of the Swedish students said.

The students had invited them to a formal dinner in one of their nations. The so-called nations were Uppsala student societies. The dinner started at 17:30 and was over by 21:00, which was the occasion to get rid of both the Congolese and Russian ambassadors. Anatoli also had to leave, as he had to meet his girlfriend arriving at the airport.

Then something happened, which was perhaps the Swedish definition of a student party. The dance floor had so far remained empty, despite the loud music and the blinking lights. Suddenly, some girls started dancing, forming a circle, while all the guys remained sitting and drinking.

Tintin thought it was funny and decided to break the girls' formation, dancing like crazy. Thierry joined in, and more girls, and perhaps a few courageous guys. Most of the young men stayed sitting, drinking, and chatting.

At a certain point, the music changed to slow, and suddenly, all the guys sitting got up and started to look for a dancing partner. Thierry was a mathematician and a modeler, and he thought it was fascinating. Could he design a program to predict the behavior of Swedish male students?

Five minutes later, the slow music stopped, and all the lights were switched on. They were told the party was over. It was 01:00.

Thierry noted that many pairs had formed during the five

minutes of slow music, and everybody was now queueing for the cloakroom to retrieve their coats. In the queue, the remaining single students were desperately trying to find a mating partner. Except perhaps Tintin, who was engaged in a crash course in quantum physics with some drunk Swedish nerds.

After he had retrieved his coat and put his cap on, Thierry found himself outside, and it was freezing. He had lost Tintin. Damn it! His phone was not working in Europe. He was hungry, and he saw lots of people queueing to buy hot dogs. He bought a French hot dog with fries and asked people around if they knew a cheap way to get back to Stockholm. Two young drunk blond girls grabbed him, and one said:

"The cheapest way is to stay with us."

"Yeah. You are the Nobel Prize in Physics? You stay with us," the other one said, sounding even drunker.

Thierry protested it was a mistake, but the two girls took him to a flat nearby, where they were joined by other students. There was a lot of vodka and even more tequila. One of the girls kissed him several times. Then, they left the flat and jumped in to a taxi. Thierry remembered they were two guys and two girls. They arrived somewhere, and he found himself in the room of the girl who had kissed him.

The next morning, the girl told him he was in a student corridor, a little way outside Uppsala. He asked the way to the station.

There was a bus, but it was too complicated to buy a ticket. One needed a European smartphone, which he did not have. He decided to walk.

At the train station, he met Tintin. He was in a very good mood. He had solved it, he said. Drinking a lot with mathematicians was helpful. He now knew how to make a spaceship travel at warp 100.

Later that day, Tintin and Anatoli had to give another conference at Stockholm University.

Then on Friday, they had to go to the academy, but Thierry stayed at the hotel, as he had caught a cold.

On Sunday 10 December was the formal ceremony. Male participants had to wear full evening dress. Swedes were funny, Thierry thought. Both modern and conservative at the same time. A country full of paradoxes.

The official ceremony took place in the Concert House where the Swedish president would call all of the laureates of the four different prizes and give them their Nobel medals.

Alice Fù was awarded the Nobel Prize in Chemistry 2095 for the discovery of the green matter. The slim black-haired lady of medium height shook the President's hand as she accepted the Nobel medal. She was the first Afro-Chinese person to ever receive a Nobel Prize.

Anatoli Govorov and Tintin Mutombo were awarded the Nobel Prize in Physics 2095 for their now proven unified gravity theory. A few hand-shakes with the Swedish President and it was over.

In his guidebook, Thierry had read that it used to be the king or queen of Sweden who awarded the prize. Sweden had become a republic in 2060 after the monarch herself had called a referendum and asked her subjects to vote for the establishing of a republic to prevent her spoiled son from becoming king. A unique case in history.

When the other European monarchies had collapsed, it had been in completely different contexts. In Spain, it had been the repeated affairs involving the royal family, and their inability to prevent the independence of Catalonia that led to their fall. In Belgium, sexual abuse of minors by members of the royal family had marked the end of their monarchy, and of the country with it. Belgium had since then been divided into two different states, Wallonie and Flanders, as well as an independent district: Brussels C.E., the capital of Europe.

In Norway, the Netherlands and Luxembourg, the monarchy had also been abolished in the aftermath of numerous affairs and scandals. Only in Sweden had a monarch asked for the abolishment of monarchy, in order to have it end with dignity.

After the prize ceremony, they went to the banquet in Stockholm's city hall. It was a bit too grandiose for Thierry's taste, but he had the chance to briefly meet Ralf Åhman, the director of WARSEC. The latter was an Afro-European in his late thirties with his right eye never completely open. Ralf was sorry Thierry had failed the entrance exam to WARSEC Young Professional Program, but encouraged him to apply again next year. If he got through, he would start directly as a level 5 with a chance to become level 6 after two years, quite a senior rank within WARSEC. As a comparison, Ralf Åhman himself was a level 10.

Thierry was not missing much, should he join only the next year. WARSEC was currently making progress with the design of a first interstellar spaceship and the setting up of a lunar base, but there would not be much action before 2097.

At the banquet, Thierry was seated next to Anatoli's mother and got to know more about his family. She was a physics teacher. Her husband, Anatoli's father, had not been able to come, as he had, sadly, been suffering from cancer of the pancreas for 7 years now. Immunotherapy was doing miracles in keeping cancer in check, but it was never checkmate.

Anatoli's father had been an NCO onboard a Russian submarine. Twelve years earlier, there had been a nuclear incident onboard the *Novosibirsk,* and he had been irradiated. Anatoli's mother was certain it was what had caused the cancer, but they had received hardly any compensation from the Russian state.

After the banquet, some students wanted to take the Nobel Laureates to a party at the Stockholm School of Economics. It was a party thrown by businessmen and for businessmen.

Tintin was not interested at all and suggested that they should go to the movies and watch Star Wars episode 27, instead. Anatoli and his girlfriend, Liisa, were interested, and so were Ralf and Alice Fù.

They went to the movies, of course followed by journalists. The movie was good but not great. At the exit of the theater, Tintin was interviewed by a Swedish TV reporter in a memorable sequence:

"Frankly," he said. "*Star Wars* is not as good as *Star Trek*. This is science fiction, yes, but with too much fiction and not enough science. It's much more like fantasy. Just look at the holographic skype-like conversation they are having while they are on planets located far, far away from one another. How could it work? Radio waves cannot travel faster than light. So if you communicate by radio waves between two star systems located fifteen light years apart, it will take thirty years to exchange two sentences. And believe me, you don't need a Nobel Prize in Physics to find that out!"

06: The Cambridge Four
(March-May 2096)

Sanne van der Maas, Samir Benyamina and Magnus Li had all obtained their driving licenses in December 2095. Carsten Nielsen had failed the driving test, but he still had five hours of free driving lessons at his disposal, and his friends were prepping him to pass on the next attempt.

The cleaning situation had consistently improved in Barrack 5. A few days after they had received the piece of advice from the caretaker, Samir had gone down to the first floor, at a time when Johan Staël and his three rich corridor friends were home.

Carsten and his corridor mates had brought the four into the kitchen. Samir had politely asked them to help with the cleaning. Everybody would clean together, including Samir, who did not even live on that floor. Should they refuse, he would punch every single one of them until they accepted.

They had laughed.

Samir had punched Johan Staël straight in the jaw, grabbed

his neck, kicked him in the face with his knee and pushed him onto the floor. He had reiterated his request to the other three. They had hesitated. He had punched Édouard de Birran in the face, a straight left and a right hook. He had fallen to the floor. The other two had then agreed to help with the cleaning.

Carsten's corridor mates had promised to co-finance the fine Samir would have to pay. To their surprise, neither Johan Staël nor Édouard reported them to the police. In fact, they even received chocolates and a thank-you note from Johan Staël's father for Christmas. Samir decided to quit trying to understand the logic of the world.

Life in Cambridge went on more less the same into 2096, with a few changes in the sleeping arrangements. Ingrid had dumped Johan Staël and moved into a student room on the university campus, where her new boyfriend lived. Magnus had moved into Ingrid's room, which was also Camilla's, his new girlfriend. Samir had taken advantage of it to bring Emily in, as she was all too happy to move out of her father's flat. All hoped that Ingrid and her dude would not break up too early. Though Sanne insisted they were a couple, Samir and Emily would keep referring to each other as 'fuck buddies'.

Emily was rather thrilled when she started an internship at the Emergency Room ("Rather blood than shit"), but she rapidly got disillusioned:

"Oh my god, Samir," she said one night, as she was cuddling

him in bed. "You have no idea how some people get beaten up in South Cambridge. It's indescribable… Now I understand why you get only a minor fine for punching somebody. Those who go to jail do much worse…"

"I know…" Samir replied. "I grew up in Beaudotte."

"That's where you learnt to fight?"

"Yes," Samir replied. "When I was thirteen, there was this guy who would pay us, kids, to attack football supporters, every time the PSG was playing. I never liked football. But I liked fighting…I was young and stupid."

"Who was giving you the money?"

Samir remained silent.

Sanne had somehow managed to get her hands on a broken cleaning robot, from the school she was working in. It was up to them to fix it. Sanne greatly appreciated Samir's systematic approach to error finding. He was definitely better at this than she was, even though she had grown up in a robotic environment. She suggested that Samir should try to apply to the nearby community college to study robotics, after his second year of Civil Service. That way, he could stay in Cambridge with Emily. He needed to obtain better grades in mathematics, but she could help him if he took an evening class the following year.

By the end of February, the robot was working properly, and Barracks 12 and 5 used it alternately. The robot was efficient at cleaning the bathrooms, the corridor and part of the kitchen. It could not do the dishes, but Samir did not mind.

However, it was a pity it could not take their clothes to the laundry and bring them back once they had been cleaned. Samir hated to do the laundry, and so did Emily, who was used to having her dad doing it for her. As a result, Samir complained he was doing all the chores, cleaning the kitchen and doing the laundry, while Emily stated that she had been doing all the rest, and it was not her fault if the robot had taken over her chores.

At the old people's home where both Samir and Carsten were working, things were as bad as ever. Supply was scarce, and they all tried to be careful with the use of plastic gloves. Once in a while, a few residents pegged out, and Samir had stopped being affected by it. He was becoming as cynical as Dr. Green. The trick was to pretend one was sorry when the family was coming, to be left in peace.

The only resident Samir had real empathy for was Gareth Fraser, the 97-year old English man who had all his mental faculties, but had asked to be put in the dementia department so as to be able to remain in Cambridge and not be sent elsewhere. In the 2030s, he had been one of the leading authors of *A European Dilemma*, a comprehensive sociological study in Europe that had concluded that a mandatory European Service for Europeans was the best way to favor 'integrationism' over 'congregationism' in the European liberal societies. He had thereafter become a very respected professor in political science at Cambridge University and was still sometimes consulted by his former students.

He was always in a good mood and helped all the slavants to feel more positive. Samir's English had improved considerably and he even caught a kind of UK accent. Gareth thought Samir ought to thank the European Service for this. Not being able to speak English properly meant, at the end of the twenty-first century, that it was almost impossible to find a decent job in Europe.

"You see, Samir," Gareth said once, as Samir was bringing food to his room, "When I grew up, at the beginning of the century, only exchange students, among young Europeans, were given a chance to discover other countries. Only those who were already better-off were given a chance to feel even more European. The European project just forgot about the working classes. EU leaders believed that everybody could just go to university and obtained a master's."

"Did they really believe that?" Samir queried. "Even I know that only half of the population has an IQ above 100. That's the definition of IQ measurement."

"Indeed," Gareth smiled. "European leaders believed nonetheless that everybody else in the continent was like them. They failed to see and understand the diversity of the social structure of our societies. They failed to see our liberal democracies were encouraging economic, intellectual, and ethnic congregation rather than large-scale social integration.

We paid a high price for this."

Meanwhile, Amina Dörflinger was quite satisfied with herself. She had passed the first term with only As and one B, despite spending most of her time at the climbing gym, where she was either working or training.

Of course, she had had a limited social life and had not got laid in eight months, but that was not the point. When she was competing at the Riga Olympics, she would make up for that. She was keeping a list of which athletes she wanted to nail the following August. The Italian swimmers were at the top of it.

She had started to like Cambridge, its university, its old stone buildings, where one could try to look for fossils. There were fossils on the walls in the middle of the city and passersby would just ignore it. People had no taste. What could be more thrilling than stones?

At the climbing gym, Amina was doing great. She was now lead-climbing all the most difficult routes, which some of them graded 8c, on the first attempt.

By the end of the 21st Century, the French way of grading climbing difficulties had become the world standard. Beginners usually had little difficulty climbing 4a to 4c. Competent climbers would climb 5a to 6a, good climber 6b to 6c, excellent climbers would manage 7a and Amina was at east climbing 8c.

She would end each session by doing thirty pull-ups with twenty kilos (44 lbs) hanging from her harness.

The irritating part was that everybody in the gym was glaring at her. Some were looking at her in awe, but some males were also looking at her as though she were sexual prey. She did not like that. Sanne's ex-fuckbuddy, the handsome, tall, tattooed topless climber, had made several advances, but she had sent him away. A climber with no interest in stones was not worth sleeping with.

One Saturday in March, Amina, Sanne, Emily, and Samir were having a lunch break in the climbing gym's café, after having climbed all morning. They were sitting on a sofa in the corner of the café, eating sandwiches.

"This was a very weird dude," Sanne said, biting into her sandwich.

"You should not sleep with students in economics," Amina remarked, "they are all weirdos, and they don't climb. Try a student in geography instead. Even a biologist is better than an economist."

Sanne swallowed her mouthful and said: "You know, next September, I start a master's in economics here in Cambridge. So, no, not all economists are weird."

"Did he really have bed linen with Margaret Thatcher's portrait on it?" Emily asked

"Yes."

"Did he lick you?" Amina asked.

"Sadly, no," Sanne replied. "He was only thinking with his dick. But the worst was that he was already saying he wanted kids!"

"What a douche!" Amina said and bit into her sandwich.

"With so many idiot men," Emily replied, "I'm happy we have this no-child benefit. Sadly, I'm already turning 21 in September this year… I'm only entitled to it for another four and a half years."

"You women are lucky," Samir said. "Between 15 and 25 you get a no-child benefit for not having children."

"You men are lucky," Amina replied. "You cannot get pregnant at all".

Sanne drank from her bottle of water and said: "Too many men used to make too many young women pregnant and not take their responsibilities. Studies showed that women having kids too early were more prone to becoming single mums, missing out on higher education opportunities and living in poverty. Even if it affected only 8% of all women, it led to too high a number of kids growing up in poverty in the first half of the century. With this no-child benefit for young women, you encourage them to think of their careers before even considering getting a baby. It has worked pretty well."

"The best is not to have any babies at all, ever," Amina stated and she bit into her sandwich.

"What do you mean?" Emily asked.

Amina took some time to chew and swallow her food before she explained: "We live in a pretty fucked-up world. Say you get a child in 2110 when you are in your thirties. It will have a decent chance to live until 2200. Believe me, you don't want to be alive or to have any of your relatives alive in 2200."

"Why is that?" Samir asked.

"We know for sure that the Anthropocene will be the shortest geological period on Earth," Amina answered. "It started with human industrial activities, and it will end when mankind cannot live on Earth anymore. By 2300 at the very latest."

"Is it so bad?" Sanne asked.

"The Little Ice Age that started in the fifteenth century was most certainly a real ice age. It was cancelled out by the Industrial Revolution and the greenhouse gas emissions."

"The Little Ice Age? What is that?" Samir asked.

Amina explained: "Well, between the 1400s and early 1900s, the climate was much colder than now. All the rivers in England and Flanders would freeze every winter. In 1912, a passenger line, the Titanic, was sunk by an iceberg on parallel 41. Same latitude as northern Spain. Have you seen many icebergs at this latitude nowadays?"

"There are not many icebergs left, are there?" Sami said.

"No. The industrial revolution, combined with exponential population growth, going from 1.3 billion in 1850 to 10.4 billion today, offset the consequences of the slower sun activity and the Milankovitch cycles."

"Ooh lala," Emily said, shaking her hand. "I had forgotten we had a geologist in our company."

However, Sanne had an objection. "It's not that bad. Mankind has practically eradicated industrial greenhouse gas emissions since 2050."

"True," Amina admitted. "But the CO2 concentration in the atmosphere is still too high. Living beings still breathe out carbon dioxide. Acidification of the oceans, urbanization… 40% of the known species that existed in 1990 are now extinct. Of course, everybody talks about the extinct pandas, or bonobos, or gorillas. But the most important species that have disappeared are those that, for some reason, the media don't mention. It is impacting all our ecosystem."

"I've heard about the book *Feedback of the Earth*, by Sheldon Cooper," Sanne said. "Is he your professor?"

"You mean *Doctor* Sheldon Cooper," Amina replied. "Yes, he is one of my teachers. His thesis is simple: Global warming has re-allocated water masses on the surface of the Earth, through the melting of ice caps and the thermal expansion of the oceans. The shift is increasing the magma convection in the mantle. The result: more earthquakes and volcanic eruptions. Think of the Big Two in California in 2081. It surprised all geologists. If the frequency of major volcanic eruptions also increases, it may generate a global cooling within a hundred years. In the event of a super-volcanic eruption, it would be even worse. In any case, within a hundred years, 70% of the species present on Earth at the start of the 20th century will have become extinct, and within 200 years, 90%, including mankind."

The climbers sat still and silent a moment. Only Amina was peacefully drinking from her bottle of mineral water.

"So, you mean," Sanne finally said, "that it would have been less than half a millennium between the start of the industrial revolution and the end of mankind. What about space colonization? WARSEC is working on it."

"I doubt it will ever work," Amina replied. "As to mankind's fate on Earth, it's geologically and geophysically certain. You cannot cheat geology. In such circumstances, all you ever want to do is enjoy life while you can, enjoy skiing while there is some snow left, and never, repeat, never, have any children. They would only live in hell."

Sanne had been glancing at the latest issue of *The Chained Palmiped*, a European weekly satirical paper still printed on actual paper. It was the sister newspaper of its French speaking counterpart, *Le Canard Enchaîné*.

"Well," she said, "Without being over-dramatic, things may get bad as soon as this year."

"What is it? Samir asked.

"Phosphate peak," Sanne replied. "As you know, Morocco has a monopoly on the production of phosphate, which is needed for fertilizer and farming. They constantly increase the price, and other countries are unhappy with that. Including our President. According to the *Palmiped*, President Bonavita has just asked the EU Military Headquarters to prepare contingency plans in case of a crisis with Morocco, including an invasion of the country."

"You can't be serious!" Emily exclaimed.

Sanne was reading further in the article and added: "Of course, state officials say that this is just routine, and they regularly devise contingency plans. Twenty years ago, there was such a plan to study the possible invasion of Switzerland."

"You see," Emily retorted, "This is just bullshit. Generals must be employed to do something to earn their salary after all."

The risk of a European-Moroccan war was indeed very remote, and did not stop the four of them enjoying their time in Cambridge. In April they also started climbing outdoors.

Amina was training very hard for the coming Summer Olympics in Riga. It did not even affect her study results. She was mostly getting As, which, in England, was not that easy.

Seeing that her climbing friends were getting better and better, Amina decided to organize a road trip to the Lofoten Islands, in Norway, where there were some legendary climbing routes.

None of them had been there, and they were all thrilled. They scheduled it for the week of the Ascension, between the 19th and 27th of May, as both Samir and Sanne managed to obtain a few days off, while Emily and Amina had no class.

They rented a little hydrogen powered car and packed all their climbing equipment and Amina's two tents in it. Carsten, who had just obtained his driving license, also joined them, though he planned to just stay at the camp and not follow the climbers.

They drove north to the Scottish border, which was complicated to cross: south of it, one would drive on the left, while on the Scottish side driving on the right was the rule. They drove on to Edinburgh, where they boarded a night ferry to Trondheim in Norway.

The following day, they set out on a 14-hour drive to Lofoten Island, where they arrived on Monday 22nd. Driving was easy as nights were short at this time of the year. On the road, they enjoyed the blue fjords cutting through the green coast and carving into steep grey cliffs.

Emily and Samir, who had never been to the mountains, were really impressed by the Norwegian landscape. When they stopped to buy food, Carsten would speak Danish to Norwegians, and they would answer in their mother tongue. It was funny. Carsten spoke as if he were constantly about to puke, whereas the Norwegians sounded as if they were constantly overwhelmingly happy.

For Sanne, it was the first ever true holiday she had ever taken in her life, and it was unforgettable. In Norway, they could pitch their tent anywhere they liked. They did it as close to their intended climbing routes as possible.

For Sanne, Samir, and Emily, it was the first time they climbed long walls and they had to practice how to abseil down. Amina had first climbed a long pitch, installed her belay station and secured Samir and Emily on one rope, and Sanne on the second rope.

The four of them were hanging uncomfortably in their harness attached to the belay with slings and carabiners arranged in what was called 'cow tails'.

Amina was smiling at the splendid fjords in the background. "You like it?" she asked, "Nothing can beat that, can it?"

The three other climbers did not answer. They were mostly focused on the fifty meters (165 ft) of void beneath them. It did not feel as safe as on an in-door climbing wall.

Amina was handling the ropes like a mountain guide. She had put a sling around a spike and added a quick link to it. She passed one of the ropes through the quick link and tied the two ropes with a fisherman's knot.

"Rope," she yelled, and threw away the blue rope.

Samir felt sudden anguish as he saw the rope fall away. Eventually, the fisherman's knot stopped it, and he felt relieved, but Amina was already yelling "Rope," and throwing away the yellow rope.

"OK," Amina said, "Now it's easy peasy. Put all your belaying devices on the rope. Sanne, at the top, you will be last. Then Emily, and Samir."

The three climbers set the two ropes through their belaying devices and into their locking carabiners, which they locked onto their cow tails, the slings attached to their harnesses.

"Good," Amina said after doing a thorough check. "Now the prusiks. Install them so that I can check. I will be securing from below, but I want to be sure you can handle it."

Prusik loops were thin cords of rope meant to be twisted in a special knot around an abseil rope. When a climber pulled on the prusik, it would grip the rope and hold on to it. They were efficient safety mechanisms. The three climbers each took their prusik loops, rolled them around the rappelling ropes and clipped them into their harnesses, using locking carabiners. Amina had been ready for a long time.

"OK. See you down there," she said, and jumped backwards.

Samir felt uneasy as he saw Amina disappear beneath them. They were now three first-time abseilers hanging on a belaying station in godforsaken Norway. At least the weather was fine. Finally, he heard Amina's voice:

"Clear."

Samir was next to go. He wanted to start abseiling down, but he could not. Something was holding him back.

"Samir," Emily said. "Your cow tail: you have to unlock it."

As Samir unlocked his cow tail from the belay station, at first he had a moment of doubt. Would the belaying device hold him on the rope, or would he fall fifty meters? The belaying device held. He was on the rope. He was very scared to begin with, but as he was abseiling down, he fell more and more confidently, using his two legs to push his body away from the cliff. It was like jumping away from it. Finally, he had done it! He had done his first abseil down!

Sanne was the last to abseil down, and when she had made it, she said: "Climbing is at least as scary as being in space. I admit I have never spacewalked, but for all my time on Mars, I have never been so scared."

That made Amina smile: "In short, you are saying that if I fail my career in science, then I can still be a space geologist?"

After the abseiling, Amina declared that Emily and Samir were good to climb on their own. She would climb with Sanne, who could follow her on harder routes.

From the 23rd of May onward, the sun didn't set anymore. While Sanne and Emily were very much impressed by the midnight sun, Samir and Amina were rather amazed by the possibility of climbing at any time of the day or night. If it was raining during the day, they would go into their tent, rest, and wait for the rain to stop. If the rain stopped only at eleven in the evening, it was not an issue, they would wait 2 hours for the cliff to dry and climb from one in the morning until the next rain clouds came.

At the camp, Carsten had his computer, and he had brought a solar panel to charge it. One afternoon when it was raining cats and dogs, they had a very good time watching the horror movie *The Lone Hiker*. The story was set in Swedish Lappland, and French and German tourists were inexplicably disappearing, immortalizing the expressions 'It's a Froggy trap!' and 'It's a

Jerry trap!' A sequel to that movie, *The Lone Hiker Hikes Again*, was expected in late September that year.

The holidays went way too fast. On Friday 25 May, it was already time to leave. On the ferry boat taking them back to Edinburgh, they realized they had completely missed the news for a whole week.

While they were happily climbing, there had been a major earthquake in Nice, southern France. On TV, *Bollox News*, as the news broadcast by the Bolloré Media group had been nicknamed, mentioned at least 20,000 killed and 340,000 homeless.

07: MOUNTAIN TROOPS (MAY 2096)

The Chained Palmiped had once written that the army was the most conservative branch of the European Armed Forces. It was indeed very attached to the tradition and the history of the regiments that composed it.

When the European Union had created the EU Armed Forces, the respective navies and air forces of the Member States had been quickly merged into a single EU Navy and EU Air Force. The stakes were indeed too high in terms of cost saving.

However, the financial pressure on the army had not been remotely close, as the European Parliament had been content with equipment standardization and a centralized chained of command. As a result, the European Army regiments got to keep their names and were, even in 2095, more or less the same as they had been seventy years earlier. Regiments were only reminded of their European obedience through the divisional order.

The 2nd Foreign Engineer Regiment (2nd REG – *2ème Régiment Étranger de Génie*), which was located in Saint-Christol, about 120 km north of Marseille, belonged to the mountain troops. On the EU divisional level, it belonged to the Arctic and Mountain Warfare Division (AMWD), a division that regrouped Arctic rangers from northern Europe, Alpine rangers from continental Europe, mountain artillerymen and mountain engineers.

Besides its logistic and support companies, the 2nd REG had three combat companies, each consisting of 130 combat engineers.

The 2nd Company was commanded by Captain Antoine Léger, a short, slim 26-year- old French Officer who had just joined the Mountain legionnaires after four years in an armored regiment. He wanted to be in an army outfit "*slightly more multinational than the European army average.*"

Aisha Barjaoui had been assigned to the 2nd Company's 3rd platoon, under the command of Lieutenant Guido Hoffman, a tall, strong young German officer. Each platoon had a 6-man command group, four drivers and three 7-man combat squads. The first squad was led by Sergeant Paul Uwilingiyimana, a tall Rwandan, whose name was often shortened to Uwil.

Corporal Singh from India, Private First-Class Tran from Cambodia and Private Gonzales from Argentina formed the squad's A team. Corporal Lee from China, Private First-Class Jean-Claude Rheinfeldt from Luxembourg and Private Aisha

Barjaoui from Morocco formed the B team.

Aisha noted that, besides her, there was only one other woman in the whole platoon, a certain Karen Brown, from the USA. She was a corporal, and the platoon's medic. She had served in the Legion for almost four and a half years, and her contract would be terminated by the end of August. She had been quite satisfied with her service. Not only had she obtained a driving license for free, but also, she had been given the opportunity to train as a medic and to take some extra courses to get the equivalent of A-levels; she, who had been a high school drop-out, back in the States. In the spring, she meant to apply to all the EU military med-schools and hoped to be accepted by one of them.

Aisha wondered if she would be able to do as well as Karen and take the equivalent of A-levels. She was not at all interested in becoming a medic, though. She was more interested in fighting, or perhaps mountaineering.

From December to January, Aisha trained in both urban warfare and explosive techniques. In February, she was sent to Savoie for a three-week basic course in military skiing, together with all the new recruits, including Torbjørn Eriksen, who had been assigned to the third squad of Lt. Hoffman's platoon.

It was the first time she had actually touched snow, and it was wonderful. The mountains around Bourg-Saint-Maurice looked more impressive than those she had been on in the

Pyrenees or those she had seen from quite some distance, back in Morocco.

Most of the new recruits were completely new to skiing, with the notable exception of Torbjørn, who seemed to have skied all his life. By the end of the first week, she was the second-best skier, though far behind Torbjørn in terms of speed and agility.

It was the first time Aisha had been instructed by regular soldiers, and not legionnaires. Most of their instructors were Alpine rangers of the regular army, and they were quite patient with the newbie mountain engineers Aisha and her fellow legionnaires were.

On the second week, they started ski touring. They would hike up slopes with skins under their skis, carrying their military equipment. On the top, they would remove the skins, tighten their boots and bindings and ski down. Of course, with all the equipment, most of the new recruits were falling quite a lot, but overall it was fun.

When she was back in Saint-Christol, Karen asked her:

"So have you seen them?"

"Seen who?" Aisha asked.

"The Alpine rangers, idiot," Karen replied. "Your instructors. What did you think of them? Did you fuck any?"

"No… there was no time for flirting."

"Come on, there are hardly any women among the Alpine rangers. When you are there, you can have who you want, when you want. Just try to avoid the officers, it could lead to a situation."

"Why, have you seen a lot of…action?" Aisha asked.

"This is the army, not the Vatican. You are seventeen! Believe me, there won't be much action for you if you only look in our regiment. First of all, with a motto such as *honor and fidelity*, do not expect the men in the regiment to hit on you. The officers will see to that. And even if they did, it would probably be the worst sex in your life… probably. I have my sources. Many legionnaires only think with their dicks and do not use their tongues and fingers. Outrageous!"

"You seem to know a lot."

"Come on, more than four years in the army! I have not tried any legionnaires, honestly, but I have met dudes from various armed forces, even from the US. Don't waste your time with navy seals, too big chests, horrible when they are on top of you. Delta forces are nice, a bit shy, but you can tame them. The best are the French Alpine rangers. They are certainly the slimmest rangers on Earth, but they are muscular, and their buttocks, my god, their buttocks… always so firm! And they know their stuff."

During March and April, Aisha got a chance to practice her ski touring skills as her platoon did several mountain exercises. At the weekends, Sergeant Uwilingiyimana usually called for volunteers to do some civilian ski touring excursion. Aisha always volunteered, and so did Torbjørn, who would spend more time with the first squad than his third squad. Lieutenant

Hoffman sometimes joined in, as would a few NCOs from the support company.

First and second squads shared the same dorm. Since Aisha was always away skiing at the weekend, the others blamed her for never cleaning the room, and Corporal Singh would have her do some extra cleaning duties.

Karen explained to Aisha that the main reason she was ordered to do all the cleaning was that she was a girl. In Corporal Singh's male supremacist view, if there was only one girl among twelve soldiers, then she should be the one doing all the cleaning. In the end, Sgt. Uwilingiyimana sorted this out, and Cpl. Singh changed his attitude.

In that same period, Aisha started her driving lessons. Once again, she proved to be more able than many other recruits. Torbjørn found driving lessons particularly difficult, and he put the blame on French civilian drivers, who were, in his opinion, a menace to road safety.

Aisha was the first of the new recruits to obtain her driving license. She got it on the day she turned 18, on 22 May 2096. As she was sitting in the driving school car, waiting for the instructor to deliver her temporary driving license, the ground started to shake.

"*Putaing, ça commence à bouger pas mal, heing ?*" the instructor said ('Bloody hell, it's starting to quake a lot, isn't it?').

Aisha and her instructor went out of the car and waited in the village square, where most of the inhabitants had gathered. The earthquake lasted for five minutes. Apart from a few flower pots falling from the windows, not much damage had occurred in Saint-Christol.

When she was back at the military camp, the ground started quaking again. This time it lasted sixteen minutes, and all the legionnaires stopped their activities and grouped in the assembly area. This second earthquake, though longer than the first one, was only slightly stronger, and there was very little damage done to the regiment quarters.

Suddenly, the colonel turned up and shouted:

"There has been a major earthquake in Nice. The major axes of communications have been cut. The 2nd REG has been called in. Support company and 2nd Company: officers and NCOs briefing immediately. Rally in 15 minutes. Pack your gears. No weapons needed, but take extra water supply."

Jean-Claude Rheinfeldt, the tall and bald Luxembourger from Aisha's squad explained the reason for the water: "When there is an Earthquake, water pipes break. The whole city may be several days without any water. When I was deployed for an Earthquake in Italy, it was for ten days."

A moment later, the twenty-eight men and two women of second platoon rallied around Lieutenant Hoffman.

"It's pretty bad," he said. "The motorway is completely cut

off; several tunnels have collapsed. All the bridges over the Var river are in the water. The airport and the harbor are the only ways into the city, but they expect a tsunami any time. The 3rd EU Fleet has been mobilized. As far as we are concerned, the support company will make a dash by road to St-Laurent-du-Var to repair the sea road and cast a bailey bridge over the river. They will be supported by first platoon, who will clear the sea road at Cannes. The sea road shall become the emergency road from Cannes to Nice, as the Motorway is cut."

"What about Tsunami?" Rheinfeldt asked.

"According to the seismologists," the lieutenant replied, "it should occur before the support company arrives with all their trucks and bulldozers. They will need at least five hours to get there. The first platoon will have been dropped by choppers before that to clear the way at Cannes. The third Platoon will clear roads of obstacles North of Nice. We will clear the roads East of Cannes, to open an emergency road to Monaco and Italy. Helicopters will take us there…"

Aisha did not listen to the rest. She was going do a ride in a helicopter! How lucky she was! They would even use explosives in a real situation. She was really excited.

A moment later, six helicopters landed, and Lieutenant Hoffman's platoon boarded two of them. Before they took-off, the colonel saluted and shouted:

"Engineers clear the way!"

"Of course, we clear the way", Jean-Claude screamed so that

Aisha could hear him through her noise cancelling headset. "We are engineers, either we block the way, or we clear the way."

In Aisha's helicopter, the first squad sat with Hoffman's command squad and two drivers. After a twenty-minutes flight, they arrived above the sea in the vicinity of Cannes, and Aisha saw the two helicopters transporting the first platoon break formation and head for a road section near the seaside on which some rocks had collapsed.

The remaining helicopters kept flying eastward, toward the city of Nice, which they reached in a couple of minutes. Past the Airport, Aisha's helicopter descended a bit, and she saw how devastating the earthquake had been. At least half of the houses below seemed to have collapsed, columns of people were walking on the streets inland or toward the castle hill and Mount Boron.

The helicopters left the coast and flew inland toward the motorway leading to Italy. She could soon see that the motorway had had been cut off with the destruction of two bridges. A few dozens of cars had been trapped, and their passengers seemed just to wait by the side of the road. Some were perhaps wounded, she thought.

Beyond the motorway was the *route du Laghet* running parallel to it. Aisha could see the two sections that had been cut-off by rocks falling from the northern hill flank.

Aisha's helicopter landed on the road close to one of the

roadblocks, where a car seemed to have been caught by the falling rocks. The mountain engineers stepped off rapidly, and Karen made a dash for the car.

"Karen?" The Lieutenant asked.

"A mother and her two children. All of three dead. The airbags worked, but it was not enough. Aisha, can you help me to extract the bodies?"

Aisha helped. It was the first time in her life she saw dead bodies, and she was not feeling thrilled anymore. The helicopter ride had been fun. What was at the end of it was not. The mother was missing her head, and there was blood everywhere. One of the young kids seemed to have been killed instantly, but the other kid seemed to have bleed for a long time, alone in the car, with the blood of her mother all over him. It must have horrible for him.

At that moment, they heard some sirens.

"That must be the tsunami warning," the Lieutenant said.

The first Earthquake had occurred at 11:07, the second earthquake at 11:42. The engineers had landed at 13:10, and the tsunami must have occurred a short while after. The *Route du Laghet* was too far inland for the engineers to have any sight on the coast. The tsunami was not their issue, they had to focus on their mission.

They started clearing up the roadblocks, blowing the bigger blocks in smaller blocks. On several occasions, Aisha had to correct Jean-Claude who was putting way too much explosive at once. No wonder he was only Private First class after seven years in the Legion, Aisha thought.

Rheinfeldt was a European citizen from Luxembourg and he had joined the Legion, because none of the regular branches of the EU Armed Forces wanted of him. Jean-Claude Rheinfeldt had served all his seven years in the 2nd REG. When he renewed his five-year contract two years earlier, they finally made him Private First Class.

However, he was still making basic mistakes when putting charges, and Aisha would not trust him to defuse a bomb. Perhaps was it the reason they had put him in charge of the light machine gun.

Around 14:30, they heard the sound of jet engines. A moment later they saw paratroopers jumping from four cargo planes above the back-country.

"The 2nd REP", Corporal Lee said. "They are probably providing assistance to people in need more inland."

Later, the Lieutenant came back with some lighter vehicles equipped with front-hoes as well as a handful of construction workers he had commandeered.

It was late in the night when they were finally joined by the bulldozers the support company. Captain Léger was with them. The bailey-bridge over the Var had been properly assembled, and the emergency road between Cannes and Nice had been opened. The bulldozer platoon was to continue to clear the road until Monaco so that assistance from the Italian side could be received.

At 04:00 in the night, the Eastern emergency road was also open and the engineers were to head for downtown Nice, to help with the search and rescue operations.

Aisha was now exhausted and acted automatically, following the orders from Sgt. Uwil. She remembered hearing agonizing sounds and seeing a lot of bodies, many of them had not been covered.

The engineers were tasked with gathering the dead bodies and putting them into corpse bags with their personal belongings so that they would be identified. They also had to mark where each of the body had been found. Temporary morgues had been set up.

It was a particular ungrateful mission. While Aisha tried to show respect to the dead and handled the deceased as delicately as possible, she noted that Jean-Claude Rheinfeldt just wanted to get over with it. In the beginning, she insisted that he be more respectful, but in the end, she was too tired to complain to him.

When dawn finally came, Aisha realized that there were a lot of military ships off the beach. Some of the wounded were being evacuated by boat.

Around lunch, the Lieutenant had the platoon gathered on the Castle Hill for a longer break. They had been up for thirty hours. As they were trying to get some sleep, they were disturbed by a middle-aged man wearing a suit.

"*C'est une catastrophe, c'est une catastrophe. Tout ça, c'est la faute du gouvernement.*" ('It's a catastrophe. All this is the government's fault')

"Who will you be, disturbing us?" The Lieutenant asked. "My platoon needs some sleep."

"I'm Christophe Estrosa, the mayor of Nice. All this damage… it's the government's fault. They should have forced us to build with earthquake-proof standards."

"Look at the bright side," Rheinfeldt told him in French. "Everything is destroyed. Next time you build up stuff, you can use earthquake-proof standards."

"*C'est la faute du gouvernement,*" the mayor went on ('That's the government's fault').

"Let us sleep, now, *petit con* [small ass]," The Luxembourger retorted. "*Dégage, écrase et barre-toi!*" ('Back off, shut up and fuck-off')

All the legionnaires laughed as the mayor of Nice was sheepishly walking away.

The 2nd Company remained six days in Nice until they were relieved. They worked mainly with the collection of the dead bodies. They had a chance to come across the legionnaire paratroopers of the 2nd REP who were working with the search and rescue. On one occasion, Aisha met Preshti Ahma, with whom she had been in Castelnaudary. She had become a certified paratrooper and proudly showed her parachute insignia on her uniform.

The earthquake had happened on a Tuesday, and the 2nd Company left Nice on the following Monday. By then, electricity and running water were available again in key districts. A working network of emergency roads had been set-up, and most victims had been found. The authorities believed that they would not find any further survivors. The search and rescue efforts were halted, and the missing were reported as dead. The earthquake in Nice had claimed 21,000 dead, 70,000 wounded, and caused more than half of Nice's population to be homeless. It had been the most dramatic earthquake in France's history.

In the news, the firefighters, the EU Navy and the paratroopers got all the credit for the rescue operation following the earthquake. Not a mention was made of Aisha's platoon of mountain engineers. Captain Léger reminded the mountain engineers that it didn't matter. The 2nd Foreign Engineers had cleared the way to Nice, opened emergency roads and helped with the identification of victims. These had been very important tasks, and they all knew it. The way the events had been covered by *Bollox News* would not change it. By 'Bollox News', the captain was referring to Channel 8 from the Bolloré Media Group. It had been nicknamed so because of its usually biased coverage of events.

In June, while Karen went to Lyon to take competitive exams to try to go to military med-school, Aisha and Torbjørn were sent to the southern Alps with the other new recruits for a three-week course in mountaineering. After the Nice earthquake, it was a welcome change of air.

They were trained by Alpine rangers certified as mountain guides. Though they were all higher ranked, they considered the recruits as trainees rather than troopers. They always gave constructive feedback, answered questions, and ensured that the recruits would learn as best they could.

After the first week, both Aisha and Torbjørn proved to be proficient enough to be paired in an autonomous rope team. She loved it. As she felt more confident than Torbjørn, she would lead the rope team most of the time. She loved moving on a ridge. She loved lead-climbing steep sections. She loved that feeling of being committed, though still in control, in such a majestic environment.

Each summit had an identity of its own, and she became quickly familiar with the summits of the area: La Barre des Écrins, le Pelvoux, les Agneaux, Roche Paillons, la Grande Ruine, le Râteau, and the most beautiful one, La Meije. "I want to climb this," Aisha said, pointing at the Queen of Oisan.

Aisha was ranked as the best of the new recruits, and the instructors recommended she should take another course to be certified rope team leader in alpine terrain.

Captain Léger decided she would take the rope-leader

course in the last two weeks of July, which she would complete with a ski-touring course the following winter.

08: Alpine Excursion (June 2096)

At the beginning of June, Emily Chapman obtained her nursing degree. She would start working at Addenbrooke's hospitals in July.

Amina Dörflinger had taken her second term's final exams just after the week spent in Lofoten and obtained only As, with this time not even a single B. Dr. Sheldon Cooper encouraged her to pursue a career in science. "Don't waste your life into the mining industry," he said. "You are too good for that."

As for the slavants' holiday arrangements, both Samir Benyamina and Sanne van der Maas were given the third week of June off.

Amina was trying to convince everybody to spend that week in Chamonix, in the French Alps. Mountaineering conditions were currently good. As far as Amina was concerned, it was also the perfect occasion to have a short holiday before the last stage of her intense training program in Switzerland. The

Summer Olympics, in which she would compete as a Swiss climbing athlete, would take place in Riga in the first fortnight of August.

Even though Samir's situation was financially tight, their holidays did not have to be expensive. Since his father lived in Paris, Samir was entitled to a free train ticket to Paris, from where it was affordable to continue to Chamonix. Public transportation in the valley was free, and they could camp in Montroc, the cheapest camping site in the area. By becoming members of the French Alpine Club, they would get 75% off the night price in the mountain huts, as they were all under twenty-five. Besides, they were strong enough to carry their own food and save the cost of a meal in the hut.

In terms of equipment, Amina could get brand new rucksacks from her sponsor Mammut, while she could provide the whole teams with crampons and ice axes. They would only need to rent or buy mountaineering boots.

As her friends were procrastinating and not committing to any decision, Amina finally said: "Come on, I will show you the movie *Chamonix can't wait*, and then you will decide yourself."

Later that day, the four climbers packed into Samir's room, in Barrack 5 of the slavants' containers, and watched the film on Sanne's computer.

The film started with the usual sensitization message about demographic growth: *The story of this movie is set in 2030. Back then, the world population was about 8.5 billion. In 2096, the world population is about 10.5 billion.*

Chamonix can't wait started in the post-Brexit UK as a group of young English men suddenly realized there would be two weeks of snow in Chamonix for Christmas. Already a rarity in the 2030s. They decided to rent a minivan and get there before the snow would melt but went through a great deal of ordeal: the French customs personnel on strike who would not let English tourists in, mechanical trouble, having to eat frogs on the motorway, and complaining about the French not being able to make a proper cappuccino: those ignorant would use cream instead of milk, even though Italy was their neighbor country! They eventually made it to Chamonix with their minivan but got hit sideways by a base jumper, whose parachute had failed to deploy. When they finally got out of the hospitals, the snow had melted too much already, and they had to ski on rocks. The movie was British and silly. They loved it.

"You saw the mountains, at the end?" Amina said. "Don't tell me you don't want to climb them!"

They left Cambridge on Thursday 14 June early afternoon. While Amina took a flight to Zurich, in Switzerland, where she would meet her childhood friend Daniela, Samir, Emily, and Sanne took the train to Paris, where they arrived shortly before midnight.

The plan was to smuggle the two girls into Samir's father's apartment while fat Ali was snoring and sleeping. Samir's little brothers, Karim and Abdelkader, were at home and helped him with the enterprise.

"The toilets are clogged," Emily whispered. "What shall I do?"

"It's always like that," twelve-year-old Abdelkader whispered back. "Dad is so fat that his poop is enormous. The pipes can't handle it. You have to use the plunger. I can do it."

They did not get much sleep that night. Sanne was sleeping in a bed too short for her, while Samir and Emily were sharing the single bunk bed on top of hers. Samir's father snored heavily throughout the night.

At five, Sanne, Emily, and Samir silently evacuated the flat and made it to the commuter train and to the Gare de Lyon.

The journey across France was pleasant, and all three were wide-eyed when the train entered the Chamonix Valley. The sky was blue, except for a little cloud above the highest summit. The solar reflection on its snowy top was so strong that they had to put their sunglasses on.

"Why does Mont-Blanc have two boobs on its ridge?" Samir asked.

"So that you get more fun when climbing it," Emily replied.

Later that afternoon, they pitched their tent in the Montroc camping site, where Amina and her friend Dani had already pitched theirs.

"The toilets are in horrible shape, here," Sanne complained.

"Don't tell me it's better at the school you are working at," Samir retorted.

In the evening, Amina just laid all the climbing gears on the ground between their tents and allocated the equipment.

"Adjust the crampons now. Check they fit your boots," she said. "Emily, you will be with Daniela. I will rope up with Samir and Sanne. I don't like to have a couple in the same rope team. They always bitch with each other."

As they went through the climbing gear and cooked dinner on the camping stove, Amina said: "I've prepared a hard-core program. I need to be fit for the Olympics, please bear with me."

Later that night, after a short sleep, they woke up at two, ate a quick breakfast made of tea and energy bars and headed for the nearby village of Argentière, through a path in the wood, with their headlamps on. From there, they took a path up the mountain, toward the Aiguilles Rouges massif.

Amina was leading the way, setting a sustainable pace for the team, moving silently under the starry sky. Soon, as dawn was nearing, they could switch off their headlamps. It was already daylight when they made their first break and put their harnesses and helmets on.

They resumed their hike, and Samir's legs were feeling quite heavy when they finally reached the start of the ridge.

"Traverse of the Aiguilles Crochues," Amina said. "It's six in the morning, which means we will be alone and in peace."

That was where the fun part began. Daniela quickly climbed up the first dihedral cliff section and belayed Emily up, who was immediately followed by Amina. Amina placed only three protections, a sling and two quickdraws, and made it to the first pitch before it was Samir's turn to climb, followed by Sanne.

From there, the two rope teams swiftly moved forward on the ridge, the leader at the front. They always ensured that the ropes between them went safely around any rocky spikes.

"So far, you are only climbers," Amina said. "It's about time to upgrade yourself to mountaineers. Many climbers shit their pants when they are on a mountain. Many mountaineers cannot climb even 6b. Try to be a better mix of both."

They had a short break at the top of Aiguilles Crochues. From there, Samir could see the whole valley beneath. In front of them, the Aiguille Vertes, Les Drus, Les Grande Jorasses and of course, Mont Blanc. An Alpine chough landed close to them, looked at them intelligently, and picked up some fallen crisps with its yellow beak.

On the way down, they had to walk on a narrow ridge ledge with the void on either side. Samir loved it. When they had come off the ridge, Amina showed them how to glide down with their boots on the snow slopes.

"We have to take advantage of it," she said, "it's not often there is snow left in June."

They were back at the camp site at 13:00 after racing down

the mountain, and Samir was exhausted, but the day was not over. They jumped into the car Daniela was leasing, a little Fiat, and drove up to the village of Le Tour. From there, they took a steep and eroded path to the refuge Albert Premier.

"It's a shortcut," Amina explained. "They don't want us to use it, because it erodes the mountain. I don't care."

It was Saturday evening, and the mountain hut was overcrowded. Many locals were there to enjoy the weekend, but there were also mountain guides with their clients. After a quick dinner made of noodles they had carried with them, Samir, Emily, and Sanne went to bed immediately, while Amina and Daniela still had the strength to chat with some mountain guides.

The following morning, they climbed on the Aiguille du Tour, by the *couloir de la table*. There were quite some bad rocks, and a large boulder ricocheted only fifteen meters (50 ft) left of Sanne.

Daniela and Emily were first at the top, followed by Amina.

"It was stupid to do that route," she said as she was belaying up Sanne, followed by Samir. "I did not know it was so bad so early in the season."

"This time, we were on the right side of the statistics," Sanne acquiesced as she arrived to the top, "But I don't want to provoke the random functions of the universe too much."

"If we attempt Mont Blanc by the normal route," Daniela

said as she was putting sun cream on her face, "we will end up on the wrong side of the statistics. The Grand Couloir is a bitch. I'm not going there ever again."

"We will test them on ice and snow," Amina suggested. "Perhaps we can do it through Bionnassay. But if they aren't at ease on ice, then we won't do Mont Blanc. I will still have managed to boost my red blood cells anyway."

That afternoon, they made it down to the car just as an evening thunderstorm broke out.

The following day was a rainy day, and they took advantage of it to take the train to Chamonix and have a peek at the city. In the cemetery, Amina showed them the first grave:

"Edward Whymper, the greatest of all English mountaineers. He was the first to climb the Aiguille Verte and the Matterhorn."

They then visited all the sports boutiques and marveled at expensive climbing gear they could not afford. Amina also insisted on going to the geology museum, and the others followed reluctantly.

One of the advantages of the Montroc camp site was that one could obtain a ski pass at a very good price. On Monday, the sun was not shining, but at least it was not raining, and they took the cable car to the Aiguille du Midi.

Sanne and Samir were happy to have Amina hold them on a short rope as they walked down the snow arête to the Vallée

Blanche. The wind was strong, and the mountaineers almost had to squat when moving forward, so as not to be blown sideways. There had been a hail storm in the night, and hail stones were lying all over the glacier. The wind would blow them off the ground and the hail stones hit everything from below. It hurt, especially for Samir, who, for the first time in his life, thought it was perhaps an advantage to be a woman in mountaineering.

"You can stand and pee," Emily yelled in the wind. "Why do you complain you have too big balls?"

They made it to the Pointes Lachenal and started to traverse on an ice slope. It was good practice. They had to use the front teeth of their crampons. In terms of protection, Daniela, who was leading the first rope team, was placing ice screws with carabiners in the ice slope and clipped the rope into them. Sanne, who was last in the second rope team, was removing the screws as they cramponed forward.

As they reached the top of Pointes Lachenal, the wind stopped.

"Let's do the Arrête des Cosmiques," Daniela said. "There is hardly anybody on it, and it leads back to the cable car by a more interesting way than the glacier."

Their next project was very close, and they soon started to attack the ridge. The first part was easy, and they arrived at a spot where they had to abseil down. They had now become quite good at it, and it went fast. Further away, there was a breach where one had to do some more advanced climbing, but mountain guides had carved foot holes for the crampon teeth, and it was not even complicated.

The worst part was the loose ladder they had to use to come back to the cable car station, as they had reached the top of the ridge.

"That way, stupid tourists don't try to go on the ridge without any protection," Daniela explained.

Back at the camp site, they checked the weather forecast. The following day would be rainy, but Wednesday and Thursday would be sunny. Amina and Daniela decided the others were good enough to attempt Mont Blanc. They would take a long way there, but it was the safest road.

The following morning, they took Daniela's car and parked it close to the Aiguille du Midi's cable car. From there, they took the train to Saint-Gervais and the bus to Contamines-Montjoie. The hike to the Refuge des Conscrits was arduous and seemed endless under the pouring rain. Luckily, there were many fewer mountaineers in this mountain hut than in the Albert Premier hut.

The following morning was sunny, and they really enjoyed the traverse of the Dôme de Miage, a hilly snow arête. There were drops on both sides, and if one of the rope mates should lose balance and fall, the other ones were supposed to jump on the other side. In theory. Sanne wondered if it ever worked.

Only mountain guides had the reflex to do that. The best was just not to fall at all.

They arrived at the Refuge Durier in the early afternoon, where the host's welcome compensated for the terrible state of the toilets. The next morning, they woke up at 1:30 and attacked the rocky south ridge of the Aiguille de Bionnassay under a moonless but clear night sky.

After an hour's scrambling, the silence of the night was broken by Emily, whose hands and feet felt freezing.

"Shake your arms like this," Daniela replied, raising her arm and quickly throwing her fist downward.

"Gravity will pull your blood back to your fingers. You will feel warmer."

Despite this technique, they all felt really cold by the time they made it to the top at five in the morning. The sun was about to rise, and they could not wait for it to show itself.

They went on and followed the northeast arête, which sank majestically below them, with a drop on each side. When they reached the Dôme du Goûter, the sun was shining, and they were not freezing anymore. From there, they went past the bivouac Vallaud, an old hut used for emergencies only, and attacked the arête des Bosses, named after Mont Blanc's two boobs, as Samir had described them.

It was now eight in the morning, but the arête was packed with slow rope teams of tourists, ascending from the refuge du Goûter. There were also the faster rope teams, already climbing down.

With the exception of Amina, all were too tired to really enjoy moving forward on the ridge, and Amina almost created an incident, as she impolitely asked a group of slow Czechs to either move their asses or move away.

They finally reached the culminating altitude of 4797 m (16,329 ft), on Thursday 21 June at 9:45.

"Mont Blanc used to be higher," Amina commented. "Global warming. The top glacier is melting down. It will keep losing altitude over the next century."

The other four climbers were too exhausted to really enjoy their achievement but Sanne said, panting:

"Well, at least that was good training to become an astronaut!"

"Why is that?" Samir asked, his gaze on the Chamonix Valley below.

"Besides the commitment grade and the focus on safety, the low oxygen level," Sanne replied.

"How is that relevant to becoming an astronaut?" Amina said.

Sanne gave a short explanation: "Space suits can only be pressurized up to a third of an atmosphere, otherwise the astronauts could not move. Two decades ago, there was even less pressure, and the suits were filled with 100% oxygen to let the astronauts breathe normally. The problem was that astronauts had to prepare their bodies for two hours before doing a space sortie. I had to do it myself when I got out of Mars, as I was using an old space suit. Not very convenient."

"How is it done today?" Samir asked.

"They fill the spacesuits with only 40% oxygen at a pressure of 300 millibars. In short, you get an oxygen amount equivalent to what you would get at 4000 m [13,200 ft]. This is still more than what we breathe here at the top of Mont Blanc. Since the orbital station is pressurized at 700 millibars with 30% oxygen, you only need fifteen minutes to prepare for a space sortie. Quite an improvement."

"What a well invested day," Amina concluded, joking. "We all qualify for a space sorties, if we ever become astronauts. Now careful on the way down."

The descent turned out to be a nightmare. They made it without any trouble as far as Mont-Maudit, but from there the descent was only ice. One section was so icy that even Daniela had trouble holding on. The exhaustion induced by the thin air did not make things any easier.

Seeing how tired her companions were, Amina built a belay station with three ice screws and two slings, and started lowering the other four down. She then installed a V-thread in the ice with a quick link and abseiled down on it. After she had repelled the rope, the group resumed their descent.

When they finally reached the Vallée Blanche, they looked like a company of zombies, and they all felt the discouragement as they saw they had to go up the final ninety meters (300 ft) to the cable car station.

When they were back at the campsite, Daniela thought that they all deserved a cheese raclette.

"I can't," Amina said. "The Olympics are in six weeks, and I can't eat too much fat before then. Besides, French raclette cheese is not as good as Swiss raclette cheese."

That did not stop the others taking her to a raclette restaurant in Agentière, and she ended up eating the most cheese of all of them.

"Today, we burned 15,000 calories, easy," Daniela said. "There is nothing wrong eating some melted cheese."

The Cambridge Four had been very happy with their alpine week. Sadly, it was already over. On Friday, they relaxed at the municipality's swimming pool, and on Saturday, it was time leave. Amina and Daniela to Switzerland, the rest to Cambridge.

09: THE LAST KING OF ENGLAND (JULY 2096)

During the summer, when most Cambridge students were at home with their families, it was easy to find a temporary part-time job. It took four days for Samir Benyamina to obtain a zero-hour contract as a cook at The Honourable Schoolboy, a pub located by the Cam river, in downtown Cambridge. The idea was to earn a few extra euros under the summer, as he had no money left after the week spent in Chamonix.

Sanne van der Maas, because of her status of 'immigrant from Mars', had only one year of Civil Service, instead of the regular two for EU citizens. She was therefore also looking for a summer job before starting a master's in economics the next September. Using Samir's connection, she managed to get hired as a part-time waitress in the same pub as him.

The following Tuesday, Sanne was notified that her WARSEC acquaintances would spend the end of the week in Cambridge. Theoretical physicists Tintin Mutombo and Anatoli Govorov had been asked to hold a conference on the unified gravity theory, while the WARSEC director, Ralf Åhman, and his global safety director, Glover Johnson, had been invited to the Political Science Institution to discuss the future of WARSEC. Sanne suggested they have lunch at The Honourable Schoolboy on Saturday.

Saturday 14 July was a warm, sunny day in Cambridge, and Sanne found the four WARSEC colleagues a table on the terrace giving on to Bridge Street. Not far from the terrace was the Cam river, flowing under Magdalena Bridge, and young families and couples were queueing for the punting boats nearby.

The last time Sanne had seen Ralf and Tintin had been in Burkina Faso, more than a year and a few months earlier. The tall Congolese theoretical physicist in his mid-twenties was wearing too-short green trousers and a white polo shirt, while the forty-year old WARSEC director simply wore jeans and a yellowish short sleeve shirt, revealing his pale brown arms.

She had not met up with Anatoli and Glover since just before Christmas 2094, during the Vienna conference. The tall Russian physicist, in his early thirties, wore shorts, revealing his once white but now rather red, sunburnt hairy legs, in contrast to Glover, the only one in the group wearing a suit, though no tie.

Glover Johnson was a short but muscular black man, now in his late thirties, with an impressive chest circumference. He had originally been an officer in the US Navy, and a specialist in nuclear safety and compact fusion reactors, reaching the rank of rear admiral at thirty-two. According to him, this was mostly because he had written *the* book. The book in question was entitled *How US Navy nuclear safety standards could be used for nuclear deployment in space,* and had led Glover to be detailed to NASA, while retaining his rank, and even being gradually promoted in the US Navy. His work had been decisive in the deployment of the first nuclear reactors in the orbital station back in 2091. After the first successful warping of spacetime in September 2094, when the *Alcubierre* made her first faster-than-light trip, Glover had been detailed to the UN before becoming a permanent WARSEC employee in the position of the Global Safety Director.

After taking the orders, Sanne had to rush to the kitchen and wait on other customers. It felt nice, however, to see her WARSEC friends again, and she wanted to keep a kind of connection to them as she really wanted to work for WARSEC after her studies.

After all, she was the one who had coined the term WARSEC in the first place. WARSEC for World's Agency for the Regulation of Space Exploration and Colonization. She had come up with the name during a brain-storming session with both Glover and Ralf in the latter's office, at the United Nations Vienna Center.

Despite her being kept busy with other customers, Sanne

therefore tried to catch up on what was happening with WARSEC every time she had the occasion.

"Progress on interstellar exploration?" Ralf repeated. "Tintin, that's a question for you."

The tall Congolese man, who had been working in Vienna since January, answered succinctly:

"We are basically ready with the design of the Forward class. We will only be able to start production next year, though. First exemplars should be ready by 2098, and the first interstellar journey may happen as soon as 2099."

"You wish," Glover retorted. "I will not allow any interstellar journey before all the safety standards have been properly verified. It may not be before 2100."

That was typical Glover, Sanne thought. The ex-US admiral came from the submarine branch and with him, it was always safety first.

"We are also working a new class of starship," Anatoli announced. "The *Ambassador* class. Will be 240 m [787 ft] long and 80 m [262 ft] in diameter. An interesting challenge."

"That big?" Sanne was surprised.

"The size of an aircraft carrier," Glover confirmed. "It will be for colonization purposes, provided a suitable spot is found."

Sanne was perplexed: "Is WARSEC looking into interstellar colonization already?"

Ralf smiled: "Not very seriously yet. But if we want to have colonization spaceships in ten to twenty years, we have to start looking into their design now."

Sanne had to wait on a few other tables but came back and poured some water in Ralf's and Anatoli's empty glasses.

"What about WARSEC Ventures?"

Ralf drank from his glass and said:

"All the stakeholders, Boeing, Airbus, et al., have agreed on the design of two aerospace shuttles."

"The Space Hound, initially a dropped Boeing project," Anatoli added, "and the much bigger Space Bear, an abandoned Airbus project. They are pretty cool."

"We will be able to manufacture them on the Moon. Only the high-tech components will be shipped from Earth," Tintin pointed out. "Five tons of components per spaceship. The rest will come from minerals extracted from the Moon."

"As we speak," Glover announced, "the space elevator in European Guyana is working at full speed to ship the equipment to the Moon. We think we will be able to start manufacturing the aerospace shuttles there as early as January next year".

Another waiter cast an evil look at Sanne for standing and babbling instead of attending to other customers. She resumed to her waiting on other customers but came back as soon as she got a chance.

"And Finland?" she asked Ralf. "When do you move to the new Headquarters in Vaasa?"

"In Q2 2097," Ralf replied. "Second quarter of 2097, I mean. Looking forward to it. We are now too many in the Vienna offices."

From the restaurant's terrace, they suddenly saw people wearing Guy Fawkes masks gathering silently and carrying cardboards reading 'United against the Quantology' or 'Don't believe their bullshit, believe in science'.

"Who are these people?" Ralf wondered aloud.

"They are the Anonymous," Sanne explained. "They are protesting against the so-called Church of Quantology, whose headquarters in Cambridge is two houses away."

"The Church of Quantology?" Tintin said, "What is that bullshit?"

"A new age cult," Sanne replied. "They make people believe that by paying for expensive seminars, they can master quantum powers and be in two states at the same time."

Anatoli started laughing.

"What the hell! They have not understood anything about quantum physics!" he exclaimed.

"Perhaps not," Sanne admitted. "But they make people believe that if they pay for these seminars, they can become true *Quantologists* and have 100% probability of winning when gambling. Not only do they cash in a lot of money on bullshit courses, but they also encourage gambling."

"Even worse, they encourage betting on dubious bets and take positions on the more likely winning side," Glover said. "I met the founder of that cult before he was a guru. He was a pilot in the EU Navy."

"Was he?" Ralf asked.

"Yes. Gerry Cruiser is his name. I met him twelve years ago on the carrier *Jean Monet*, during an exchange program between the US and EU Navies. He was a hotshot. Had no respect for safety procedures. He flew his plane under the flight deck level to impress a journalist and crashed into the sea. He was lucky, though, as he could eject just before impact. He was fired from the EU Navy, but then started his religion, claiming he had survived his accident by mastering so-called 'Quantology skills.'"

"You see, Tintin," Anatoli said, "If we want to be rich we ought to start our own religion instead. Science does not pay as much."

"Well," Tintin replied, "I am quite content with half a Nobel Prize in Physics."

Suddenly the church bells started to ring, and Samir came out of the kitchen, wearing a white apron. He turned on the TV on the restaurant's terrace:

The Queen of England had just lost her long battle against breast cancer. England was mourning.

Samir was working at the elderly home on Sunday and was surprised to see that some of the senile residents looked really saddened, as if they knew who the Queen of England was, while they could not recognize most of their own relatives.

Even Gareth Fraser, who was, constitutionally speaking, a die-hard republican, looked really sad. Later in the morning, the thin, dark-skinned Dr. Eamon Windsor dropped by. The medical personnel greeted the psychiatrist silently. His mother dead, he was the logical successor to the English throne.

He went straight to Gareth's room and stayed there for two hours. When he came out, Eamon looked confident and resolute; he greeted Samir and went for the stairs.

One week later, Eamon was crowned king in the cathedral of Canterbury, not without a certain amount of opposition. Some right extremists had demonstrated not far from the cathedral, Samir understood from the news. How could one let a colored person become the king of England? Even worse, he was a 'bastard', as his parents had never been married. The police even arrested someone calling himself a 'Ginger Supremacist' who wanted to kill Eamon so that his ginger cousin would inherit the Throne.

The following days, there were some further demonstrations in front of Buckingham Palace, and some peers of the House of Lords urged King Eamon to show courage and abdicate in favor of his cousin.

This caused King Eamon to react and give a speech which was broadcasted live on all media. That evening, both Samir and Sanne were working at the restaurant and everybody was watching TV:

"*My dear people,*" the newly crowned king said on the screen, "*over the last few days, there have been numerous* demonstrations and manifestations to question my legitimacy to the throne. My mother, Queen Lea, was the rightful queen of England. My father never had the chance to marry her. Why? Because he died during the Qatari Flu, like so many other doctors and healthcare personnel, who were on the front line to stop the spread of that pandemic. My father failed to marry my mother because he sacrificed his life for Britain."

"Now, I have also been attacked for having subversive ideas. And it is true. I am subversive. I believe that the UK should either be a constitutional monarchy, with a written constitution, through which the Monarch is not the head of the Church, or, that the UK should be, and let me use the bad word, a republic, like the Scottish one.

"I believe a decent government should give the opportunity, to my people, to vote for one of these two alternatives. Should the government organize such a referendum, I hereby swear to abdicate, whatever the outcome of that referendum. Should my people vote for a constitutional monarchy, then my cousin shall become the new king. Should my people vote for a republic, then the new president elect would become the new head of state."

"The Lords calling for my abdication recently talked about courage. Leaving now, under such circumstances, would be, in my view, a sign of weakness. Leaving after the government has organized a referendum, the outcome of which can only strengthen the future of South Britain, is the true display of courage which, I believe, is expected of me.

"Until the outcome of that referendum, I shall remain on the throne."

Most of the guests in The Honourable Schoolboy stood up and applauded and cheered, while a minority sat silently.

Reading *The Guardian* at Sanne's request, Samir later understood that the House of Lords had been taken completely by surprise. Now, both the right and the left were calling for a referendum. The right was sure the constitutional monarchy would win, so that they could replace King Eamon with his cousin. The left was sure the republic would win.

The British Government finally yielded and called for a special convention to draft two different projects for a constitution. One republican and one monarchist. The government promised that a referendum would be held before July 2097.

10: NOT ALWAYS RIGHT, BUT NEVER IN DOUBT (AUGUST 2096)

In Burkina Faso, things were progressively going Thierry's way. After Tintin had left V-Space for WARSEC, Sophie Couillard must have been worried about losing Thierry as well, for she did everything a manager could do to retain him.

His salary had been increased by 60%, and he had suddenly become aware that both Tintin and he had been underpaid for the sole reason that they were African. Being African was worse than only being black, at least in the corporate world.

His team had been increased with additional personnel from the warp propulsion department, which was still headless since the Russian director had been sacked. He had been given privileged access to two of the quantum computers. He had used them. If only they had known the truth!

Sophie Couillard and Michael Vahlroos should have known better. Thierry was planning his revenge for having been underpaid, and there was nothing Sophie could do to win back his loyalty. She seemed, however, unable to grasp it with her limited intelligence. After all, she only had a master's degree and no PhD.

Thierry had lied as best he could. At the end of June, he had shown her a new proof of concept: the V-craft would be able to travel twenty times faster than the speed of light, to travel at warp 20 instead of warp 2. Warp 20 was twice as fast as the interstellar spaceships being designed by WARSEC. Sophie had been impressed. It would put V-Space ahead of WARSEC. If only she had known.

After the night in Uppsala in December, Tintin had been inspired. Alcohol combined with the absence of sex always led to creativity. He had cracked the nut. Using the V-Space computers and Tintin's approach, Thierry had determined it was possible to reach all the way to warp 250. This was still theoretical, as the green matter would not allow it. But researchers at Harbin University in China had discovered a way of turning the green matter into a purple matter with improved attributes. The purple matter would generate a greater amount of negative energy than the green matter and, if oscillated properly, could multiply the effective power of the warp field by up to twenty. Most scientists believed the purple matter would be available for industrial uses within five years at most.

If a space-only starship could theoretically make it to

warp 250, Thierry had to accept the fact that a spaceship with horizontal atmosphere entry would be limited to warp 130. V-Space did not deserve to know that. In the design he handed over to Sophie, the V-craft was specified to reach only warp 20.

Sophie Couillard had been so impressed that she had left Bobo-Dioulasso for New York City, to show the result to the CEO of Vahlroos Corporation, Michael Vahlroos. She had promised Thierry a promotion.

Thierry did not really care. He had other plans in mind. He had also sent the new design and calculations to Tintin at WARSEC in good conscience. He secretly hoped that Tintin would be able to convince them to build faster ships. The prospect of three-year-long interstellar missions was not exciting him.

In the meantime, he was still studying for the entry exam to the UN. This time, he was practicing by writing test exams in the heat of his corridor room, rather than in the comfortable air-conditioned premises of V-Space.

Tintin had coached him. Writing about ethics and morals for a UN exam was about being as sexless as possible. It was about having no emotion, balancing all viewpoints, and being as neutral and as ass-saver as possible. Thierry was not used to it.

With some practice, he could do it, though. Being an ass-saver was not that difficult, after all and many less intelligent people had made a career of it. To start with, Brice de Robien, the irritating project director in the Hawaii shirt.

For he who wanted to master the art of ass-saving, the trick was to read random reports written by the European Union. They were neutral, insipid, and boring. Exactly the tone that was expected of a candidate to a UN agency in the test in moral and ethics.

This time, he was almost certain he would get in. He did not want to be too over-confident, though. Over-confidence usually led to failure.

In New York City, Michael Vahlroos had invited Sophie Couillard for dinner in his loft apartment, located on the top floor of a skyscraper on 5th Avenue. It was so hot outside that it was better to stay indoors and benefit from the air-conditioning. Thanks to Vahlroos Energy and its nuclear fusion reactors, there was enough power supply in New York for everybody to have their AC on.

"You're welcome, New York City," Michael joked as he welcomed Sophie in his air-conditioned loft apartment.

The CEO of Vahlroos Corporation was wearing a pale pink silk shirt, black suit trousers and black socks but no shoes. With a hand gesture, the thin forty-two-year old blond, blue-eyed CEO invited her to proceed to the large living room. She knew the way.

To Sophie's dismay, there were some candles lit on the table. She thought it was an informal business dinner. What was

Michael doing?

Mike went to the table, took the bottle of red wine, opened it and poured her and himself a glass of wine.

"*Château Pétrus 2084,*" he said as he invited her to sit on the couch. "Very expensive. The bottle costs as much as two months of your engineers in Burkina's salaries."

There was a ring on the door, which Michael opened with a voice command. A short moment after, a waiter from a catering firm brought food on a silver tray into the living room. The waiter served two plates of duck breast with green beans and chestnut purée and left two other dishes under their covers on the tray. Michael used his smartphone to transfer the waiter a generous tip before asking him politely to leave.

Michael then invited Sophie to the table and, when they were both seated, finally said:

"What was it you wanted to discuss, Sophie?"

She took a sip of the expensive wine and replied: "The V-liner and the V-craft. For the V-liner, it seems to be a no go. However hard they try, they can't find a way to handle the vertical entry safely. However, for the V-craft, we have some good news."

Michael seemed to be listening with only one ear as he chewed a bit of the duck breast.

"Do you like the duck? It's tasty, isn't it?"

Sophie was irritated. She had not even taken a single bite. She felt the conversation was drifting.

"Not as tasty as the news I have to tell you," she added firmly. "With the V-craft, we could have a horizontal entry vehicle reaching warp 20. This relies on the development of the purple matter currently in Harbin. Perhaps we may want to invest in that."

"It was an expensive duck. It melts in the mouth," Michael said. "Delicious, isn't it?"

"Are you listening to me?" Sophie insisted, "We have the possibility to develop a ship that can be faster and better than those being developed by WARSEC. If we don't jump on it, Thierry is gonna talk with Tintin, and WARSEC is gonna steal our ideas."

Michael pointed at the bottle of expensive red wine standing on the table and said:

"The *Château Pétrus* is perfect with the duck. I'm so good at picking wine."

Sophie angrily unbuttoned her shirt, opened it and bent her torso. Michael looked down at her breasts, and then up at her face.

"Do I really need to do that to attract your attention?" Sophie said. "What kind of man are you? This is 2096."

"Sorry, Sof."

"We have to push on the V-craft and put the V-liner on hold", she insisted again.

"No," Michael replied.

"Have you been listening?"

"I have. It's not as though, because I am a man, I can't do several things at the same time. You said the V-craft would be able to reach warp 20, but it would require the development of a new purple matter, probably not available before five years?"

"Yes."

"How fast could this technology transport the V-liner, if applied to it? The V-liner has no need for a horizontal entry."

"Between warp 35 and warp 40, according to Thierry," Sophie replied.

"How difficult or easy is it to change the warp propulsion on an already manufactured ship?"

"According to the warp propulsion team, it would be only a few weeks' work, provided the purple matter turns out to be as we expect it."

"Then we stick to the plan," Michael said. "We go ahead with the V-liner. It may take some more time to solve the vertical landing, but when we do, we'll have the purple matter available."

Sophie poured herself a new glass of *Château Pétrus* and drank it all.

"Thierry is convinced it will not work, never, ever," Sophie objected. "He says it's like asking to draw a square circle. According to him, we have better chance planning for a conventional atmosphere entry from orbit."

"Thierry is an engineer," Michael replied. "I used to be an engineer. Engineers have limited thinking abilities. Why do you think we pay them so little? Business people should have the visions. It's not for him to decide what is possible or not. It's for me."

Sophie looked for a moment at Michael. Had he really been the one who had invented the compact fusion reactor? Or had he stolen the design from other colleagues at Lockheed? She started to believe the rumors were true. He was there only because his parents had died in the Big Two and he had inherited a fortune at a young age. She poured herself a new glass of expensive wine and drank it.

"If we don't go for the V-craft," Sophie tried, "we will lose Thierry. He will go over to WARSEC."

"He will go there anyway," Michael replied firmly. "He despises us because we are entrepreneurs. He is an idealist. He will never understand that only private companies make the world a better place. Let him go to hell. All his work is ours anyway."

"I can't do that…"

"Why? Do you like him so much?"

Sophie smiled as she poured herself another glass of wine.

"He's kind of sexy," she said, "nerdy, intelligent, with quite some muscles, which is quite unusual for someone of his intelligence."

Michael Vahlroos suddenly stood up and asked:

"What about me? Am I not OK?"

Sophie laughed and looked down at her hands. No, Vahlroos was nowhere near as intelligent as Thierry, and nowhere near as athletic. She'd rather not answer. When she looked up again, she saw that Michael had taken off his silk shirt, showing a belly without a six-pack.

"It's the 'black man effect'," Michael said. "Black people always look sexier than white people. It's because muscles are more visible when you are black. Don't let yourself be fooled. You've been too long in Burkina."

Sophie laughed again. What a fool, this Michael!

He was now dragging down his pants and underpants, and his manhood was pointing toward the ceiling. What was he doing?

He walked toward her chair, grabbed her hands and laid them on his hips. She was contemplating his penis.

"Made in California," he said.

Damn it! She had to leave. As she stood up, she realized that her shirt, which she had unbuttoned out of provocation, was being taken off, while one hairy hand was unhooking her bra.

"Michael, you can't do that."

"I know you like me, Sof," he whispered in her ear just before sucking her earlobe.

She started breathing heavily as he lay his hand on her bosom. How long had it been the last time since she had been with a man? Too long. Intelligent men were usually scared away when they saw how athletic she was. Athletic men were scared away when they realized how intelligent she was. Only pot-bellied male supremacists were after her for sex. At least

Michael was not pot-bellied, even if a six-pack was nowhere to be found.

He had now dragged down her pants and was kissing her on the mouth as their two naked bodies stood by the table.

"Wait," Michael whispered, and he squatted down to his trousers on the floor and retrieved a condom out of them. He clapped his hands.

"*eButler at your service*," a computer voice informed him.

"Light off, romantic music," he said as he put the condom on.

Sophie let herself be led to the giant glass window. The night had fallen, and all of New York was at their feet. She felt Michael's hands on her back forcing her to bend forward.

"Michael," she yelled, "What did you learn at school? Lick it before you stick it."

He did not. It hurt as he forced himself into her.

11: EUROPEAN JUNGLE (SUMMER 2096)

During the first weekend of July, Lt. Hoffman and Sgt. Uwilingiyimana invited Aisha Barjaoui and Torbjørn Eriksen to follow them on a three-day ridge raid over Pic de la Grave, Le Râteau and La Meije. Aisha was roped with the sergeant while Torbjørn was teamed with the lieutenant.

It was one of Aisha's fondest memories from her time in the 2nd Foreign Engineers. The weather was fantastic. The approach on the glacier to Pic de la Grave was pleasant, and the subsequent ridge walk to Le Râteau was elegant, though the rocks were, in some places, in very poor condition. It gave her a total sensation of freedom. Only the Alpine choughs flying above could experience more freedom, she thought.

They bivouacked at the top of Le Râteau. It was the full moon, and the sky was cloudless. "*Que la montage est belle!*" Aisha said, contemplating La Meije, to the east, and the Écrins range to the south. The next morning, they climbed down to the Refuge du Promontoir and the next day, they attacked La Meije, the Queen Mountain of the region.

They reached the Grand Pic at noon but did not stay long because of white clouds forming in the west. They continued the traverse down to the Meije Orientale and the Refuge de l'Aigle. By then, the clouds had turned dark grey. The afternoon thunderstorm suddenly started, and they all got pretty much drenched by the time they made it back to the car in La Grave.

Aisha had hoped they would also go on a mountaineering tour the next weekend, but the weather was too bad that time.

The following weekend, she was leaving for Chamonix, where she would follow a two-week course at the army's mountaineering school. Karen was right. Alpine rangers were "totally fuckable". With nobody there from her regiment to judge her, it was easier to make a move. She was determined to nail the instructor sergeant, and she strived to be as good as possible.

She turned out to be excellent on rock and was very comfortable when they scrambled in the Aiguilles Rouges. By the end of July, all the snow had melted and the four-thousand-meter (13,000 ft) peaks dominating Chamonix were covered with blue ice, on which cramponing was much harder.

In order to test their limits, the instructors were packing their rucksacks with a lot of unnecessary gear, which Aisha did not appreciate much.

She was the only woman in the group, and the male alpinists seemed to be ignorant of the fact that women could simply not carry as much on their backs as men. What was the point of carrying an anti-tank mine to the top of Mont-Blanc? The crampon hike on the icy Arête des Bosses could certainly have been interesting, if it had not been for that excruciating unnecessary weight on her back.

On the way down, she complained to the sergeant that it had been a very stupid exercise and said she would at least expect a massage from him when they would be back at the casern. He accepted.

"How was it?" Karen asked when Aisha was back in Saint-Christol

"It was a fucking A," Aisha answered.

"Only fucking?"

"Also licking A, fingering A and sucking A, you name it. You were right. Very firm buttocks!"

Karen informed Aisha she had been accepted at Med School. She would study in Lyon, in southeast France, to become a military doctor. Aisha was a bit sad at the thought that Karen, the only other woman in her platoon, would leave the regiment by the middle of September.

"Well, we still have August together." Karen reminded Aisha. "You perhaps missed the news, but we will spend four weeks in European Guyana."

"Guyana?"

"You know, in South America. That European overseas territory, bordering Brazil."

"Why are we going there?" Aisha asked.

"Well, it's mostly a thankyou from the Colonel for collecting dead bodies in Nice. We deserve some holiday."

"You are kidding?"

"Yes and no," Karen said. "Some foreign gold panners have mined larger areas to protect their illegal gold mining activities. The governor of Guyana has asked for support from engineering troops. The colonel is sending our platoon. The best part: we will be missing the Summer Olympics. No TV in the jungle."

Before their departure, Aisha Barjaoui got a chance to read a little about European Guyana. It used to be a French overseas territory called French Guyana. When the European Union became a federation back in 2054, the EU took over the administration of all the French overseas territories, as French rule had proven disastrous for the local populations.

The 2nd Platoon arrived in Kourou, European Guyana, on Saturday 4 August 2096. They were quartered at the barracks of the 3rd Foreign Infantry Regiment, also from the Legion. At quite some distance from the military camp, Aisha noticed what looked like a shining cable that went up right through the sky.

"What is it?" she asked.

"That must be the European Space Tether", Torbjørn suggested.

"You mean the space elevator?" Aisha asked.

"You can use my binoculars," said Karen, handing her a pair, her eyes on a paper, which Aisha identified as *The Chained Palmiped*.

Aisha took the binoculars and looked. It was in fact not one cable but two, perhaps two kilometers from one another. On one cable, containers were climbing up to the sky. On the other cable, containers were coming down.

She handed the binoculars to Torbjørn and said: "There seems to be a lot of traffic up to space."

"Yes, there is," Karen confirmed, reading *The Chained Palmiped*. "They are currently shipping a lot of equipment to space for transit to the Moon. For the lunar factories they plan to build up there."

"You don't look impressed," Aisha noted.

"I know Guyana," Karen replied. "That's how I came to Europe. As a teenage girl, I ran away from Texas, through Central America to Brazil and European Guyana. That's where I joined the Legion."

"You fled from your parents?" Torbjørn asked.

"Yes, a bit more than five years ago. I was a high school dropout. Only seventeen at the time."

"If you were under age," Aisha remarked, "how could you

join the Legion? I needed a consent letter from my parents."

"Ever heard of digital image editing?" Karen replied, her eyes still on the paper. "Quite useful."

"What's so interesting in the *Palmiped*?" Aisha finally asked.

"Nothing. It's about the upcoming elections in the States. I'm still a US citizen. Now the voter enrollment is automatic, I will be able to vote. First time ever."

"What do they say?" Torbjørn asked.

"In short, the Republicans have a candidate, Ted Blackswan, running for "*Freedom and Responsibilities*", as his slogan reads, against sitting Democrat President Shannon Fang, with the slogan "*Americans first*".

"Who will you vote for?"

"I have not decided yet. I don't like the Republican's stance on abortion, though. He sounds like a male supremacist."

Over the following week, some elements of the 3rd Foreign Infantry took the Foreign Engineers to the jungle for a crash survival course in the equatorial forest. Since Caporal Lee had terminated his contract in June, Torbjørn had been assigned to Sgt. Uwil's B team and was now together with Aisha, and Jean-Claude, the Luxembourger. The sergeant did not want to entrust Jean-Claude with any leadership duty and had made Aisha a private first class, and the team leader of the group.

Training in the jungle soon turned out to be much tougher than Aisha had expected. It was hot, wet, and the air felt constantly heavy. There were snakes, and none of the engineers was fond of them, though the foreign infantrymen showed how they could be caught, cooked, and eaten. Aisha's two teammates were constantly whining.

"Who is stupid enough to put mountaineers in the jungle?" Torbjørn complained.

"Traditionally, it's the Legion that is supposed to serve in overseas territories," Aisha explained. "They needed engineers, so it was either us or the 1st Regiment."

"They should have sent the 1st Regiment."

"What I don't understand," Jean-Claude said," is why the government absolutely wants to preserve this jungle. We should wipe it out with napalm and defoliants!"

"How would we breathe, with no forest to turn carbon dioxide into oxygen?" Aisha asked.

"I don't care," the bald Luxembourger replied.

Torbjørn was constantly sweating and Aisha had never seen anybody losing fluid so fast, no matter how many salt pills he took. The Norwegian legionnaire was always thirsty, and Aisha and Jean-Claude did what they could to save as much fresh water as possible for the poor devil.

After the exercise week, 2nd platoon was deemed fit for jungle duties. The following Monday, they were shipped upstream the Oyapok river along the Brazilian borders. They were sitting on small motor rafts, and Aisha really hoped that no gold panners would open fire on them from the Brazilian bank.

The Foreign Infantry had discovered a gold panner's camp on the river's left bank, and its surroundings had turned out to be heavily mined. Lt. Hoffman's engineers were to clear up the areas.

Since it was only a clearing operation and the surroundings had been assessed safe, Aisha had left her individual mortar at the camp and only taken her secondary weapon, a twelve-round pistol. A squad from the foreign infantry was protecting them, anyway.

As soon as they arrived, Aisha was assigned an area to clear, and she set her team to the task.

Torbjørn was handling the mine detector while Aisha and Jean-Claude were supporting with their knives, probing in the soil. Every time they found a mine, they marked it with a flag.

It took only half an hour before they ran out of flags and Aisha decided it was time to get rid of the mines. For each mine, they would dig slightly around it, place a small explosive charge and attach it to a thread.

It was a meticulous task and sweat was dropping down from Aisha's forehead. Torbjørn was covered with water, with not only huge rings under his arms but also all over his back and buttocks. Aisha could not help laughing at it. Finally, they were done, and Aisha linked all the threads to a master cable, which she drew back to the river bank.

"Already, Barjaoui?" Lt. Hoffman said. "Keep up the good work."

Aisha connected the cable to the detonator.

"Fire in the hole," she yelled.

All the legionnaires took cover, she put her earplugs in, and she pressed the button. There was a violent set of explosions, and she could feel the shockwave.

Aisha, Torbjørn, and Jean-Claude stood up in the cloud of dust, keeping their buffs on and went on to work the next area. This time, they were not as fast as they had been in the first area. Every so often, a team would shout "Fire in the hole", and there would be a new set of explosions. She decided to keep her earplugs and buff. It was noisy, and there was dust, earth, and sand flying everywhere. Her eyes were itching, her hands were sweating, and she started to feel thirsty.

As they had finished marking their second area, all the teams had cleared their first sectors, and she decided to take a break.

"*Putain, Torbjørn!*" she exclaimed, "You really need to drink."

The poor Norwegian looked as if he would collapse. Aisha took out her gourd and handed it over to Torbjørn. Jean-Claude joined them. With the blade of his knife, he started drawing on the ground. It looked like a penis.

"Bigger than yours," Torbjørn commented

"What are you drawing now?" Aisha asked.

"A clitoris," Jean-Claude replied. "Special tribute to you."

They were sitting in the jungle, about sixty meters from

the river bank.

As she was playing with the blade of her knife, Aisha looked for an instant at the jungle in front of them. The trees were so tall that the sun rays did not hit the ground. What a horrible place to live! She was happy she grew up in Casablanca.

Suddenly something moving attracted her attention. It was one, two, three snakes swiftly moving as they were scared away. She looked more carefully and spotted a man, who was hiding fifteen meters (49 ft) away.

"Jean-Claude," she whispered.

He was still absorbed in the drawing of his clitoris.

"Your light machine gun?" Aisha went on.

"In the boat. Why?"

"*Merde*," she said ('Shit'), "He has a grenade."

As the man was raising his hand to throw the grenade, Aisha jumped four meters forward and threw her knife at him. She hit him in the shoulder.

Behind her, she heard Jean-Claude shouting: "À terre! Down!" as he was grabbing Torbjørn's assault carbine and pointing it at the man.

"*Non, non, non,*" Aisha shouted. "*Debout*! Stand up and up with your hands! Keep the grenade visible, don't drop it."

Aisha went quickly to the man. While she grabbed the hand holding the grenade with her left hand, she confiscated the explosive device with her right hand, holding it firmly. As long as she was holding the grenade, it would not explode, but the safety pin was nowhere to be seen.

She looked calmly around her, still holding the man with one hand, aimed for a bush twenty meters away (65 ft) and threw the grenade. She immediately dragged down the man to take cover from the explosion.

The sound of the grenade detonation was stunning. She had just removed her earplugs for the break. Stupid!

A second later, Torbjørn was on her to help retain the man. As Jean-Claude was also coming to help, Aisha asked him to cover them and watch out for other potential threats around.

A moment later, Lt. Hoffman, Sgt. Uwil, and Karen had joined them.

"What the hell is going on?" the lieutenant asked.

"This guy," Aisha answered, "he was about to throw a grenade at us."

"Was it you who threw your knife at his shoulder?" Karen asked, starting to tend the wounded man.

"Yes," Aisha answered.

"That was stupid," Sergeant Uwil commented, "You could have missed."

"*Oui, sergent*," Aisha replied ('Yes, sarge'), "But I had my knife at hand. My gun was in my pistol pocket."

"Where did you learn how to throw a knife?" the lieutenant asked.

"In Casablanca."

Aisha had first thought that Uwil and Hoffman had been unhappy with her handling of the incident. It turned out that they were not. She had demonstrated the kind of leadership and initiative that was expected of NCOs, and they, therefore, wanted her to become a corporal. When they got back to France, she would take a four-week course in Castelnaudary to become an NCO.

12: THE RIGHT SIDE
OF THE ROAD
(AUG - SEPT 2096)

The first two weeks of August 2096 were those of the Summer Olympics in Riga. Be it at the old people's home, where Samir was working most of the days, or at The Honourable Schoolboy, where Samir and Sanne were working most of their evenings and weekends, people were glued to the TV screens.

Samir and Sanne were mostly interested in climbing competitions, especially women's climbing, as their friend Amina was participating as a Swiss athlete. Emily, who could not do much climbing on her own anyway, would spend most of her evenings at The Honourable Schoolboy, especially when they were broadcasting the climbing competitions. All three cheered for Amina, and some customers rolled their eyes in disapproval as the EU youths waved Swiss flags.

In bouldering, Amina was eliminated in the semi-final. In lead climbing, however, she made it to the final. Out of the eight finalists, she was the second to climb. Amina made it almost to the top, but lost grip two meters above the last clip.

"Damn it!" Emily cursed.

It now depended on how bad the other climbers were. The third, the fourth, and the fifth finalist did not reach as high as Amina had climbed. The sixth climber, a girl from the Czech Republic, reached the top.

So far, Amina was second. It depended on the seventh and the eight climbers.

The seventh climber was a girl from Japan, and she reached the top even faster than the Czech. She would probably win the gold.

Amina could still win the bronze, if the last climber, a girl from Thailand, could fail beneath the point Amina had reached.

In the restaurant, Samir, Sanne and Emily were standing in front of the TV and screaming "Fall, fall, fall!" as the Thai climber ascended the wall.

Some customers were laughing, other looking at them in disapproval, but they did not care.

The Thai climber was good, however, and was pursuing her ascension, climbing like a leopard.

Finally, she failed to catch a grip properly and lost balance half a meter under the position Amina had reached.

Emily, Sanne and Samir all cheered. Amina had won bronze. The Czech Climber had won silver, which counted as a medal for the European Union and the Japanese girl had won gold.

Johan Staël von Trollstein happened to have been sipping a beer in the bar with a male friend.

"What are you cheering about? It was only a bronze medal she won. The EU won silver. EU beats Switzerland. In your face."

Amina Dörflinger was back in Cambridge in the first week of September. By then, Samir had quit working at The Honourable Schoolboy, as he had earned back the money he had spent during his holiday in France. Meanwhile Emily was now a nurse with a decent salary living for free in the slavants' barracks. Sanne van der Maas had kept her part-time job as a waitress at The Honourable Schoolboy, as she was about to resume her studies. She had had only one year of Civil Service, and she had now started a master's in Economics at Cambridge University.

Sanne and Amina had moved into a small three-room student flat, and they had a mini housewarming party with only Samir and Emily as guests.

"I'm a bit sad for the Thai climber," Amina said, sipping some Génépi liquor she had brought from Switzerland. "She deserved the bronze more than I did. She is clearly a better climber than I am. She just happened to be menstruating on that day."

"Come on," Emily said. "You deserved that bronze."

"Also, for her," Amina added. "It meant less sex than for me…"

"What do you mean?" Sanne asked.

"The Olympic village," Amina explained. "It's A-MA-ZING. Imagine a place like a university, with only young people, except that they are all extremely athletic and good-looking. It's the only place in the world. It happens only once every four years!"

"Is it really so good?" Samir asked.

"You have no idea," she said. "I nailed all the guys I wanted. Three Italian swimmers... You should have seen their bodies... and their techniques..."

Emily and Sanne were smiling and laughing, while Samir looked embarrassed.

"Anyway, I got what I wanted," Amina said. "Sex in the Olympic village: check. I'm gonna stop with climbing competitions, now. I really don't like the pressure. It does not rock as much as geology anyway."

The following week, Samir started high school evening classes in mathematics, and Sanne promised to help him if needed. That way, he might be able to start a bachelor in Robotics at the Cambridge community college.

On Monday 17 September 2096, all the slavants, university and high school students had been requisitioned by the South British government. At eleven o'clock in the morning, all of South Britain would switch from driving on the left to driving on the right.

Samir was standing in the street close to the elderly people's home with Carsten. At 11:00, they heard a siren, and all the cars, in all the United Kingdom of South Britain, stopped. It was a historic moment.

Samir's and Carsten's task was simple. They just had to remove the covers from a few newly installed traffic signs on the right side of the road and put them on old signs on the left side of the road, which would be removed later. Samir had to do the switch for only five road signs, and it barely took ten minutes.

At 11:15, the traffic police officer in the street blew her whistle and waved at the cars to switch sides. Suddenly, all the cars waiting on the left side of the road slowly drove to the right side.

It was a very organized chaos. The sight of it was impressive and both Samir and Carsten had a good time looking at it.

At 11:30, they heard a siren again.

The United Kingdom of South Britain was now driving on the right side of the road.

Later that evening, when watching *Bollox News* in the Barracks, they realized it had not gone smoothly everywhere. In Oxford, an old man had obstinately refused to move to the right side and kept driving on the left side until the police interfered.

In the following days, the number of road accidents increased significantly, and Emily, who was working at the E.R.

was complaining about the extra workload. According to her, the worst part was that most of the accidents had been caused by the car computers that were supposed to help the drivers. The update had not been properly executed on all vehicles. Since most drivers of self-driving cars did not actually have a clue as to what attitude to adopt in the event of such system failure, they had just sat and prayed, and waited for their vehicle to eventually crash.

Those car computers had become both figuratively and literally a real pain in the neck for their drivers.

The end of September was not all bad, though. It was when the sequel to *The Lone Hiker* was released in the movie theaters.

Sanne, Amina, Samir, Emily, Carsten and Carsten's hook-up at the time, went to the cinema on the release date. *The Lone Hiker Hikes Again*'s opening scene was a poop gliding down from a squatting hiker and the all audience laughed like kindergarten children, except Sanne. The rest of the movie was no intellectual masterpiece either. It was silly, it was Swedish, but they loved it.

13: UN CRISIS (OCT 2096)

Ralf Åhman had spent the third week of October 2096 in New York. Officially, it was to answer a few questions for the Fourth Committee, which was the Committee of the United Nations General Assembly in charge of colonization issues and outer space affairs. It consisted of representatives of all the member states of the United Nations, though some representatives were more present than others.

The Fourth Committee was the UN legislative body supervising the work of the World's Agency for the Regulation of Space Exploration and Colonization (WARSEC), of which he was the director.

Ralf had been questioned for two days. There had been questions about the hiring process of the new employees and the migration to the new information system. Were they meeting the cost-effectiveness criteria set by the UN? Yes, they were. Ralf bit his lips.

His very presence in New York was, in his opinion, a waste of money. He could have answered the question by video-conference. However, Ralf had not been in New York for a year, and they had requested his physical presence. He did not mind. He liked New York in October. The leaves were turning to orange and red, and the weather was usually pleasant. It was better than rainy Vienna.

He had, however, decided to stay another three days in New York, with the hope of having a one-to-one meeting with the UN Secretary-General, Mrs. Dr. Hira Dorjee-Sherpa.

Originally from Nepal, Hira Dorjee-Sherpa had been a diplomat within the South-Asian Union, the large political federation covering the Indian subcontinent. She had become the United Nations Secretary-General shortly after the successful testing of warp-drive technology in September 2094. Back then, Ralf Åhman had been the Director of the United Nations Office for Outer Space Office. Shortly after the Hira's appointment as Secretary-General and under her sponsorship, Ralf had chaired the Vienna Conference, which had given birth to WARSEC. It was Hira Dorjee-Sherpa who had then appointed Ralf to the head of this newly created United Nations space regulation agency.

However, the UN secretary general had been kept very busy lately, with no time to spare on outer space affairs.

The EU president, Mrs. Bonavita, had turned out to be rather inexperienced in international diplomacy and had uttered more and more open threats to invade Morocco, which she accused of jacking up the phosphate prices. The UN, as always, was trying to find more diplomatic approaches, and had been succeeding so far. The EU had still not invaded Morocco, and Ralf was sure President Bonavita's manifestations were nothing but empty threats. But it cost time. The secretary general came back from Brussels first thing on Thursday 18 October.

She had agreed to have an informal dinner with Ralf, to discuss the recent development at WARSEC. They would be served dinner in the VIP room of the UN cafeteria at 20:00. Ralf was looking forward to it.

The situation had become slightly more complicated in Finland, where WARSEC was having their new headquarters built. The mayor of Vaasa had suddenly decided to build a new runway for the airport, and the decision had been taken by the municipality council. Ralf had, at first, welcomed the decision. A bigger airport would make it easier to handle aerospace operations within a couple of years when both the Space hounds and Space bears would be available. They would be able to fly directly from Vaasa to the orbital station where WARSEC would have established its Orbit Control.

That silly mayor had, however, authorized the start of the construction work without waiting for the impact study to be done by an environmental committee, and the proper green light given by the Finnish Government. This had upset some Vaasa citizens, who had started a large protest movement. This was not really Ralf's problem, except that these discontented citizens seemed to believe that WARSEC was behind the decision, whereas in fact the mayor had acted on his own. The consequence of this misunderstanding was that demonstrators were now targeting the WARSEC construction site, causing some delays.

Ralf was a diplomat, and he was confident he would be able to handle this situation eventually, even if the mayor turned out to be completely incompetent. But still.

What he truly wanted to talk about with Hira Dorjee-Sherpa was the upcoming interstellar exploration schedule. Tintin Mutombo had convinced him that within five years, it would become possible to travel at warp 250 rather warp 10. Because WARSEC did not have quantum computers and because there were some extensive test procedures to follow, this would mean that no such spaceship would be operational for exploration duty before 2103, at best, if the development were started now.

On the other hand, traveling at warp 250 meant that one would be able to reach Alpha Centauri, the closest star to the Sun, in about six days, instead of five and a half months. It was substantial.

Financially speaking, it would indeed be wiser to wait. By then, WARSEC would have amassed a decent treasury from the sales of aerospace shuttles by WARSEC Ventures.

However, it would imply giving up the idea of attempting to complete the first interstellar journey before 2100. For reasons

Ralf could not really grasp, there seemed to be an untold pressure from all member states to perform the first interstellar journey in 2099.

Ralf wanted to debate with the secretary-general the possibility to get rid of that pressure and commit themselves to 2103 instead. If they did not, they would not be able to have operational ships with warp 250 capabilities before 2110 or even 2113 because of their resource limitations.

It was silly to slow down all the subsequent exploration and perhaps even colonization programs, just because one wanted to race too fast to the first interstellar journey.

When Ralf Åhman showed up in the VIP room, the dinner was about to be served. But Hira Dorjee-Sherpa was nowhere to be seen.

She had clearly been delayed. He decided to wait.

Twenty minutes later, she was not still there, and Ralf thought about the dinner, which was going to be cold.

Finally, the door of the VIP room opened. It was not Hira. It was her aide.

"Hi Mr. Åhman, sorry for making you wait," he said, "There has been a crisis. I mean a real crisis with real UN diplomacy at stake, not just a space meeting."

"What happened?" Ralf asked.

"The UN Security Council is now in an emergency meeting," the aide replied. "It may take the whole night, and perhaps two days. Hira will not be able to come for dinner."

"You should go back to your hotel and enjoy being only a diplomat of outer space affairs," the aide added, "my girlfriend is going to kill me when I see her, in… four days only… perhaps."

The aide left the room, and Ralf wondered why Hira had hired him. He sounded like a douchebag. Since he was in the VIP dining room, and since the dinner was served, and since he hated wasting food, Ralf decided to eat, while browsing for the news on his tablet. What kind of crisis could have happened?

Had the European Unions bombed Morocco? A quick browse told him it was not the case. He exhaled in relief, poured himself a glass of wine, and took a sip. What kind of emergency crisis had happened? He browsed down and saw that there had been some massacres in southern Kirghizstan. Could it be linked to them?

He remembered that his old friend Esko Punainen was serving as the ambassador to the EU in Bishkek. He decided to call him. No answer. What time was it in Kirghizstan? He checked. It was 05:27. If there was a crisis, Esko was not sleeping.

He called again. Somebody answered the call, but all he heard was the intense sounds of firecrackers.

"Esko? Esko? What's happening? It's Ralf".

"Ralf? Don't you hear what's happening? People are shooting with assault rifles all around the embassy."

"Are you kidding?"

In the background, he heard the muffled sound of an explosion.

"*Saatana perkele vittu,*" Esko swore in Finnish ('Bloody fucking hell!'). "You never used any firearms in the fucking navy?"

Suddenly, memories from his short basic training under his military service came back. Real gunfire sounded like curt firecrackers, not like echoing movie-like rounds.

"What's happening, Esko?" Ralf asked urgently. "There is an emergency session of the security council happening as we speak."

"Thank, God," Esko yelled. "It was about time. Some right extremist groups, the Interkirghiz militia, are attempting a coup d'état against the prime minister and slaughtering the Uzbek minority."

"*Helvete,*" Ralf said in Swedish ('Holy hell!').

"Exactly," Esko replied. "Now, the Kirghiz prime minister has asked her representative at the UN to ask for an intervention in the country. We need a peacekeeping force here and now."

"Can I help you in any way?" Ralf said, loudly enough to be heard despite the shooting in the background.

"Well, since you ask," Esko replied, "President Bonavita.... Even though I am her ambassador, she refuses to talk to me, the bitch..."

In the background, he heard a long machine gun fire volley which Ralf thought he identified as being of .50 caliber. When the belt had been emptied he could hear Esko again:

"I fear the EU is reluctant to send soldiers in a hypothetical peacekeeping force. If no real army is sent over here, it won't work. Don't say that to the SG, but I don't think Bangladeshi or Pakistani blue helmets could do a good job over here. We need the Chinese and the EU. The US won't budge anyway because of the pending elections."

"Copy that, Esko," Ralf yelled in the mobile phone. "I will go to the permanent mission of the EU and do some lobbying in the back door."

"Thanks, man."

"Good luck, man".

Ralf drank his glass of wine, poured himself a new glass, drank that too, drank some water, and rose to his feet. He grabbed his coat and rucksack and made it to the exit of the UN building. His Radisson hotel bike was parked not far from the entrance. He unlocked it and pedaled away in the night, to Dag Hammarskjöld's plaza, where the EU permanent delegation was quartered.

14: UN Deployment (Oct 2096)

Aisha's platoon had left European Guyana just in time to avoid some major tropical storms that hit the European islands of the Caribbean. Instead, the EU High Command had sent the 1st Foreign Engineer Regiment to assist the local population. The men and Aisha were happy about that. After the earthquake in Nice, they had had enough of natural disasters for at least a year.

In September, the whole 2nd REG took part in a two-week exercise in urban warfare together with two other infantry regiments. It was noisy, dusty, sweaty, but thrilling. Aisha liked it. It helped her forget that Karen had now left the regiment.

As combat engineers, one of their tasks was to blow up house walls, so that the infantry could move forward from one house to the next without being slaughtered by machine gun fire in the adjacent streets. They were also helping with clearing mines.

At the end of the exercise, while most legionnaires went on leave, Aisha had to go to Castelnaudary to take a four-week NCO course. When she was back in Saint Cristol, the evening of Friday 19 October, Aisha Barjaoui had earned the rank of corporal. She was told to report immediately to her company.

All of the 2nd Company had gathered in the regiment mess and were watching TV. Cans of beer and bottles of alcohol were everywhere.

On TV, she recognized US President Shannon Fang talking to her supporters: "*What matters is not the supremacy of the American flag, but the welfare of the people living under it. The Republicans call us "globalists" because we strive to cooperate with the United Nations. I say we are realists. The future of the American people is linked to the future of all mankind. Yes! Americans first means mankind first. The sea level has….*"

Somebody turned the TV off. It was Rheinfeldt.

"Boring," he said, holding the remote control in one hand and a bottle of Ricard in the other. He started singing instead, standing in front of the TV:

"*J'ai deux amours, la Kanterbräu, la Kronenbourg. J'ai deux espoirs: le Martini et le Ricard. J'ai deux ennemis…*"

"*Ta gueule, Rheinfeldt.*" Sergeant Uwilingiyimana shouted ('Shut up, Rheinfeldt'), "Put the TV back on."

Jean-Claude Rheinfeldt switched the TV back on, but it was another channel.

"Oh yeah," he said. "That's Wolf Welsh, he has swum across

the melted glacial Arctic Ocean. Let's watch it instead."

"I would like to see him ski off-piste instead," a voice said. "I guess he is worse than you and you are the worst in the whole regiment, Rheinfeldt."

The legionnaires laughed. It was Lt. Hoffman. He was accompanied by the Captain and the other officers of the company.

"*Garde à vous*," Sgt. Uwil shouted ('Atten-tion').

"*Repos*," the Captain said ('At ease'). "The colonel will come in an instant. Please clean up the cans and the bottles. From now on, I need you sober."

"*Oh, non*," some legionnaires complained but they resigned to clear up the mess.

Aisha found Torbjørn.

"What did I miss?" she asked.

"Hi, corp," Torbjørn replied. "No idea. They asked the 2nd Company to gather here."

"And when I was away?"

"Spent two weeks' holiday in Chamonix. I did Mont Blanc with Sergent Uwil."

"I was in Marseille. Nailed some nice chicks there," Jean-Claude said, as he had overheard them.

"Last week we had a few exercises with the new gliders," Torbjørn added.

"The gliders?"

"You know, the Chough glider, from Airbus Military,"

Jean-Claude clarified. "They are stealthy, silent, and have small electric engines so that they can even land and take off vertically."

"You mean these gliders can also fly?" Aisha was impressed.

"Yes, but at the magnificent speed of 140 km per hour [76 knots]," Jean-Claude replied. "You'd better want to have them towed."

"We practiced being dropped on some hills," Torbjørn said. "Though I don't really see the purpose of it. Helicopters are easier, especially when it's windy."

"Torbjørn threw up in one exercise," Jean-Claude added as he placed his bottle of Ricard on the bar.

"*Garde à vous,*" the sergeant major shouted.

The colonel had entered the mess with some of his intelligence officers. They joined the other officers and stood in front of the TV.

"*Repos, legionnaires,*" the colonel said. "As you clearly don't know from watching the news, there is trouble in Kirghizstan. A resolution is being examined at the UN Security Council to send blue helmets over there. The European Government will contribute with two companies. South of Kirghizstan is mountainous. Mountain troops will be sent. One company of the 27th Alpine ranger battalion, and one company of mountain engineers. 2nd Company, you are now on alert, all leaves cancelled."

"*Putain,* I had a date tomorrow," Jean-Claude ranted.

The captain took the floor:

"If the UN Security Council decides to send UN troops, we will know the detail of the operations by tomorrow morning, probably for deployment as soon as tomorrow afternoon. I want you to be ready to be deployed. Tomorrow, wake up at 06:00 and transfer to the airport base. The only thing I know so far is that winter equipment will be needed. For the rest, we will give you more information when we get it."

The next morning, the 2nd company of mountain engineers arrived at the nearby air force base in Orange at about 08:00.

An hour later, the 3rd company of the 27th battalion of Alpine angers joined them.

On the tarmac, the 192 Alpine rangers distinguished themselves from the 133 mountain engineers of Aisha's company with their peculiar large black berets, the *tarte*.

They were told to wrap their helmets with pieces of UN blue tissue and had to sew a UN badge on their shoulders. Aisha hated sewing, but so did all the other men in the company, except perhaps Torbjørn. He was good at knitting, he had said. It was a national sport in Norway.

As a corporal, Aisha was called with the rest of the officers and NCOs to a briefing by Capitaine Léger in one of the hangars. He revealed the situation:

"All right, there has been some ethnic unrest in Kirghizstan. An extremist party, named Kirghiz Power, has been attempting to seize power. According to them, Uzbeks are potential Islamist terrorists, ergo all Uzbeks should be killed. Over the last two days, there have been some skirmishes in the capital between the Interkirghiz militia and the troops loyal to the government. There have been reports of massacres of Uzbeks in the south of the country. The current Kirghiz government fears it may lose control of the situation, as a growing part of their police and military seems to now be more loyal to the Interkirghiz militia. They have called the UN for help. All the background information is summarized in this little booklet, copies of which we will hand out."

"The UN Security Council has passed resolution 19940406 and answered the call of the Kirghiz government to deploy UN troops. We will be under the order of a General Kurosawa from the Japanese defense forces. There will be troops from Japan, China, and the South Asian Union, totaling 3,000 UN. As for us, we will be deployed in the south, where some massacres have occurred over the last week.

"The Kirghiz do not want any European plane to land on their soil, so we have to wait for a transporter from the Russian Air Force that will take us there. We will be the first to land in Bishkek. We wait for the Chinese to secure the Kirghiz capital and we go to the south with the Japanese. Any questions?"

"What is our mandate?" Sgt. Uwilingiyimana asked.

"General Kurosawa made it clear to us that it was an operation under Chapter 7 of the Charter of the United Nations.

We should not hesitate to use force to stop the massacres."

"Use force?" Lieutenant Kowacz asked. "Do we know the strength of the Interkirghiz militia?"

The captain read some notes and said: "Kirghiz Power has at least a million active supporters. Their militia is assessed to be 200,000 strong, while the Kirghiz military is only 50,000 strong."

"Do we know how many in their military are loyal to the government and how many have joined Kirghiz Power?" Aisha asked.

"Unfortunately, we don't know," the captain replied.

"3,000 UN troops for one million fanatics and potentially a quarter of a million armed militia," Lt. Hoffman commented. "Isn't that a bit thin?"

"It will be challenging indeed," the captain noted.

Aisha hated the word 'challenging' already.

"However, according to UN headquarters," Capt. Léger added, "the militia are not well trained, and not heavily armed. They have hunting rifles and axes. Our Japanese commander is confident that if we show calm and determination, they will not dare make a move."

"If the Europeans are sending the Legion, it cannot be safe," Lt. Kowacz commented.

"Come on, they're also sending the Alpine rangers," Lt. Hoffman kidded, "it won't be a suicide mission".

Just after lunch, a gigantic Russian cargo plane landed on Orange's air force base. There was enough room onboard for the 335 Mountain troopers and their equipment. They boarded the plane over the next half hour, while the tanks were being refueled.

The plane took off at 13:17 French time.

In the plane, Aisha read the booklet she had received. While most of central Asia had blossomed with the construction of the silk-road railway linking China to Europe, Kirghizstan had been left out. She noted that the poverty index there was worse than in Morocco. Kirghizstan had had no integration policies, and different ethnic groups had been encouraged to congregate with one another. The usual blame games played by irresponsible politicians had fueled a new kind of inter-ethnic hatred that had recently turned deadly. The current government was well aware of the situation and wanted to implement a kind of Civil Service to integrate Kirghiz society more deeply. However, they had met instead protests from extremists among the majority ethnic group, who had organized themselves as "Kirghiz Power". Aisha had personally no idea how 3,000 UN troopers could make a difference in this chaotic situation.

"Legionnaire Rheinfeldt," she asked Jean-Claude, who was sitting in front of her. "You served as a peace-keeper in Greenland six years ago, is that correct?"

"Correct, *mon caporal*" Jean-Claude Rheinfeldt answered.

"What happened there in the first place?" Torbjørn asked.

Jean-Claude looked at the two young legionnaires and explained:

"Greenland: 90,000 Greenlanders, but also 50,000 Chinese miners, as the Greenlanders sold their mineral resources to China. Some Chinese miners happened to rape some Greenlandic girls. But the Chinese government always protected the suspects. The Chinese just said that their miners believed that raping was legal in Greenland, for whatever reason."

"You're kidding me?" Aisha said.

"Then, there was that rape too many," Jean-Claude went on.

"What happened?" Aisha asked.

"All the Greenlanders are armed," Sergeant Uwilingiyimana jumped in. "Seal hunting, and polar bear watch. They started to wreak their own justice on Chinese suspects."

"China threatened to invade Greenland", Jean-Claude went on. "So, the UN set up a peacekeeping mission. The whole regiment was deployed."

"How was the mission?" Aisha wanted to know.

"First two weeks were uneasy," Jean-Claude said. "But then, it was mostly fun. Snow scooter driving, shooting seals, and polar bears."

"You killed polar bears just for fun?" Aisha was shocked.

"Of course not," the sergeant said. "They are protected."

"I did," Jean-Claude said. "A mother and her cubs. That was fun. I managed to smuggle their hides home. I also shot a minke whale with a bazooka. It just turned the water around red. Really cool."

"*Quel con de Luxembourgeois*," Sergeant Uwilingiyimana said ('What a Luxembourger asshole'), "You were lucky you were not in my platoon."

As the plane flew east, the sky turned into night. Aisha hoped the landing at the airport would go well. Troops loyal to the government were supposed to have secured the international airport.

She was pulled out of her thoughts by the plane's intercom:

"Troopers. We will land in half an hour."

It was the crew of the plane who had spoken, with a heavy Russian accent.

As time went by, the tension increased in the plane. Even Jean-Claude kept quiet.

Aisha prayed silently that God would help her in the trials to come. They had to show calm and determination. It was their only plan. They had to behave like an alpha German shepherd in a courtyard full of crazy Chihuahuas. She took a deep breath. It would be tough, but OK.

Aisha was uncertain how much time had elapsed before another message from the pilot came through the intercom. Still the heavy Russian accent.

"Troopers," the voice said, "We have been so far unable to contact Bishkek International Airport. UN HQ has, however, confirmed we are clear to land. They may have trouble with their radio. Be ready for a landing in five minutes."

Aisha felt suddenly really nervous.

«*Ça m'a l'air foireux, cette histoire*,» Jean-Claude commented to himself in French. ('This whole affair sounds fucked up to me.')

"The pilot should abort the landing, god damn it" Sergeant Uwilingiyimana exclaimed.

Suddenly there was a scream in the plane.

"Two missiles 5 o'clock. Two missiles 5 o'clock, *bordel de merde*" ('for fuck's sake')

"*Putain, on va tous crever! Dégage dégage bordel!*" ('Fuck, we're all gonna die! Brake, brake, for fuck's sake').

"*Il fout quoi le pilote ? C'est qui ce connard de Russe?*" ('What the fuck is the pilot doing? Who is this Russian asshole?')

Aisha was dead scared. Being shot at by missiles had never been part of the plan. Alarms were blipping all over the cabin.

She was going to die in an instant in a Russian plane in some godforsaken place. She felt the plane veer violently to the right. A moment later, all the passengers sitting in the dark cabin were blinded by a violent explosion outside the aircraft. The plane then climbed steeply upward, and her ears started to hurt.

"Thank the Lord," Sgt. Uwil said "The elusion maneuver has worked. We are still alive."

"It seems that the government does not control the airport

anymore," Aisha grumbled.

An hour and a half later, the Russian Antonov landed in Urumqi, in western China. The European soldiers were quartered in a large hangar.

They were told to wait for instruction. Aisha slept very badly.

The next morning, it was still unclear what they would do. Japanese UN troops had also arrived at the base, and some Chinese paratroopers were gathering around.

At two in the afternoon, while walking on the tarmac, she saw five large European cargo planes land. They each unloaded what looked like two peculiar light planes. Once they were assembled, Aisha noted that these aircraft had four wings, two larger at the front, and two smaller at the rear. Each wing was equipped with ducted fans that could rotate up to 90 degrees downward, giving them vertical take-off and landing capabilities. The wings were covered with solar cells.

"Those are Chough gliders," Torbjørn explained.

"Why are they here?" Aisha asked.

"I guess the European Government wants to use them to do a demonstration, and hopefully sell them," Sgt. Uwil said. "What is good for Airbus Military is good for the European Union, as one of the Airbus CEOs once said."

"Demonstration? What kind of demonstration?" Aisha asked.

"We will find out soon enough. Look, the officers are going to a briefing with the Japanese general. My guess is that the Russians did not like to have their plane fired at. The UN intervention is going to escalate."

Sgt. Paul Uwilingiyimana proved to be quite right. The situation in Bishkek had become more confused. Kirghiz militia had taken over the three airports of the city, and massacres had been reported in the southern district. The government had taken refuge in their building, the Kirghiz White House, defended by some loyalist troops, but the Interkirghiz militia was now surrounding them.

An emergency meeting of the UN Security Council had led to the decision that the airports of the city should be taken by force by the UN troops, and the Kirghiz government rescued. The Europeans were putting ten Chough gliders at the disposal of the UN force, and the Chinese had mobilized two parachute regiments, while the Russians were providing additional transport aircrafts.

The plan would be the following: taking advantage of the cover of night, the European mountain troops would land in six gliders on the military helicopter airport south of the international Airport, just at the northern limit of the city. They would destroy the helicopters and air defense systems as well as provide cover for the subsequent landing of two Chinese parachute battalions.

The mountain engineers, including Aisha's squad, would then make a dash, under Chinese escort, for the international airport twenty-five kilometers (16 miles) away, to clear the runway and enable the landing of the large Russian transport planes carrying the Japanese and South Asian UN contingent. Four gliders carrying French Alpine rangers and Chinese special forces would also land on the Spartak stadium and secure it as a refugee compound while assisting the Kirghiz government currently surrounded in the nearby White House.

They would take off from Urumqi at 01:00 and land in Bishkek at about the same time, because of the time zone difference.

In the evening before the assault, Aisha tried to rest a little bit in the hangar, but she could not get much sleep. Neither could Torbjørn, but Jean-Claude the Luxembourger seemed to sleep like a baby.

In one corner of the hangar, she saw some Muslim soldiers discreetly praying toward Mecca. She realized, she had not prayed once since she had left Morocco for Ireland for her abortion. She asked the men if they did not mind her joining them for the Isha, and they replied she could. They joked they were not Saudis. No problem mixing women and men for prayer.

She washed her hands quickly with a bottle of water, and turned herself toward Mecca. Before softly praising God, she thanked Him for having the plane survive the missile attack, twenty-two hours earlier, she submitted to His will, and hoped to have the strength to be brave and upright in the hours to come.

As she went back to her sleeping pad, she noted that Sgt. Uwilingiyimana was also discreetly praying. He was Catholic.

She did her best to get some rest, but it was soon time to get up and pack her bag.

At midnight, the soldiers started to gather on the tarmac with the equipment.

Further away, she caught a glimpse of the Chinese paratroopers getting ready for battle. They would jump twenty minutes after the initial glider assault. They were as tall and well-built as Deng Hoang, the Chinese expat she once had an affair with, in Casablanca. How ironic that a poor quality Chinese condom used with a Chinese man could have led her to China, she thought. She was in China! She had barely realized it, as she had only seen Urumqi Airport, which looked like any other airport. And now she was going to Kirghizstan, a country she had barely heard about before.

Aisha, Torbjørn, and Jean-Claude assembled with the rest of the squad: Sergeant Uwilingiyimana, their driver Private First Class Kowalski, and the A team: Corporal Singh, Private First Class Tran and Private Gonzales.

The eight mountain engineers were soon met by the rest of their glider chalk: 13 alpine rangers divided in to an assault squad and a command squad, as well as a Chinese air commando who was to guide the second wave of the airborne assault by the Chinese paratroopers.

Aisha noted there would be only two women in the glider, the other one being an Alpine ranger. The chalk leader was a lieutenant from the Alpine rangers, and they went through the assault plan one more time.

At 23:45 Bishkek time, the twenty-two soldiers boarded their Chough glider, parked with two other gliders behind a large Chinese transport aircraft.

At 23:55, the aircraft started its engines.

At 23:58, Aisha felt her glider start to roll forward on the runway as it was being towed.

A moment later, their glider was airborne.

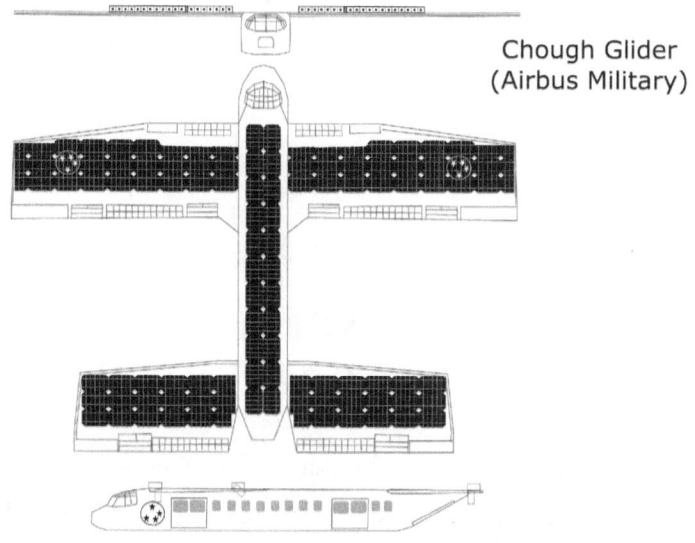

Chough Glider
(Airbus Military)

Figure 1: The Chough glider is stealthy and can be towed at supersonic speed. Equipped with ducted fans, it can do a vertical take-off and landing and fly at 140 km/h, powered by solar energy. Here with the insignia of the EU Air Force.

15: BISHKEK (OCT 2096)

The Chinese transport aircraft was towing the European gliders above the cloud ceiling. It was a dark night, as the Moon had set early, and the stars were clearly visible. They were flying westward, and Aisha and the ten other soldiers sitting on her seat row were facing the glider's left windows.

The silence in the cabin was suddenly broken by an Alpine ranger.

"You see the bright star over there, to the south?" he asked.

The name on his combat vest read: *E. Legrand*. He was a sergeant.

"What about it, sarge?" Aisha asked

"It's Sirius. 8.6 light years away," the ranger replied. "It will certainly be one of the first stars where mankind will travel to when they start interstellar exploration."

"Alpine rangers are so nerdy," Jean-Claude Rheinfeldt said. "You have your heads in the stars, you know the names of all summits in the Alps, and so on. But can you fight at all?"

Tran and Gonzales laughed.

"*Je t'emmerde,*" the sergeant said to Jean-Claude ('Fuck you').

"Look at the Chinese dude, instead," Rheinfeldt went on, pointing at the Chinese air Commando. "He looks like a tough guy."

The Chinese soldier sitting close to the glider's back door was ignoring the European soldiers. His face was painted in green and brown camouflage.

"Hey, Chinaman," Jean-Claude said. "Who are you? Wolf Warrior forty-seven? Are you gonna kill all the baddies on your own?"

The Chinese Air Commando gave him a hard look and showed his middle finger.

All the soldiers laughed.

Suddenly, there was a gentle shock, and they heard the aircraft fading away. They were now gliding. Everybody had shut up, and the silence was oppressing.

Through the window, Aisha could see they were heading for the cloud cover. The other gliders were flying in formation nearby. She would have thought of it as thrilling if there was not the prospect of getting killed upon landing.

"Gentlemen, I just got a kind reminder from the pilot," the lieutenant said. "It will be shaky in the clouds."

And shaky it was. Aisha almost felt sick. Luckily, the cloud cover was not too thick, and they soon saw they were gliding toward a city underneath.

"The city lights are still on," Jean-Claude noted. "Something is wrong."

"Negative," the lieutenant said. "It's not 1:30 yet."

One minute and a half later there was a blackout, and all the lights on the ground vanished.

As the glider was silently descending, Aisha was observing the ground beneath them. There had been some frost. In some places, there was snow. They all had their khaki clothes on. Wrong camouflage.

Suddenly, the four doors of the gliders opened, and a biting chill engulfed the cabin. Aisha wished she had put on a cap beneath her helmet. She had her gloves in her pocket. She put them on.

As they got close to the ground, the ducted fan engines started and the red lights above each door went on.

Aisha could now clearly see below them the military helicopter airport they were to seize. It was located at the northern edge of city of Bishkek. The two large rectangular landing pads looked like broad runways.

The troopers unfastened their seat belts and stood up. Most of them, including Aisha and Sgt. Uwil, had ropes coiled over their shoulders.

Aisha saw the ducted fans on the front wings rotate downwards. They were going to land vertically on the hangar roof.

That was it.

The glider did not touch the hangar roof. It remained in a geostationary position for less than ten seconds, which was enough for the 22 soldiers to exit the aircraft through all four doors.

Aisha was third to exit the glider through the rear right door, and she headed immediately for the edge of the hangar roof. As she was installing a rappel, the glider slowly flew away, and she was happy not to be on it. It flew at less than 140 km per hour (76 knots) and was not very maneuverable. Their only chance for safe return was to avoid detection, which was not completely impossible as the sky was pitch black, and the Chough glider had been designed to be stealthy to radar detection.

Aisha was now ready to throw her ropes down. She looked around. The glider chalks had been dropped on the roofs of all the five hangars, and one chalk had landed on the top of the control tower.

The Alpine rangers had already set their ropes and were silently abseiling down from the roof of the hangar. Sgt. Uwil cast his rope, and she did the same.

She was first to abseil down on hers.

She did it 'Dülfer' style: no harness, no belaying device. She was only sitting on the rope, which was going around one thigh and behind her back.

It burnt a little in the neck, but she was quickly down on the tarmac, where she crouched holding her assault carbine to cover for Torbjørn and Jean-Claude, who were following her.

She spotted the military helicopters she had been tasked to destroy.

Sergeant Uwil led the way.

Once they reached the helicopters, they heard some muffled grenade explosions and gunfire. Aisha adjusted her earplugs.

"It's OK," the sergeant said. "The rangers have captured the garrison's quarters. Hurry."

Aisha's team was tasked to set explosives on nine helicopters. Jean-Claude was providing support with his light machine guns, watching out for potential threats, while Aisha and Torbjørn were placing light charges in the cockpits of the helicopters. They were not detected, and the operation went quickly.

After five minutes, the 1st and 3rd squads had placed charges in all helicopters, and Sergeant Uwilingiyimana had them quietly move away toward the grass field by the runway.

They heard some gunfire around the control towers and the hangars, but it was nothing worrying. The Alpine rangers seemed to have the situation under control.

"OK," Sergent Uwil said. "Detonate."

Aisha pressed her detonator, and so did the other team leaders, and it triggered a series of explosions. When the smoke cleared away, they saw that all the helicopters had been destroyed, except one. Torbjørn had not set one charge properly.

"*C'est pas grave*," the sergeant said ('Never mind'). "We move on."

The 3rd squad went east to check for possible opposition troops coming from the road, while Aisha's 1st squad continued north to the end of the helicopter airport, to check for possible air defense systems. The eight engineers moved quickly and quietly forward on the frozen grass.

Suddenly, they saw blinding flashes, and heard heavy cannon fire. They took cover on the ground. It was hard and cold.

"40-mm AA shooting at the control tower," the sergeant said. "Kill it."

Immediately, Aisha helped Torbjørn get his 51-mm individual mortar ready and load his weapon. The target was 200 m (660 ft) away.

Meanwhile, in the A team, Corporal Singh was helping Tran with his anti-tank recoilless rifle.

Torbjørn fired his first mortar round, and Singh and Tran dashed forward, followed by Gonzales and the sergeant. It took 12 seconds for the mortar round to reach the target, but the 51-mm individual mortar had the advantage of not giving away the position of the shooter.

There was an explosion, followed by a series of other

very powerful explosions.

Torbjørn's round had missed the 40-mm AA canon but hit an air defense missile system a dozen meters behind. With the blazing in the background, the 40-mm AA canon vehicle was now showing a perfect silhouette. And so were the A team, now standing 80 m (260 ft) away from Aisha.

Tran fired a rocket at the anti-aircraft vehicle, which was hit and caught fire. Two men jumped out of it and ran away.

Aisha gave the signal to her team to stand up and run forward.

Shortly after, some tracers came toward the three of them, and they all plunged back to the ground.

Aisha pointed at a building at the end of the airport.

"The house over there. At least two heavy machine guns."

"*Merde, Merde, Merde,*" Jean-Claude was whispering.

"Torbjørn, your kit bag," Aisha said.

Aisha went through the different kind of shells for his individual mortar, took forth three high-explosive rounds, one illumination round, and one smoke round.

She helped Torbjørn reload his mortar as he fired the three explosive rounds followed by the illumination round.

The first round exploded on the target only one moment after they had fired the illumination round. Aisha loaded the mortar with a smoke round. When the illumination round finally triggered, Jean-Claude opened fire with his light machine gun.

"OK, Torbjørn, now fire the smoke," Aisha ordered.

It took ten seconds before the smoke grenade exploded in front of the house, and another four seconds before the smoke curtain was thick enough.

"Jean-Claude: suppressing fire on the right. Torbjørn: forward."

Aisha dashed forward while Rheinfeldt's tracers were flying past them. Sergeant Uwil and the A team were now also running forward to the house from their previous position.

Aisha and Torbjørn stopped at sixty meters (220 ft) from the house, as the A team was already by the building. Fifty meters to the right of it, the 40-mm anti-aircraft gun and the missile defense system were burning.

"Rheinfeldt!" she shouted, "Cease fire!"

Caporal Singh threw a grenade into the house. There was a muffled explosion and Tran and Gonzales stormed the building.

"Clear!" Gonzales said.

"Set a defense perimeter around the house," Sergeant Uwilingiyimana commanded. "Hey, who is this guy?"

Somebody with a camouflage net was moving a dozen meters behind Jean-Claude, who was now arriving at the house.

"That's our friend Wolf Warrior Forty-Seven," Jean-Claude said. "He's gonna lead his parachuting friends."

"I got a message from the Captain," PFC Kowalski said. "The south end of the airport is cleared."

"Tell him the north end is also clear," the sergeant replied.

Kowalski was one of the platoon's drivers, but he was now accompanying Sergeant Uwilingiyimana as a radio operator.

A moment later, they heard the sound of jet engines. Twenty-four large transport airplanes arrived low above the ground from the east. The first paratroopers started jumping down over the helicopter airport from their open cargo back doors.

"They are also dropping armored vehicles," Jean-Claude said. "Watch out not to take one on your head."

Four companies of parachute infantry and two companies of mechanized paratroopers landed over the military airport. It was an impressive sight.

The Chinese parachute infantry took over the control of the helicopter military airport, and the Alpine rangers could now head downtown. Meanwhile, the legionnaires climbed on the vehicles of the mechanized paratroopers: they were heading for the international airport. Air support was provided by Chinese drones.

It took them forty-five minutes to make the 25 km from the military airport to the international airport. They took the long way round in order to drop by a construction area and requisition a few earthmoving vehicles.

The Chinese armored vehicles with the UN flags created great confusion at the international airport as the drones bombed the anti-aircraft positions. As a result, the column met little resistance on its way into the airport.

A Chinese major started to shout *"Engineers, clear the way! Engineers, clear the way!"* and Aisha's company set to their tasks to remove obstacles from the runways.

At five in the morning, the runway had been cleared, and the Japanese UN contingent started to land. It was Monday 22 October 2096. It was to be a long day.

While the Chinese had secured both airports and waited to be relieved by the Pakistanis and Indians in the coming days, the Japanese and European UN soldiers had to stabilize the situation downtown in Bishkek. Later in the morning, the Foreign Engineers hitch-hiked the Japanese battalion who drove them back to the helicopter airport, which was at the entry of the city. From there, they set out on a march to the Spartak stadium downtown, where the other four gliders had landed and where the Alpine rangers had already regrouped.

It was an 8 km (5 miles) march across narrow streets, while the Japanese battalion advanced with their armored vehicles on the main arteries. A mixture of rain and snow was falling. Aisha wanted to put her cap on under her helmet, but she was scared she might be hit by a sniper if she removed her helmet, even temporarily.

There was sporadic gunfire everywhere. Aisha hated it. On the ground, they saw some bodies, mostly in civilian clothes.

There was a lot of blood. The second time, Torbjørn had to stop and throw up. Sometimes they heard people screaming in despair. There would be some heavy fire, and the screaming would stop.

It was impossible to know where the shooting was happening. Sometimes it was on the left, sometimes on the right, sometimes behind, sometimes ahead.

On two occasions they happened to scare away some militiamen armed with axes and hunting rifles, but there was nobody to save. Only dead corpses on the snowy street. It was mid-afternoon when Aisha's squad finally reached the Spartak stadium, which was located in the vicinity of the governmental house.

The Japanese had been taking some government officials into their UN white armored cars and asked them to broadcast appeasing messages using their trucks' loudspeakers. In the evening, the situation seemed to have calmed down, and Aisha hoped she would be able to rest a little bit. It was a mere wish, she understood, as Lt. Hoffman and Sgt. Uwil came by.

"The Kirghiz prime minister, Mrs. Olga Kudaybergenova," the lieutenant started, "wishes to go to her home to pack up some things. We will escort her."

The lieutenant was confident ten legionnaires were sufficient for an escort. He would accompany Aisha's squad with his own platoon sergeant.

A moment later, the ten UN soldiers stepped into a white armored vehicle with the UN colors (courtesy of the Japanese battalion). Madame Olga was with them. The prime minister, Mrs. Kudaybergenova, had a too complicated Russian sounding name, Sergeant Uwilingiyimana thought, so Madame Olga it was.

As the ten UN soldiers drove to the eastern part of town, where Madame Olga's flat was located, they realized it was a very questionable idea. The night had fallen and it was pitch dark, as a curfew had been declared.

Everywhere, menacing militiamen were surrounding their vehicles, but the prime minister insisted on reaching her home. On several occasions, the lieutenant ordered warning shots to be fired at the mob.

They eventually reached the prime minister's home.

The squad stayed to guard the armored vehicle, while the lieutenant and his platoon sergeant escorted Madame Olga to her flat.

The way back would be more complicated, Aisha thought.

After a moment, they heard a heavy engine sound.

"*Putain*," Jean-Claude swore. "They have tanks."

"Tran, get the Bazooka ready," Sergent Uwil yelled. "Eriksen, the mortar."

Three tanks emerged from the crowd, as Madame Olga and her escort reappeared from the building.

"*Mon lieutenant, c'est pas une situation d'avenir,*" Jean-

Claude said to Hoffman. ('Sir, we have no great future ahead of us')

As the prime minister raised her hands, the ten UN soldiers understood they had no other choice than to surrender to the militia men. Aisha just got the time to throw an incendiary grenade into the UN armored vehicle so that it would not be captured by the militia, before she was hit with a rifle butt on the shoulder. The legionnaires and the prime minister were being taken prisoner.

They were put on a truck and driven to a Kirghiz military camp nearby, which had obviously rallied to Kirghiz Power.

They were led to one of the camp's buildings and their equipment, boots, and wrist watches were taken away and locked in a room. The legionnaires were taken to two separate classrooms, while the prime minister was locked in the commandant's office.

Then, some Kirghiz soldiers came back and started beating them up.

Aisha did not like it. She kicked one soldier in the head and broke the arm of another one. That pissed the other soldiers off.

Three of them grabbed her and took her to the bathroom in the nearby corridor. They removed her belt and dropped down her pants.

They were going to rape her.

"Wait, wait," Aisha yelled in despair. "Let me at least remove my pants completely so that I can spread my legs."

They released the pressure on her. She rose her right ankle, to get her foot out of the trouser leg.

Except that she did not.

Instead, she grabbed the knife that was inside the trouser leg. The three soldiers behind her did not see it before the one on the left had his throat cut, and warm blood flowed onto the other two.

Aisha had pivoted around and was already stabbing the second soldier in the heart while grabbing the third soldier's left hand with hers. He was whining "Noooo," but it was too late. Aisha got her knife out of the second soldier's chest, shoving his body with her knee, and used it to cut the third soldier's throat.

There was blood everywhere. Warm blood. It felt rather pleasant after being cold so long in the streets.

Talking about cold, she felt like peeing. She was in the bathroom. Her pants were already down. The bodies were on the floor. She peed on them.

The soldier she had struck in the heart still had his eyes wide open, and it felt as if he was looking at Aisha.

"You disapprove, rapist? I just hope none of you had blood diseases."

When she was done, she dragged her pants back up and put her belt back. She took one of the pistol belts and the bayonets of the three dead soldiers. Fire shots were to be avoided if she did not want the whole army camp to rush into the building.

She went carefully into the corridor.

There was nobody.

The door of one of the two classrooms was open, and she could hear the agonizing screams of men being beaten up.

She approached carefully. She glanced inside the room.

Six Kirghiz soldiers were beating up Sgt. Uwil, Kowalski, Rheinfeldt, and Eriksen. They had been particularly violent with the sergeant, presumably because he was black.

She threw a bayonet at the throat of the soldier closest to her, and another bayonet at the throat of a soldier standing further away, looking in her direction. The other soldiers had not noticed her yet.

Holding the third bayonet in her left hand and her knife in her right hand, she dashed for the two men kicking Sergeant Uwilingiyimana and cut their throats simultaneously.

The two remaining soldiers finally realized what was happening, but she threw her two blades at them. She hit the soldier on the right in the heart but missed the one on the left.

She should not have cast the bayonet with her left hand! Luckily, Jean-Claude, who was on the ground, picked up the bayonet and stuck it in the soldier's leg. He let out a deep scream, Jean-Claude retrieved the knife, dragged the soldier to the ground, and stabbed him in the heart.

"*Problemet er løst,*" Torbjørn commented in his mother tongue ('Problem solved'.).

Aisha quickly shut the door and helped the legionnaires up.

"*Putain*, Aisha. That's the spirit of Cameròn," Sergeant Uwil said weakly.

The poor sergeant was in very bad shape. His nose and jaw were broken, and there was blood dripping from his left eyebrow. He complained he had some broken ribs, too.

Aisha ensured that Jean-Claude, Torbjørn, and Kowalski stood up and equipped themselves with the bayonets and assault rifles of the neutralized guards. Kowalski stayed in the room with the sergeant, while Aisha, Torbjørn, and Jean-Claude went to the other classroom, where the other legionnaires were being beaten up.

Aisha kneeled down in front of the door, holding her assault rifle. Jean-Claude stood slightly behind her, while Torbjørn opened the door violently.

"Everybody stands still!" Aisha shouted calmly.

The eight Kirghiz soldiers in the room looked surprised to see this little girl soldier covered with blood. When they saw the three assault rifles pointed at them, they slowly raised their hands. Aisha commanded them to strip down completely.

A moment later, Lt. Hoffman, Privates Tran and Gonzales, and the platoon sergeant had tied down the eight soldiers using their laces and their clothes. Corporal Singh was lying lifeless on the ground.

"That was nicely done, *caporal*," the lieutenant eventually said to Aisha. "Do you know where the prime minister is?"

"I think in an office, at the other end of the corridor, close to the room where they locked up our gear and shoes."

The legionnaires searched the corridor and captured a few other Kirghiz soldiers. In an office room, they found the prime minister. The poor lady had been beaten up pretty badly, and raped. Aisha helped her to put some clothes on.

After a few moments, Torbjørn entered the office with two pairs of shoes:

"These are your boots, Aisha, and your shoes, Madame Prime Minister."

Aisha helped the prime minister to put her shoes on. Suddenly they heard some gunfire.

"*Putain, le lieutenant est touché.*" ('Fuck, the lieutenant is hit').

The lieutenant's platoon sergeant was now in command and gave calm instructions.

"Everybody, take cover and be ready to shoot back. Eriksen, help the lieutenant."

The ten UN soldiers had managed the take control of the buildings where they had been initially brought in as prisoners, and they even had captured a dozen Kirghiz soldiers. However, they were still in the Kirghiz military camp and surrounded by at least six hundred soldiers who were shooting sporadically at their building.

"Now what?" Aisha asked, as she squatted under a window, holding a Kirghiz assault rifle.

Kowalski replied: "Before he was hit, the lieutenant was able to use a radio and contact the UN troops at the stadium. The Japanese blue helmets are coming for us."

The wait in their besieged building seemed to last forever. Sergeant Uwil, Corporal Singh and Lt. Hoffman had all been wounded, and were in no condition to fight. The lieutenant had been shot in the left collarbone. The bleeding had been stopped, but he was in great pain.

It took a whole hour before the legionnaires heard some gunfire at the entrance of the military camp. Then, they saw four white armored vehicles flying the UN and Japanese flags driving through the military camp. Somehow, the rebel Kirghiz soldiers were letting the UN Japanese soldiers come through without firing at them.

The four vehicles parked just outside the previously besieged building. Japanese soldiers stepped out and formed a perimeter. General Kurosawa, a short but imposing figure, took the prime minister to the second armored vehicle.

The ten legionnaires were shown the third armored vehicle. Inside it was sitting a man in a suit, wearing a light blue helmet and blue flak vest, matching his grey eyes. He had a bottle of alcohol. The vehicle drove away, and the man handed the bottle over to the legionnaires.

"*Koskenkorva*," he said, "Finnish vodka. I thought you may need some."

"I would have preferred some Russian vodka," Kowalski

said. "But today, I can make do with a Finnish one."

The radio operator grabbed the bottle and drank from it, before passing it to Jean-Claude.

"How many dead?" the man in the suit asked.

"Three wounded," Aisha replied.

"But no dead?" the man checked. "Good. We lost one European soldier already."

"Who?" Aisha asked.

"Some guy from your platoon, from the third squad. Killed by a sniper, I heard. Luckily he was only a legionnaire."

"*Fuck you!*" Jean-Claude exclaimed. "Who are you?"

"I am the European ambassador to Kirghizstan."

"Rheinfeldt did not mean 'fuck you', Mr. Ambassador," Aisha said. "He is just tired."

"Perhaps he meant it," the ambassador replied. "I don't care: I'm a Finn. What I care about is that if we lose too many of you, President Bonavita will pull out the EU forces. And this will be a mess. So, please, don't get killed."

Aisha grabbed the bottle of vodka from Jean-Claude and took a few sips as the vehicle was driving back to the UN headquarter.

Listening to the EU ambassador, Esko Punainen, it seemed that Kirghiz Power had deliberately aimed at capturing and killing European soldiers, with the hope of the EU president subsequently pulling the European troops out of the country. Thanks to Aisha's knife work, the legionnaires had managed to set themselves free and wait for their rescue by the Japanese. Had she not fought, she would have just been coldly murdered and been nothing more than another piece of collateral damage of the world's geopolitics.

16: LOST ASSET
(NOV 2096)

Sophie Couillard was tired and had jetlag. She had just spent ten days in Montreal, Canada, paying a visit to her parents, who she had not seen in a while. On that Friday afternoon of late November 2096, she was back in Bobo-Dioulasso, but only after an annoyingly long journey.

She had first taken a seven-hour flight from Montréal to Brussels, in the European Union, followed by a six-hour flight to Ouagadougou, the capital of Burkina Faso. There, she had boarded a little propeller plane taking her directly to Bobo-Dioulasso airport, where the V-Space premises were located.

She hoped it was the last time she had to endure such a long commute between the American and African continents. In a few months, V-Space's sister company, Vahlroos Travel, would operate an Albaspace air service on the route between New York and Bobo-Dioulasso three times a week.

The Albaspace manufactured by V-Space was equipped

with a scramjet and four CUBIC-R engines, all running on liquid hydrogen. CUBIC-R engines were modular hybrid air-breathing rocket engines able to switch between three kinds of configuration: reaction jet mode, up to Mach 3, ramjet mode up to Mach 7 and rocket mode, up to Mach 30, by injecting liquid oxygen. In atmosphere flight, the Albaspace would, however, prefer its air-breathing scramjet over the rocket engine, which still gave it a decent speed of Mach 17. It was able to connect New York to Bobo-Dioulasso in less than forty minutes.

The Albaspace was a good aerospace shuttle. Sophie knew it, she had been the project director behind its development. It could reach the orbital station in eight hours and, using its suborbital capabilities, could travel to anywhere on Earth in less than an hour. The US president had chosen it as Air Force One, while the EU president had picked it as EU Flight One.

The future was bright, obviously. But the present was foggy, and she seemed to have lost her grasp on it.

Directly after landing, she had headed for her office on the seventh floor of the main V-Space building and asked her assistant to bring her a double expresso.

The general manager of V-Space had sat down on the sofa in the corner of her office, gazing through the window at the airport beneath it, as the sun was heading westward toward the horizon. She had just thrown her trolley bag on the little sofa opposite hers, and, on it, her Canada Goose jacket, scarf, and cap. The temperature difference between Montreal and Bobo-

Dioulasso was fifty-degrees Celsius (122 °F).

As she sipped her double expresso, she pondered over the recent developments at V-Space. She had sexual encounters with Michael Vahlroos on not one, but three occasions. She was uncertain if she had really been willing every time, but she had felt it had been a necessary ordeal to go through. It had been bad sex all three times.

What had it led her to? On the plus side, her salary had been increased by thirty percent. On the minus side, Michael Vahlroos had refused to listen to her, and even decided to cancel the development of the V-craft. All resources had been re-allocated to the V-liner, which she feared may be a dead-end.

As it now stood, the V-liner would be able to warp at 40 times the speed of light using the purple matter instead of the green matter. It would also be able to take off from Earth, but there was no progress as to finding a way of having it land safely back on our planet. Elon Musk and Space X had once developed ways of having a rocket safely and vertically land back on Earth or Mars but their work could not be applied to the larger cylindrical V-liner, as it was too wide and subjected to a too high amount of turbulence when coming out of warp within the atmosphere.

This was one of Sophie's major issues. It was not the only one. She had also lost her best developer, it seemed. Thierry Diakité had taken again the competitive exam to enter the

WARSEC Youth Professional Program, and this time had been called to the interviews in Vienna, where the UN agency was still quartered. He would not know the results before the middle of December, but there was no reason to doubt that the engineer who had developed the Martian robots during his PhD and had produced a proof of concept of the now cancelled V-craft would indeed be hired by the World's Agency for the Regulation of Space Exploration and Colonization.

Sophie looked at her watch. It was 16:57. Speaking of the devil, she had a one-to-one meeting with Thierry scheduled in three minutes.

Thierry knocked on the door at the appointed time. He was wearing a navy-blue suit and a white shirt, which was very unusual for him. He had no tie, but ties were banned from the dress-code throughout the Vahlroos Corporation and its daughter companies. Sophie was only wearing jeans and a T-shirt with the V-Space insignia and it felt weird to have a subordinate better dressed than herself.

Sophie showed him the sofa where she had been previously seated and sat down herself on the couch where her Canada Goose jacket and trolley bag were piled in chaos.

"How was Vienna?" she asked, forcing herself to smile.

"Rainy and cold," Thierry replied.

Sophie clarified her question: "I meant the interview at WARSEC. You will get the job, won't you?"

"Very likely. I would be surprised if I did not get it. For the WARSEC Ventures, they want to use modified versions of the robots I developed for the Martian rescue. They want to use them to manufacture their aerospace shuttles and interstellar ships on the Moon, but they are stumbling upon difficulties. I am confident I could fix their issues pretty fast."

"So am I, unfortunately."

Using her smartphone, Sophie called her assistant, asking him to bring two double-expressos. She looked at Thierry:

"I have to ask. It's the protocol. Why do you want to leave V-Space? Was there anything you disliked in particular?"

Sophie saw how Thierry bit his lips. He would not answer and they were shortly disturbed by Sophie's aide bringing two double expressos and putting them on the sofa's side table. Thierry told Sophie it was too late for him to have coffee. She replied the two expressos were for her. When the assistant had left the office, Sophie reiterated her question:

"Please, be honest. I need to know. Were you discontent with your salary? Why leave the leading space corporation for a UN agency? I suspect your new salary will be lower than your current one."

"It will," Thierry admitted. "At least the first two years, but if I deliver, I may soon be on the same level."

"Except you won't get any bonus or stock options," Sophie retorted. "What can the UN offer that our company can't?"

Thierry thought about it a moment and finally said:

"A better world. Or at least giving me the opportunity to serve an organization that genuinely wishes to make the world better."

Sophie sipped her cup of double expresso and retorted: "V-Space also strives to make the world a better place. The Albaspace has vastly reduced intercontinental travel time. We are based in Burkina Faso, contributing to the prosperity of your home country. The V-liner will enable to mine extraterrestrial resources and bring them back to Earth at an affordable cost."

Thierry gazed silently at Sophie who was now lifting the second cup of expresso to her lips.

"Are you so naïve?" he eventually said. "The only thing V-Space genuinely wants is to maximize profit. The Albaspace is a convenient way of traveling, I admit, but it's for the happy few 0.1%. If you ever manage to develop the V-liner and make it work, it will only serve the purpose of large capitalistic corporations, probably putting them in an advantageous oligopolistic situation. Are you kidding yourself into believing you make the world a better place? Perhaps the new generation of millennials will buy this nonsense, but I won't."

"Well," Sophie admitted, as she put back her empty expresso cup on the side table. "Corporations still need to make profit. We are not the Red Cross either."

"Profit at whatever cost!" Thierry exclaimed. "I have seen enough of it and I am tired of it."

"What do you mean?"

"My father was killed by armed Chinese security guards when I was ten. He was demonstrating against a Chinese farming corporation seizing lands in Kodala, the village where I was born. Burkinabe families evicted from their lands, demonstrators killed, and for what? To maximize the profit of a Chinese corporation! What about the Martian colony? A private company sending thirty-four people to colonize the red planet and abandoning them as soon as they met the first difficulties, making the enterprise non-profitable! I designed the robots that built the rocket that brought the last Martian survivor to Earth. I know what I am talking about!"

"There will always be immoral capitalists," Sophie retorted. "But good entrepreneurs also exist! I don't see myself as an immoral business woman."

Thierry calmed down and said:

"Sophie, there are a few in your teams I dislike, to start with that Brice de Robien. I have nothing personal against you. As far as I am concerned, you are the best general manager I have ever met."

Sophie smiled vaguely.

Thierry added: "Don't take it as a compliment, though. You are the only general manager I have ever met."

They both laughed.

Then, Sophie said more seriously: "You know, Thierry, if all the disgusted people leave the corporate world, then the corporate world will only be made of disgusting people. Keep that in mind, while your go on your crusade to make the world a better place."

Thierry acknowledged her point, and when the two V-Space future ex-colleagues parted, they were in good terms despite everything.

After Thierry had left her office, she went to her desk, set her laptop in the docking station, turned it on, and gazed at her large screen.

It was the problem with idealist employees. They could be very conscientious workers, but as soon as their conscience was slightly troubled, they could become a true pain in the ass. However, her conversation with Thierry had inspired her. To attract and retain more talent, she had to position V-Space as a company serving mankind.

The only issue was Michael Vahlroos, the CEO. He was totally opposed to a deeper cooperation between V-Space and WARSEC and, as a result, V-Space had suffered from a negative image.

Yet, in the short term, cooperation was unavoidable, and even beneficial for V-Space, and its sister company, Vahlroos Travel. Since the development of the V-craft had been cancelled, and she was personally convinced that the development of the V-liner would take much longer than Michael seemed to believe, it made sense to redefine V-Space's growth strategy.

She had ideas, and the fact that she was having occasional

sex with Michael Vahlroos may help her steer the company back to the right trajectory.

As she was about to start drafting a PowerPoint presentation, she was disturbed by a news alert on her screen. It read: "*Situation under control in Kirghizstan, UN spokesman says.*" She did not really know what was happening over there, and she did not really care: it had no impact on the future of V-Space.

17: PEACEKEEPING
(DEC 2096)

The Spartak stadium in Bishkek had become a UN base, where Aisha's company was quartered. Lt. Hoffman, Sgt. Uwilingiyimana, and Cpl. Singh had been evacuated to France, and Hoffman's platoon sergeant had been appointed leader of 3rd platoon. There was only one other sergeant left in the whole platoon, as the legionnaire killed by a sniper on the first day mentioned by Esko Punainen had been the team leader of third squad.

As a result, Aisha had been appointed leader of what was left of 1st squad: Damian Kowalski, their driver, Gabriel Tran, and Pedro Gonzales, from the A team, and Torbjørn Eriksen and Jean-Claude Rheinfeldt from the B team.

Meanwhile, the UN Security Council had passed a resolution giving a mandate to the UN forces to arrest all the leaders of Kirghiz Power in order to have them tried before the

International Crime Court. General Kurosawa had been sending the Alpine rangers and the Japanese battalion to raid throughout Bishkek to capture war criminals. Engineers were helping with the destruction of found weapons.

Aisha's squad had been out on the first day of the operation only. They had done such a bad job, accidentally blowing up a whole building while demolishing a weapons cache, that the Captain had forced them to remain at the stadium to rest.

They were bored, but it was better than being fired at by snipers. Aisha still had to put up with her squad. Despite, and perhaps because of, what they had been through, they were always bitching with each other.

"Have you read the news?" Tran asked, "The UN has easily secured the capital and peace has been restored. I wonder what they mean by easily."

"It's because you are reading *Bollox News*," Torbjørn replied. "Fuck Bolloré and his media group."

"Fuck yourself, Torbjørn," Jean-Claude retorted.

Regardless of how frustrated they were, it was better than being out. Twelve UN soldiers were killed during the week the operation took to complete. Among them two legionnaires from the 2nd squad of Aisha's platoon.

Aisha started to think there was a curse. 3rd platoon was taking all the losses. Sgt. Vasiliev, the platoon sergeant, was the only remaining senior NCO. The captain put 3rd platoon in reserve.

Somehow, the massacres and fighting completely stopped in the Bishkek area. Joint patrols of UN soldiers and loyal Kirghiz soldiers seemed to have restored peace.

At about the same period, the EU mountain troops eventually received their vehicles: Swedish-made tracked, articulated, all-terrain carriers called 'Bandvagn 708'. They had been painted in white with large black letters reading 'UN'.

The second phase of the peacekeeping operation began. The two EU companies formed a column with the Japanese battalion and a newly arrived Chinese armored regiment and moved southward to the Osh province, where the massacres had started.

The first two weeks in Osh were very demanding. There was half a meter of snow, the wind was always strong and cold, but the operation continued. The UN soldiers had received information about weapons caches. The engineers and Alpine rangers were sent on patrols to find these caches and destroy them while trying to capture local ringleaders of Kirghiz Power.

Aisha's platoon was in reserve, which meant they had to do an even worse job. Here and there, the UN would receive information about mass graves of Uzbeks who had been slaughtered, and her platoon would have to help UN investigators and the Red Crescent to recover the corpses.

The corpses were usually in pieces, though preserved because of the cold. One would stumble upon a head, an arm, a trunk, not knowing to whom it belonged. Jean-Claude would just throw away body parts with a total lack of respect, while Torbjørn had to throw up several times.

Aisha was also close to throwing up on one occasion. Even though the body parts were frozen, she could not get used to the stench. It was worse than retrieving the bodies after the earthquake in Nice.

One day, she became so angry at Jean-Claude's lack of respect that she provoked him into a fight and he took up the challenge. The two UN investigators, in their white jackets, were looking helplessly at the two legionnaires fighting in the middle of the corpses. Finally, Aisha knocked Jean-Claude's head against a stone and walked away from the mass grave. She saw that one of the UN investigators was crying. She did not care.

The European mountain troops were dependent on the UN logistics to get their food supply. The EU army logistics were not the best in the world: Aisha was still waiting for the rucksack specially designed for women she had been promised. But the UN logistics were even worse.

They had to go hungry in the cold, all the more since the captain was keeping more of the supplies for the platoons searching and destroying the weapons caches.

After a whole morning spent in a mass grave, the platoon was back at the camp for lunch. There was no food left. They would have to wait until the evening. Jean-Claude punched the store's door, while Torbjørn, Gabriel, and Pedro broke a table in the cantina.

The only officer at the camp, a lieutenant from the Alpine rangers, looked at Aisha in distaste:

"This is your squad, Barjaoui. You are a leader, act like it."

Aisha did not care.

The legionnaires were saved by their platoon sergeant, running into the cantina.

"*Mon lieutenant,*" he said, "According to UN intelligence, there is a massive concentration of weapons in a hamlet south of Shohimardon. Some members of Kirghiz Power may also be found there if we act quickly. Got a message from the captain, he is busy in Kezel-kia. He wants us to go there."

"*Putain,*" the lieutenant said ('fuck'). "I have only three squads of Alpine rangers plus your platoon. Assemble the men."

The hamlet was forty kilometers away from the base, and the five UN tracked, articulated carriers were driving slowly up the snowy road. The Alpine rangers' three Bandvagn 708 were closing the convoy. Aisha's squad was in the trailer compartment of the second vehicle.

"*J'ai faim,*" Rheinfeldt complained inside the trailer ('I am hungry').

"*Ta gueule! Hold kjeft! Shut up!*'" Torbjørn replied in French, Norwegian, and English.

"What does UN intelligence know anyway?" Aisha asked.

"UN and intelligence don't go together," Jean-Claude provoked.

"Their intelligence platoon has some guys of ours," Tran objected.

"What guys?" Aisha asked.

"From the Human Intelligence Company," Gonzales explained, "of the Mountain and Arctic Warfare Division. They are based in France. They are the best."

"Have not seen any of them," Aisha grumbled.

"Of course not," Tran said. "They are always hidden, operating on their own. They bury themselves somewhere under the ground and remain there for weeks. They are professionals."

"What do they do when they need to pee and shit?" Eriksen asked.

"Ask them when you meet one, *connard*," Rheinfeldt said.

"*Putain, mais je vais te casser la gueule!*," Torbjørn exclaimed ('Fuck it, I am gonna beat the shit out of you').

Jean-Claude had no time to reply. There was an explosion, and the vehicle braked abruptly. They were all thrown on top of each other.

"The lead Bandvagn has been hit," Kowalski said.

Aisha opened the back-door of the trailer compartment and led her 1st squad out. They crouched carefully to take cover. The 2nd squad and part of the 3rd squad came laboriously out of the smoking vehicle. Most of them had bruises.

"It was an IED," a legionnaire informed them, "The sergeant is wounded."

"*Putain!*" Aisha shouted ('Fuck!').

The sergeant was taken out of the smoking bandvagn and laid carefully in the ditch by the side of the road. He had been wounded in the left thigh, the stomach, and the left arm.

Aisha swiftly jumped to the other side of the road, to assess the situation. The road followed a torrent river upstream. The hamlet lay a half kilometer (1,600 ft) ahead of them, against the steep flank of the valley, with cliff sections on some part. Past the hamlet, there was a half-frozen waterfall, leading to rocky foothill over the village. Above the village were a few short cliff sections.

Behind her, the legionnaires and Alpine rangers had all left their vehicles and regrouped on the left side of the road, against the trees. She was on the right side of the road, and the torrent was running beneath her.

"Kowalski," she yelled. "Bring me the radio."

Suddenly, she saw tracers coming from the hamlet and took cover on her side of the road. Snow was flying all over the road under the round impacts. She was isolated.

The next second, mortar rounds started falling around them. Snow and earth were blasted all around them. Trees exploded. Branches were torn in pieces and blown away.

She instinctively took deeper cover in the snow on her side

of the road, and put her earplugs in. By the explosions and their frequency, she guessed that the insurgents had three 60-mm mortars.

She heard Jean-Claude and Torbjørn laugh loud. Her men were getting even crazier than usual.

"*Caporal!*," Jean-Claude yelled, "*C'est pas une situation d'avenir.*" ('Corp, we have no great future ahead of us').

Aisha was in no mood to answer.

"Look on the bright side," Jean-Claude screamed on "If we get cut into pieces, President Bonavita will pull our company out of this shit-hole."

For a moment Aisha considered running into the middle of the mortar barrage to punch Jean-Claude Rheinfeldt, *ce connard de Luxembourgeois (*'This Luxembourger asshole'*).*

But she just wanted to lie there. She was cold and hungry. She was in no mood to fight.

"*Barjaoui!, qu'est que tu fous?*" Someone yelled ('Barjaoui! What the fuck are you doing?').

It was the Alpine ranger lieutenant, he was on the other side of the road, at the level of the third Bandvagn.

Suddenly, one of the Alpine rangers' vehicles exploded. It had taken a direct hit from a mortar round. No one had been wounded. The lieutenant barely took notice of it and kept yelling at Aisha.

"Why are you separated from your radio, Barjaoui? You are on that side of the road, and the radio is on this side of the road.

How can you talk to me on the wireless? You are in charge of the platoon, now. I want you to lead the attack."

Once again, Aisha considered running through the mortar barrage, but to punch the lieutenant, this time. She abstained.

"What is the plan, lieutenant?" she yelled back.

"Listen up, corp, it's pretty shitty. No air support, and the rest of the company will not be here to help us until at least three hours from now."

Aisha's heart sank.

"I will leave one squad with the vehicles. I will lead two squads through the woods on the left to fire at those fuckers on the ridge up there. I want you to lead the remaining three squads to that hamlet and take it, understood?"

"It's suicide, lieutenant."

"If we don't attack now, they will take us in a pincer movement. We can't defend this position. We have the low ground. We must move the hell out of here. Now, you take that hamlet."

"*Oui, mon lieutenant*," Aisha yelled back ('Yes, sir').

"*Engineers, clear the way!*" The lieutenant yelled and moved into the woods with his squads.

Enculé de lieutenant! ['Fucking lieutenant!'] He would pick the easy mission for himself and send the legionnaires to a suicide mission. Aisha was hungry and tired and sore. She did not care anymore.

Luckily, the intensity of the mortar barrage decreased. Only two legionnaires of the first squad had been wounded, as far as she was aware. The mortars had been firing for about three minutes, at about 120 rounds a minute. If they had not run out of ammo, their tubes were certainly overheating.

She started to act mechanically.

She ordered one of the lightly wounded men of 2nd squad to jump in her bandvagn and maneuver the remote controlled .50 caliber machine gun.

"Suppressing fire at the hamlet," she yelled, while throwing two smoke grenades on the road.

"2nd Squad, you stay in reserve here. 1st and 3rd squad, on me, come quickly to my side of the road!" she yelled as soon as the smoke had become thick enough.

One instant later, twelve legionnaires were with her. She led them through the deeper snow toward a boulder by the river.

There she stopped and gave instructions to the machine gunner and the mortar man of 3rd squad: "You stay here. You see the first house of the village? That's the only one with a firing angle on us. Machine gun, you see anything, you shoot. Mortar, place more smoke on the road."

Aisha led her remaining legionnaires quickly to another boulder, close to the hamlet's first house, which was just above the torrent. She did not want to go up on the road, as tracers were flying like crazy.

"Gonzales," she commanded. "Blow a hole in the cellar

of that house."

Pedro made a dash for the building. There, he spread explosive paste on the wall of the house close to the foundations, attached a thread to it, and ran back to the boulder.

"Fire in the hole," he screamed, and the next moment there was an explosion, adding more dust to the already smoky air.

Aisha gave a sign to the two men left behind in support to join them, while Kowalski and Tran were storming the house's cellar. She followed them in, and the smoke made her eyes itch. She heard a woman screaming upstairs. She went up the steep stairs to the main floor.

There was an older lady with three children crying and yelling. Aisha was in no mood to be nice. She just asked them to shut up. Kowalski somehow managed to calm them down and led them to the cellar, while Aisha went to the attic to observe the situation.

Some of the firing was coming from the hamlet, but most of it was coming from a cave in a cliff leading to the foothill above the village. Further on, on the left, there was a lower snowy foothill, from the ridge of which other insurgents were shooting at the Alpine rangers in the wood.

Something on the ground attracted her attention: there were threads. Threads everywhere. She looked more carefully using the sight of her carabine.

"Corporal, the whole village is mined. I could talk in Russian with the lady."

It was Kowalski. He was standing in the room behind Aisha, offering a perfect target for everybody looking at the house's roof.

"Kowalski, down, you idiot."

"Oh, you know," he replied, "When your time is up, it's up anyway."

Aisha pulled him down.

"Fuck you, Kowalski, you stay put when I told you to. I have seen it is mined. So far, they don't know we have taken this house. If they do, they will blow it up. It seems all the threads lead to the cave in the cliff below the foothill."

Aisha went quietly down to the first floor and gave instructions to the machine gunner and mortar man of 3rd squad to stay in the house with their corporal. They were to try to defuse the charges laid in the house, while at the same time shoot at any militiamen who would charge to attack their vehicles down the road. Optimally, they were to avoid being noticed.

She led the rest of the legionnaires out of the house, back through the hole in the cellar, and took the radio from Kowalski.

"CP, this is 3rd platoon engineers, over."

The lieutenant answered: "What's the situation, Barjaoui? Over."

"The whole village is mined. There are civilians in it. Don't launch an attack on the ridge."

"Don't worry, Barjaoui, we would all get killed anyway, I'm

not that stupid."

"We have taken the first house," Aisha went on. "So, we have set-up a good defensive position. Most of their forces are in a cave below the rocky foothill, above the hamlet."

"Copy that, Barjaoui."

"If we follow the river, we could make it to a half-frozen waterfall. By climbing it, we would be able to surprise them from above. But we don't have any ice climbing equipment."

There was a silence on the radio.

"*Mon lieutenant*?" she asked ('Sir?').

"I think I can find you something. Stay where you are. I'll send you a few men."

Five minutes later, they were joined by two Alpine rangers. One of them was a sniper. The other was the sergeant from their assault glider. His name was Éric Legrand. He had four ropes on top of his rucksack as well as ice axes, crampons, and several harnesses.

The hamlet was the end of the road. There were only four houses along the river bank, and they walked beneath them, almost in the torrent, without being detected. Aisha ordered the three remaining legionnaires of 3rd squad to stay at the foot of the fourth house and to blow a hole in its cellar, as they had done in the first house. They would wait for a signal. She would be blowing a whistle.

They followed the river bank past the hamlet and arrived at

the foot of the waterfall without meeting anybody. There, Aisha ordered Rheinfeldt, Eriksen, and Gonzales to set a defensive perimeter, while she and Tran put on the harnesses Legrand had brought with him.

The two Alpine rangers already had theirs on. The sergeant put his crampons on, took a pair of ice axes, and started climbing up the frozen waterfall, while the sniper belayed him on two ropes. The ice cliff was of poor quality, but the Alpine ranger was just hacking his way up, surely and swiftly. He was ten meters (33 ft) above the ground when he put his first ice screw in a more solid ice section. He added a quickdraw to it and clipped the rope.

He was damp because of the running part of the waterfall splashing on him here and there, and Aisha saw how he had trouble using his fingers. They were clearly freezing. He resumed his climbing nonetheless. Five meters (16.5 ft) higher, he put a sling around a tree and clipped the ropes again.

Aisha was scared of seeing him fall, anytime, hit by a bullet. But no one seemed to have spotted him. He eventually reached the top of the ice cliff, forty meters (130 ft) above Aisha.

A moment later, they saw the ropes shake twice.

"You can go, quick," the sniper whispered and handed over the two white ropes to the legionnaires.

As they had no ice axe or crampons, Tran and Aisha had to prusik themselves up. Aisha twisted a thin cord loop around her rope and passed it on a locker-carabiner which she clipped and locked on her harness. That was the first prusik loop. She then took another thin sling, which she twisted around the rope slightly below, passed on another locker-carabiner, which she clipped in a longer sling. Tran had done the same.

Aisha started to prussik herself up. She set her foot in the longer sling and stood up on it. As the lower prussik loop was pulling on the rope, it gripped it and held. While balanced on the sling, she slid the prusik attached to her harness up the rope as high as she could and then relaxed, and the prussik held her. She was now hanging by the harness sixty centimeters higher above the ground, and she slid up the prussik holding the longer sling. Once again, she stood up on the longer sling and repeated the whole operation.

It was exhausting, and both legionnaires were panting. Aisha cursed when she felt a rope on her head. It was the third rope the sergeant had installed. The sniper did not have an ice axe either, so he also had to prussik his way up. But he was faster.

When they were ten meters above the ground, they started to receive splashes from the running waterfall. It was cold and wet. The physical effort was harder, though, and Aisha was sweating when she first arrived at the top. The sniper was second, and Tran third.

They took a short break at the top, while the sergeant coiled one of the ropes. The two others were left, for a hypothetical, but highly probable, retreat. From where they were, Aisha could see that the lieutenant had spread out two squads of Alpine rangers at the edge of the wood, 800 m (half a mile) from their snowy ledge.

His mortar men were using their 51 individual mortars to fire at the hilly ridge, 200 m (660 ft) away from them. Aisha could now see it was from there the three insurgent 60-mm mortars were firing.

The sergeant led the group, on a snowy ledge below some trees, until they were just above the cave platform where most of the automatic fire was coming from.

Aisha, Tran, and the sergeant checked the trees and installed two belay stations, while the sniper was looking for a good position to aim at the militiamen on the ridge.

Aisha installed one of the ropes on one belay station and prepared herself to abseil down. Meanwhile the sergeant attached Tran to the fourth rope and was ready to lower him down from his belay station. Aisha took some duct tape out of her pocket and attached mags to one another.

"That's for you, Tran," she said, handing it over to the short Cambodian legionnaire. "Five mags. That's 200 rounds. There are max twenty people down there. Don't miss them."

She handed over her whistle to the legionnaire.

"Tran, when you have cleared the ground, you blow in it. I will abseil down immediately to the platform, while the sergeant will lower you right down to the ground."

Tran did not say anything, took the whistle, passed it around his neck, adjusted the strap of his assault rifle and went ten meters (33 ft) further away along the ledge.

"When you're ready, Tran," the sergeant said.

Tran looked at Aisha, at the sergeant, and just stepped into the void. Aisha saw how the sergeant gave him some slack in order not to stop his fall too abruptly. The next second, she heard firing. It was Tran's assault rifle. She was relieved.

He was now dangling over the militiamen's position, hanging on his rope and emptying his mags. They must have been completely taken by surprise.

The sniper, about twenty meters (66 ft) on the sergeant's right, was shooting at the insurgents on the hilly ridge.

As soon as Aisha heard Tran's whistle, she jumped into the void, abseiling down on the rope. She had a moment of panic when she saw that Tran had dropped his mags and was trying to reach for his pistol.

Pain followed her anguish. Pain in her jaws: the butt of her rifle had hit her. She accelerated her descent and touched the ground in a puddle of blood.

She slipped and fell.

Two militiamen were aiming at her at close range. Her rifle was still hanging on her shoulder. She rolled onto her side and kicked the one on the left before getting to her feet and grabbing her knife. She was still attached to the rappel rope.

She fell a bullet flying through her jacket under her left arm.

It was Tran, who was shooting with his pistol while hanging on the rope. When Aisha grabbed the militiamen's shoulder and cut his throat, she saw how Tran looked sorry. He hit the second man right in the head.

Aisha spotted the detonator, plunged for it, was held back by the rappel rope, remembered to unclip her belaying device, and finally reached it. She cut the threads.

One moment later, Tran was on her, panting, aiming his pistol at some wounded militiamen.

Aisha gave him two mags from her combat vest, and Tran clipped one in his assault rifle. They both cast a quick glance at the hole in Aisha's jacket sleeve. There was no blood. The bullet had missed her triceps by a hairsbreadth, though.

"Really sorry, corp," Tran said, pointing his pistol at the militiamen.

The wounded insurgents were now raising their hands.

Kirghiz Power were cowards, Aisha thought. They had no trouble killing unarmed people, but when it came to fighting, they gave up easily.

She went to the nearest insurgent and put her knife against his throat.

"Who is the boss, here?" she yelled.

The scared insurgent pointed at a well-shaved, potbellied man wearing glasses, who was only slightly wounded in the hands. Aisha grabbed him and pushed him to the entrance of the cave. She picked up a loud-hailer stained with blood and handed it to the man.

"Now, fat guy," she said slowly in English, "You ask all of your men to surrender now, or I cut your throat, in say... ten seconds. You have seen what I have done to your other men."

Aisha saw that the man's legs were shaking, but eventually, he started to yell into the loud-hailer in Kirghiz.

She could not be sure what he was saying, but a moment later, the firing stopped, and she saw men walking slowly with their hands up, holding white flags.

"*Putain, quel bordel.*" ('What a fucking mess.')

It was the Alpine ranger sergeant, who had just abseiled down. He turned to the sniper, who was rappelling down on the other rope.

"*Tu rappelles les cordes?*" ('Can you take down the rope?')

The mission turned out to be a major success for the UN forces. The main ringleaders of Kirghiz power in the Osh province had all been captured or killed. An impressive amount of ammunition and weapons had been retrieved and destroyed.

Subsequently, combat almost completely stopped in the region. Meanwhile, the two platoons had sustained only seven wounded in total.

Aisha was said to have turned a desperate situation into a success. As for her, she only remembered being sore and angry all the time, but the Alpine ranger lieutenant recommended her for promotion to sergeant. She was put temporarily in command of 3rd platoon, though she was still technically only a corporal.

At the end of November, the UN secretary-general and some other people in suits came and visited the base of the EU mountain troops. The captain took Aisha aside, together with the rest of 1st squad, and they were all introduced to Mrs. Hira Dorjee-Sherpa, a Nepalese woman who wore strange glasses, as she was blind. She was the United Nations secretary-general, and gave each of them a medal, for having been beaten up by Kirghiz soldiers in Bishkek.

It was called the *Dag Hammarskjöld* medal. It was named after an important UN diplomat who had been killed by some white mercenaries in Africa in the 1960s. As a result, UN soldiers wounded or killed under peacekeeping operations were awarded a medal bearing his name.

They also met with the EU ambassador, Esko Punainen. He offered Aisha Barjaoui and Gabriel Tran a bottle of Finnish vodka each. He seemed to like *Koskenkorva*. He also gave both legionnaires the *Jean Monnet* medal, for their heroic abseiling charge at the hamlet. Jean Monnet had been one of founding fathers of the EU. That medal was one of the highest decorations given to EU soldiers.

"I'm giving you the medal," the EU Ambassador said, "because our beloved President Bonavita would not take the trouble to come here. She does not care about Kirghizstan. Nobody in the news does either: they are only talking about

US President Shannon Fang being re-elected."

As a platoon leader, she had to take care of the 18 remaining legionnaires. Since the situation had improved dramatically, they were doing fewer patrols and there was nothing worse than bored legionnaires, especially as peacekeepers.

One day, Jean-Claude Rheinfeldt took his pistol and shot a sheep wandering nearby. He wanted to eat fresh mutton, he said, as he was tired of the military food. In his defense, the mutton he cooked was delicious, but then other legionnaires started killing farm animals around too.

Local farmers were very unhappy with this situation, and so was Captain Léger, who had to pay indemnities to them. Aisha decided to take her platoon on a long ski excursion. There was was enough snow now. She wanted to be better at ski touring, and it was a good way of keeping the men busy.

The legionnaires first complained, but when they saw that the snow was better than anything they had experienced in the French Alps, they became more positive about it. Even Torbjørn and Jean-Claude stopped bitching with each other, especially after the Norwegian started coaching the Luxembourger in improving his skiing.

On New Year's Eve, Captain Léger told Aisha that Sgt. Uwilingiyimana would become Lt. Hoffman's new platoon sergeant, to replace Sgt. Vasiliev too badly wounded in the Bandvagn at the hamlet. She would subsequently become a sergeant and take the lead of 2nd Squad, after completing an NCO course in Castelnaudary.

She would also take extra courses in skiing and mountaineering to be able to lead a whole platoon on mountainous terrain.

Aisha was rather pleased. The year 2097 was starting better than the year 2096 had ended.

At the end of January 2097, the 2nd company of the 2nd REG and the 3rd company of the 27th BCA were relieved by two European companies of the *Gebirgsjägerbataillon* 232.

None of the legionnaires were sad to leave godforsaken Kirghizstan

18: Last Month In Vienna (March 2097)

On this Friday evening of mid-March 2097, Tatjana Aydemir had taken Thierry Diakité to Ralf's office. The WARSEC temporary premises were located in the Vienna International Center, where the United Nations Office for Outer Space Affairs (UNOOSA) used to be, and where the International Atomic Energy Agency was still located.

Tatjana Aydemir, a short lady in jeans and polo shirt, with black hair but blue eyes, was the WARSEC production director, and Thierry's new boss at WARSEC. A 42-year-old German engineer who had previously worked at the European Space Agency, Tatjana had given him a picture of the situation on his first day at WARSEC, back in January:

WARSEC needed money. The contribution paid by the member states was far from enough to launch an interstellar expedition. However, WARSEC had sovereignty over space resources and could levy taxes on space activities by private corporations. It was therefore in WARSEC's interest to encourage commercial activities in space, so as to tax them.

One of the goals was to set up a shipyard on the Moon to manufacture and sell space vehicles at a competitive price. The other one was to promote space tourism.

The orbital space station was being greatly extended. By 2098, it would consist of four gravitational rings, each 150 m (492 ft) in diameter and fifteen decks thick. One habitable ring would be reserved for WARSEC and Orbit Control.

The second ring would be for national space agencies, public research institutions and universities, as well as for national delegations wishing to have representatives on board the international station. It was a matter of power. Some countries, like the EU, would pay just to have a representative on board the station.

The other two rings would be leased to private corporations. Radisson and Sheraton would each operate their hotels. A space entertainment center operated by Vahlroos Travel was to open, and it seemed that, already, a bunch of Harry Potter nerds were willing to spend a huge amount of money to play *Quidditch* in weightlessness. Vahlroos Travel would also run some hotels and start organizing space trips to the Moon's orbit.

To make space tourism and vehicle manufacturing on the Moon possible, it was vital to have a more convenient way of bringing people into space than the current two space elevators on Tarawa and in Guyana.

The Albaspace from V-Space was very expensive, and the Vahlroos Corporation had refused to cooperate with WARSEC to make it cheaper. Luckily, other space manufacturers such as Boeing, Airbus, and Comac had agreed to participate in a consortium mostly owned by WARSEC to build cheap aerospace shuttles on the Moon. It was called WARSEC Ventures.

Since the International Labor Organization (ILO) treaties did not apply on the Moon, it was allowed to use as many robots as were necessary for manufacturing there. This would enable mass production at a low cost. In theory.

They had tried to design production robots based on Thierry's robots, which had been used to build a rocket on Mars. However, the lower gravity environment on the Moon had made it much more complicated for them to operate. Furthermore, it had seemed that as soon as there were more than twelve robots on the same location, they would bug more easily. Thierry's help had therefore been more than welcomed.

Thierry's first suggestion had been that, on the Moon, it would be easier to have robots moving on caterpillar tracks rather than a set of legs. After two weeks, Thierry had proposed a new design for caterpillar robots using the same frame as his insect-like robots. Another four weeks were necessary for him to rewrite the interaction code of the robots so that they could interact in a large robot population environment.

Cooperating with the university, they had managed to test half a dozen prototypes in Vienna by the end of February. The new interaction code had been deployed on the existing robots on the Moon, and a production team had conducted some successful tests in the second week of March.

On that Friday 15 March, however, the test results had come back, and Tatjana had called for a late meeting with Ralf Åhman, the WARSEC Director, and Glover Johnson, the global safety director.

Ralf had invited them to his little office, showing them the tiny sofa section, which was large enough for four people. Tatjana began by giving a short summary of the test outcome.

"When does it mean we can have a fully operational shipyard on the Moon?" The WARSEC director asked.

Tatjana looked briefly at Thierry, and said: "The two new batches of robots will be ready by the end of May. They are being manufactured in Brazil. We will ship them into orbit with the Guyana Space Elevator in June, and then we have to ferry them to the Moon. But I guess it is reasonable to believe we can start manufacturing the Space hounds and the Space Bears by the middle of July. The first aerospace shuttles will be ready by the end of August. Then it will be up to the Boeing and Airbus engineers and pilot to start the test procedures. If we are satisfied with the quality of the aerospace shuttles, we should start assembling the first Forward class starship in November."

"That's five months behind our plan," Ralf noted.

"Better late than in time, when it comes to safety," Glover retorted. "The cost of a catastrophe would be much higher than the cost of delay."

"True," Ralf admitted, "but we are relying heavily on the mass production of aerospace shuttles to relieve WARSEC's finances."

Glover Johnson turned to Thierry: "Not disappointed to have missed the tests?"

"Partly," Thierry admitted, "On the other hand, I am not yet trained as an astronaut. I have just started."

"We move to the new headquarters in Vaasa in June," Ralf said. "But the training center over there will be operational in April."

"The safety team is moving there at the end of March," Glover announced, "Including myself. We will have our first training session on April 15th. It would make sense that you be part of that training program if we want you to accompany the new batches of robots to the Moon in June."

"Absolutely," Tatjana said. "I will arrange for Thierry to move to Vaasa in the first week of April."

"Thank you," Thierry said.

"By the way, Thierry: do you still live with Tintin, Anatoli, and Liisa?" Ralf asked.

"Yes. Not worth finding a place of my own for so little time left in Vienna."

"I guess you will welcome having a place of your own in Vaasa," Ralf said. "We are located by the airport over there, but at least we have plenty of space."

That evening, as he stood in the U-Bahn to Schwedenplats, Thierry was happy. He was going to the Moon! Of course, it was not extraordinary anymore those days, but still! Even Anatoli and Alice had not walked on the Moon. Not to mention Tintin. He had not even had his astronaut training and had never been in space. But after all, he was only a theoretical physicist.

From Schwedenplats, Thierry walked decisively to the flat located more than a kilometer away on Kegelgasse.

During his first weeks in Vienna, he had studied the traffic light pattern and calculated the most optimal itinerary and pace to adopt to walk the distance without having to stop a single time for a red light. Anatoli had called him nerdy, but Thierry could not help it. He was good at finding patterns and solving problems. That was all. And having to wait two minutes for a green light on a pedestrian crossing was a problem worth solving. Besides, one had to think of something when walking. In Vienna, one could get an expensive fine, if seen by a police officer walking with the head down, on a smartphone. They claimed that this behavior was responsible for too many traffic accidents.

The first two weeks in Vienna had been difficult, though. When he had been in Sweden for Tintin and Anatoli's Nobel Prize ceremony, Tintin had been kind enough to lend him warm clothes from his time in Russia.

This time, Thierry had had to buy a winter coat and other warm clothes, and they were not inexpensive. Housing had also been an issue. Tintin was renting a room in Anatoli's three-room apartment, and Thierry had planned to crash in Tintin's room until he could find a place of his own. It had turned out to be impossible in Vienna.

Now, they were four living in the flat: Tintin, Anatoli, his girlfriend Liisa, currently unemployed, and him. Not to mention Anatoli's and Liisa's kokoni dog, Calypso.

When he arrived at the building, Thierry saw Mikko and Valeriya walking their new husky puppy. Mikko Andersson, a brown-haired Swede with Asian-shaped grey eyes, and Valeriya Limonov, a short but stout Russian lady with brown hair, were two warp specialists. Both in their late twenties, they worked on the interstellar propulsion program, together with Tintin, Anatoli, and, of course, Alice Fù, the Afro-Chinese inventor of the green matter, who had been awarded the Nobel Prize in Chemistry as the two theoretical physicists got theirs in physics.

Alice, Mikko, and Valeriya were sharing a three-room flat just above Anatoli's and Tintin's apartment, and Thierry wondered how Alice could stand living with them, since every time they were, so to say, at warp speed in the bedroom, the whole building could hear them.

"Come, Apollo, come," Mikko said to the dog.

But the husky puppy was more interested in sniffing some canine urine.

"Good evening guys," Thierry greeted them.

"Good evening, Thierry," Valeriya replied. "So, the result of the test?"

Thierry gave a thumbs-up. "Success. I'm going to the Moon in June."

"Really?" Mikko said. "Congrats. We have not started our astronaut training, even though we qualify for interstellar travel."

"Well, you need people on the Moon to build your ship before you can do an interstellar trip," Thierry retorted.

"Hi guys, hi Apollo, you have grown up since last time."

It was Laura Martinez, Glover's girlfriend. She was dragging a suitcase.

"Good evening, Laura," Valeriya said. "Back from where this time?"

"Eight-week cargo cruise between Rotterdam and Kourou, in Guyana."

"Let me help you with the suitcase," Thierry offered.

Glover Johnson had a three-room apartment on the third floor, just under Anatoli's flat. As they all entered the building, a neighbor greeted them.

"*Hallo, die Raummenschen. Wünche Euch ein'n schön'n Habend.*" (Hi, space people. I wish you a nice evening).

"*Dir auch*" ['Likewise'], Mikko replied, as he was the only one in the company to know some German.

After helping Laura with her case to the third floor, Thierry went up another floor to his flat. When he opened the door, a little brown dog came out and started playing with Apollo, behind on the stairs.

"Come back, Calypso, come back!" Thierry said firmly at the dog, and the kokoni followed him back into the flat.

"Was it Apollo, outside?" Liisa asked.

Anatoli's girlfriend was a tall, athletic blond Estonian, constantly dressed in sports clothes.

"You are late for our Friday dinner," Tintin noted.

Anatoli and Tintin had cooked and the table was dressed.

"Sorry, had a late meeting. By the way... surprised to see that Glover stayed at the meeting while his girlfriend is just back from an eight-week mission. He's gonna get killed!"

"Glover is used to it." Anatoli said as he invited everybody with a gesture to come to the living room's small table. "So, the test: what results?"

Thierry sat down and said: "Success. The caterpillar robots are more precise than the legged robots, and the new interaction algorithm is not bugging."

"Good to hear," Liisa said as she helped herself to the salad. "At least your non-paid overtime hours were not in vain."

"I'm going to the Moon at the end of June," Thierry added

"Damn it, you go to space before me!" Tintin exclaimed. "Congrats, man."

"Damn it, you are going to the Moon before me!" Anatoli added.

A moment later the flat's door opened, and Alice, Valeriya,

and Mikko came, with the husky puppy Apollo.

"Heard that Thierry is going to the Moon," Alice said. "We've got some champagne, and we would join you gladly for dinner."

"OK, no problem," Tintin said. "We can turn our dinner into a little buffet."

A moment later, chairs had been rearranged and they were all sitting around the little side table by the sofa, raising a toast to Thierry.

"My last time in space was November 2094," Alice commented. "I've not been back up there since I joined UNOOSA and WARSEC".

"It makes sense," Liisa noted. "The current priority has been to expand the orbital station and set up manufacturing capabilities on the Moon. They need production specialists, not propulsion specialists."

Alice Fù looked at Thierry: "You are going to the Moon in June. Any idea when we start manufacturing the Forward?"

"Middle of November," Thierry replied.

"OK, that means they will not start before January 2098," Valeriya said conservatively. "It will be completed by July 2098. There will be six or eight months of testing, meaning they will give the green light for the first interstellar journey to Alpha Centauri at best in 2099."

"The only question that remains," Anatoli said, "is: who will be in the crew?"

"Whoever will be on the crew," Liisa said, "If you, Anatoli, are part of it, then you will have to take Calypso with you."

"But why?" Anatoli asked, looking at Liisa. "This is your dog, not mine."

"I just received the answer this afternoon. I will start a post-doc in Berlin, at the Wegener's Institution in June. I will have to travel a lot to Antarctica, and dogs are not allowed in Antarctica. They may eat penguins."

"Come on, Liisa. Calypso will never eat a penguin. She is too small. Apollo, perhaps, but not Calypso."

"You could congratulate me on my post-doc instead," Liisa commented.

Anatoli would do whatever Liisa decided anyway. Tintin had told Thierry stories of their time in Moscow. Anatoli's friends from the military had tried to convince him to break up with her. It was not wise, they had claimed, to go out with an Estonian woman. Baltic women were dangerous. That had made Tintin laugh heartily. In antiquity, Greek sailors were afraid of mermaids. In the twenty-first century, Russian soldiers were afraid of Baltic women.

As far as Thierry was concerned, the only issue with Liisa was how she ran the flat. Saturday was cleaning day, and the following morning, it was his turn. He hated cleaning the flat.

Where he used to live in Burkina Faso, the corridor mates paid someone to clean the corridor and the rooms three times a week. But Liisa denied them the right to hire somebody. They could use their hands! Thierry, who was an outstanding robot programmer, had hoped to bring in a cleaning robot. Liisa had vetoed his attempt.

According to her, weekly cleaning of the flats was a good way of reminding these rocket scientists of the down-to-Earth reality of life. That way, they would certainly show some respect to the people cleaning the UN offices, which she was sure they weren't.

Perhaps she was right. In the meantime, Thierry still hated cleaning up the flat; all the more since their dog, Calypso, was responsible for most of the dust. The worst was the stone collection. Liisa, as a glaciologist and geologist, had a great interest in stones, and her stone shelves were accumulating dust incredibly fast. Dusting them off was time-consuming.

The next day, Thierry was done with the cleaning of the flat by lunchtime. Since the weather was fine, he decided to take a walk in the Stadtpark. When he was back at the flat, it was already dusty again, with dog hair flying everywhere. Damned bitch, he thought looking at the brown kokoni. Anyway, in three weeks, he would be in Finland, with a flat of his own.

Later in the afternoon, he was informed by Tintin that Glover and his girlfriend Laura were getting married at the end of May at the US Embassy in Vienna. They would have a very small ceremony, but as their Viennese neighbors, they were invited.

19: VAASA
(APRIL 2097)

Glover Johnson was happy that Laura had gone to the States to visit her family. Otherwise, she would have accompanied him on this very flight to Helsinki. It was Friday 5 April, and the WARSEC Global Safety department was moving to Vaasa, in Finland.

Laura had gone to the States on March 31st. Glover had moved out of his flat on April 1st, having their furniture taken back by the leasing company and their personal belongings, including their bikes, shipped by train to Vaasa beforehand. He had crashed in Ralf's spare bedroom for his remaining few days in Vienna.

Now, they were twelve from the safety department sitting in the plane to Helsinki. The whole department consisted of seventy staff, but Glover had refused to have all of them onboard the same flight. What if the plane crashed with the entire safety department onboard? The whole WARSEC program would be delayed.

Since his years in the US Navy, Glover had been an expert in risk mitigation and contingency plans. Yet, he had failed to prevent it. His girlfriend Laura was pregnant. Damn it!

They had been on the wrong side of the statistics; that was all. As Laura was now in her early thirties, she was advised not to continuously take contraceptive pills for health reasons.

She had just been promoted to captain in the merchant navy and was now operating huge nuclear-powered cargos from the Danish shipping company, Maersk. Every time she went on a cruise, she would stop taking her pills. Sometimes a bit before, depending on her cycles.

They had done it just before she left for Rotterdam, but the condom had split. They had assessed the probability she would be pregnant was minimal. And technically it was. But the probability was not zero. God damn it! He, WARSEC's global safety manager, had made a bad call on such a trivial issue.

The worst part, however, was that she wanted to keep the baby. She was thirty-four and claimed that if she were going to have a baby at some point, why not now? She had just been promoted captain, and her career would not suffer from it, as the Danes were more tolerant toward young mothers than Americans. They had therefore decided to keep the baby.

But Glover was not particularly thrilled at the prospect of it. Ralf had said that in Finland, where they were moving, dads were expected to devote at least at much time to their children as mums. Glover Johnson had been kindly advised to set time aside to properly take care of his child, else, he would be bullied by all his Finnish colleagues.

That meant that, although her career would not particularly suffer, there was a risk that his would.

And then, Laura had insisted on getting married. Who got married these days?

Luckily, it would be a simple wedding. Just sign a few papers at the US embassy in Vienna, and a restaurant visit with their former neighbors and Ralf. The guys at the restaurant would not even know it was a wedding. They had a habit of charging more for weddings than regular dinners.

Glover was drawn out of his thoughts by a voice in the cabin's intercom informing them they were about to land in Helsinki. It was only his second time in Vaasa. The set-up of the headquarters in Vaasa had happened mostly under the supervision of the Vaasa office director, a very organized Finnish lady.

In Helsinki Airport, the signs reminded him how weird the Finnish language was. It seemed to be taken straight out of a fantasy book. Could mankind really, during its evolution, have come up with a language such as Finnish on its own? Finnish was said to be one of the most ancient languages in the world. That would imply that humans living on Earth 10,000 years ago had found a much more complicated way of communicating than modern humans. It was intriguing indeed.

A moment later, he boarded the plane to Vaasa. He took his tablet and decided to re-read some of the background information the Vaasa office director had sent him. Their arrival in Vaasa might be tricky. They had been instructed to avoid the welcome of the Vaasa Mayor at any cost, in order not to worsen the situation.

As he was reading through the briefing notes, he recalled the situation. Petri Granfalk, the mayor of Vaasa, was a peculiar individual, suffering from what could be called megalomania.

A few years earlier, a tunnel connection had opened between Vaasa, in Finland, and Umeå, in Sweden, on the other side of the Gulf of Bothnia. Some had believed it would boost the economic development of the area and the mayor had had built a gigantic arena, now called the 'Space Arena', in tribute to the newly installed WARSEC headquarters.

This arena was able to host 150,000 spectators, even though the Vaasa population was no greater than 75,000. A lot of taxpayers' money had been wasted in the process, the arena was said to be ugly, and there was a lot of resentment in the city toward the mayor.

This should not have been a problem as far as WARSEC was concerned. However, the new headquarters was located by Vaasa Airport, and the Mayor had had taken the initiative of expanding the runway, without waiting for all the proper impact studies to be completed.

As the Finnish government was currently looking into it, there were some demonstrations in Vaasa directed against the construction work by the airport, and by extension to WARSEC. Some Vaasa citizens seemed to mistakenly believe that WARSEC was indeed to blame for the extension of the runway at the airport, which was absolutely not the case.

As a result, all WARSEC personnel were clearly instructed to keep a safe distance from any of the city officials, in order to remain as neutral as possible in this local conflict between a mayor and his citizens.

When the plane started its approach to Vaasa airport, Glover noted that there was still some snow on the fields around. The new headquarters stood out east of the airport. The huge new arena under construction lay west of the airport, close to the motorway.

At Vaasa airport, they were welcomed by the mayor and some of the other town officials, who offered toasts to the arriving 'space people', as the local newspaper referred to WARSEC employees. Glover smiled politely, explaining he did not speak Finnish, even though the mayor was speaking English, and led his WARSEC colleagues quickly out of the terminal. A bus shuttle was waiting for them.

On the WARSEC campus, Glover Johnson had been given a three-room furnished apartment on the seventh floor of his building. He had a view over the WARSEC headquarters and could just glimpse the airport behind.

The next Saturday, he borrowed a service vehicle to retrieve his shipment at the train station, including the bikes. Since they were having a baby, he also decided to lease a car for their private use. He would probably not need it much, but she would.

The new headquarters in Vaasa were impressively large, and some of the buildings were still under constructions. The complete Vaasa campus was expected to be ready by 2103 and would then be able to host no less than 10,000 employees and their families. According to Ralf's calculation, when interstellar colonization started, provided a habitable planet within a reasonable range was available, there would most likely be up to 15,000 employees on WARSEC's payroll. The 'space people' and their families would probably represent an increase of 25% of the whole Vaasa population, and it was no wonder that the mayor was suffering from a kind of megalomania.

However, for the time being, the premises felt quite empty. The current Finnish employees in the administration were fewer than 100. Out of his team of seventy, twenty were currently in space, twenty were on leave, and there would be only thirty safety specialists available to train the new space construction workers.

Currently, WARSEC had only two dozen astronauts trained in space construction, and they mainly relied on astronauts from the various national space agencies. As of now, however, they would also train manufacturing workers from their corporate partners, such as Boeing and Airbus, for the lunar shipyard's venture.

On April 15th, 2097, the first training class started. In it were seventy-five students. Twenty-six were from WARSEC, fifteen from Airbus, twenty-four from Boeing and ten from Comac. Thierry Diakité was among them. It was not a selection program, just *Basic Safety Course 1*.

During the first two days, after a final medical check-up, each student was put in a centrifuge to test how much G-force they could take before passing out. The requirement was to manage 3-G for ten minutes, which most normally fit people would manage.

Thierry did not like it. He felt slightly sick. But he managed to handle a 10-G force before passing out. All the students happened to perform much better than the minimum requirement.

For the rest of the week, they had to train to dress and walk in different kinds of space suits: Red atmosphere entry suits, white space-sorties suits, pale pink lunar suits.

To Thierry's dismay, Glover Johnson put quite some pressure on them.

"Astronauts," he said, "You all have advanced knowledge in physics and know that the boiling temperature of a fluid is a function of the pressure applied to it."

Yes, they all knew that, but Glover went on:

"The Armstrong limit? What is the Armstrong limit?"

An Airbus engineer replied: "The Armstrong limit is the atmospheric pressure at which water boils at human body temperature."

"And what temperature would that be?" Glover asked.

"98 degrees Fahrenheit," a Boeing engineer answered.

"37 degrees Celsius, you mean," Glover retorted. "It's almost the twenty-second century, it's about time to use the metric system. You are going to space. Even NASA has used the metric system for a hundred years, now."

"Thank you for reminding me," the Boeing engineer said. "I'm fine with the meters, I just need to work on my Celsius."

"Good. So, what concrete consequences does the Armstrong limit have?"

Thierry decided to answer: "If our suits get torn apart when in a depressurized environment, we are in trouble."

"Please expand. What will happen to you if your suit cracks open in space?" Glover insisted.

"My saliva and the water in my lungs will start boiling," Thierry replied. "I will feel a burning sensation in my mouth before passing out and eventually die of lack of oxygen. It will take another dozen minutes before my dead body freezes."

"Good description, Thierry." Glover said, "That's why we don't mess up with safety at WARSEC."

In the second week, Thierry and the other students started spending time training in a depressurized hangar. Every time, Thierry checked his suit pressure on his wrist computer. He was so scared of the Armstrong limit. And yet, they were still on Earth. In the event of an accident, the instructors could immediately pressurize the hangar by opening large doors.

The space trainees spent the last three days in a simulated Moon Base within the hangar. They slept in imitations of Moon huts, ate dry food, relieved themselves in lunar toilets and, every day, put on their lunar suits, went through the airlock and worked ten hours in a row in the depressurized hangar.

They had to wear diapers in their space suits, and Thierry started to think there was nothing glamorous about being an astronaut. He wondered how Sanne van der Maas, the survivor of the Martian colony, had managed for eighteen years in that kind of environment.

They practiced how to react in case of fire in a lunar hut, how to evacuate a hut in emergency. The week was, overall, exhausting. In order to give them some freedom of movement, the spacesuits were pressurized at 0.3 Atmosphere, which was equivalent to the air pressure at 9,000 m (30,000 ft) of altitude. Of course, the oxygen concentration was much higher than on Earth. The oxygen concentration in their suits was at least 40% and could be gradually increased to 60%. But it still equated to being at 3,600 m (11,800 ft) of altitude. In order to speed up the inflation time of their space suits to five minutes only, the lunar huts kept an atmosphere similar to that of 2,700 m (8,900 ft) of altitude.

In the third week, Thierry and the other trainees still had to practice other maneuvers in the depressurized hangar and sleep in the Moon Base. However, they were given the opportunity to slip out of the hangars three times and do three flights in a 0-gravity plane.

The plane had been leased by Airbus for the occasion. When it reached 15,000 m (49,000 ft), it would do a maneuver which would cause the passenger to feel weightlessness for a few minutes.

For Thierry, weightlessness felt like falling, except than one would never land. He did not like it. But he got used to it, as the exercise was repeated over and over again, with and without space suits.

The last week, the 0-G plane took all the 75 students and 25 instructors to Toulouse, in southern France. Now, it was for real.

There, they boarded an Albaspace belonging to the European Space Agency. Manufactured by V-Space, the long, thin aerospace shuttle had a sharp-nosed fuselage and canard wings. Its rear delta wings were slightly curved, bearing four CUBIC-R engines. The scramjet was located on the top rear of the fuselage, under the rear overarching curved aileron.

Although the Albaspace was safe enough for the passengers

not to wear protection suits, the instructors had insisted all the students wear red atmosphere entry suits: they should not get used to unnecessary comfort.

The Albaspace took off from the long runway and climbed violently to the altitude of 15,000 meters (49,000 ft).

"*You are not wealthy space tourists,*" the ESA pilot joked in the intercom, "*You are astronauts.*"

Thierry felt how the plane levelled horizontally, but he was soon pulled back again to his seat as the Albaspace kept accelerating.

"*Mach 3,*" the pilot announced. "*Our jet engines have now switched to ramjet mode.*"

The whole cabin was silent, and he had to admit that the Albaspace was most likely the best aerospace shuttle in the world. The Space Hound and Space Bear they were about to manufacture would not be as comfortable as this.

He remembered the Albaspace shuttles being assembled at the V-space factory from his time in Bobo-Dioulasso. Now he was in one and escaping Earth's gravity. It was only a pity there were no windows for the passengers. But he could understand why.

"*Mach 6.4,*" the pilot said. "*We have now ignited the scramjet and will resume the climb when we have enough speed.*"

Thierry was still being dragged back in his seat by the acceleration force. When looking at one of the TV screens, he noted that the Albaspace was now climbing.

"*Mach 21, CUBIC-R engines now in rocket mode,*" the pilot said.

Pilots were like that. They always had to tell their life to everybody, as if their job was so interesting, Thierry thought. Though, he had to admit, it was a bit interesting.

On the TV screens, he could see the sky darkening as they were climbing fast.

They were now out of the atmosphere.

The pilot eventually turned off the engine, and then he suddenly felt a force releasing him from the seat.

They were in weightlessness! He smiled. He was in space. Not bad for an orphan from Kodala.

"*Ladies and Gentlemen,*" the ESA pilot said on the intercom, "*We will reach the orbital station in seven and a half hours. You can remove your escape suits unless your instructors are mean to you.*"

They weren't.

Thierry unstrapped himself from his seat and took off his suit.

The astronauts were now floating in the cabin, queuing to go to the cockpit, the only place with real windows. Thierry followed them. Seven hours was a long time anyway.

In the cockpit, the two ESA pilots were chatty. Thierry could understand they had to be, as flying back and forth between the orbital station and Toulouse could only be boring. He took out his smartphone and took some pictures. They were all of bad quality.

Albaspace (V-Space)

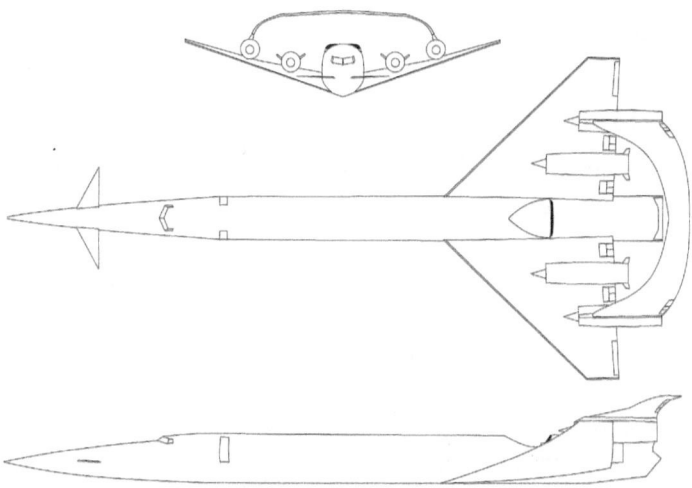

Figure 2: The Albaspace developed by V-Space has no windows, but the cabin is equipped with a multitude of screens. It is equipped with four CUBIC-R engines on the wings and one scramjet, at the rear of the fuselage. The US president has picked it as her Air Force One, and the EU president as her EU Flight One.

The orbital station was impressively big. There were four habitable rings around a thick core axis. Two rings were wider than the others. They had a diameter of 150 meters (495 ft) each, and 15 gravity decks. One ring was for WARSEC, and the other ring was for the existing space agencies and space corporations.

Two other rings were under construction and, on the TV screens, Thierry could see White Parrots and teams of astronauts working on them.

SX-White Parrots were small, space-only double decker vehicles developed by NASA in the late 2080s to assist with the construction of the orbital station. They had been put into orbit using the space elevators and could carry up to twenty passengers each. The White Parrots working with the ring construction had the colors of ESA, NASA, Roscosmos and the CNSA, the main shareholders of the station.

SX-White Parrot
(NASA)

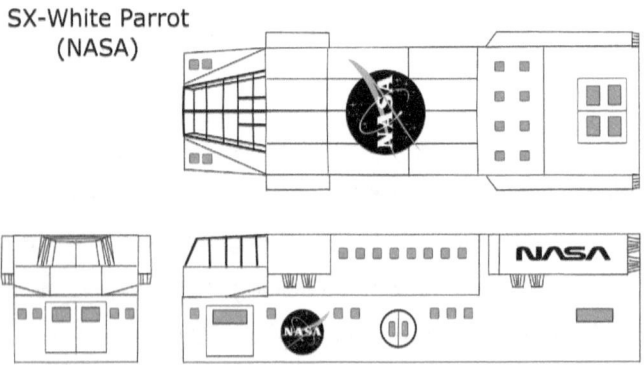

Figure 3: White Parrot

The Albaspace finally docked in the station's shuttle terminal. The astronauts floated their way in and followed their instructors to the 0-G core of the station. They were shown around the fusion reactors, a few 0-G labs, and also the place where Vahlroos Travel was building a space attraction park, with a playground to play Quidditch in weightlessness.

That was silly, Thierry thought, but that was business.

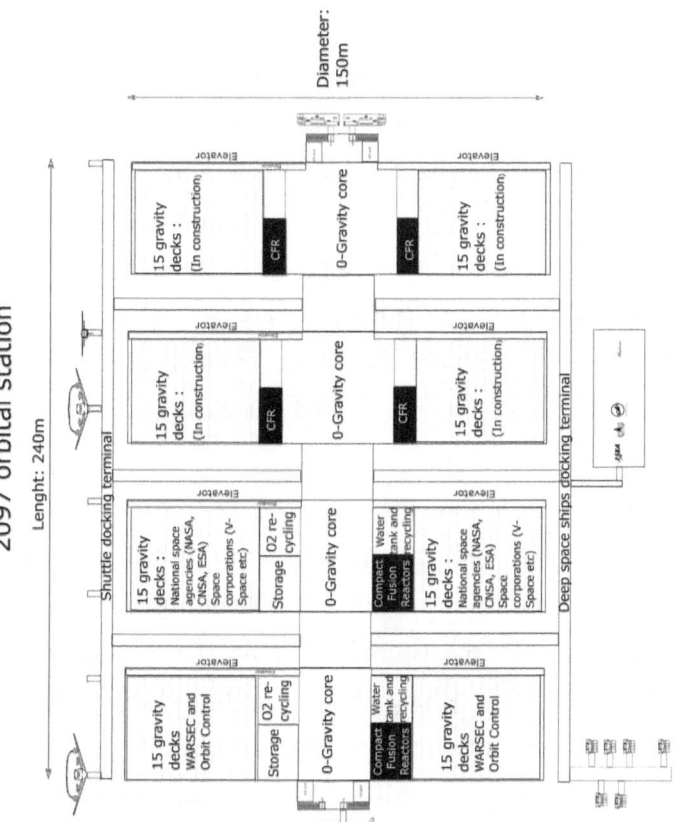

Figure 4: The orbital station in 2097

The instructors then showed the trainees their way into the WARSEC ring. The fifteen G-rings all simulated a gravity similar to that on Earth. As a result, they were not rotating at the same speed. Deck 1, which was the inner deck and whose perimeter was about 195 meters, took only 11.6 seconds to complete a rotation. The outer deck, deck 15, had a perimeter of 465 meters and would take 14.3 seconds for a full rotation. The gravity decks were grouped in sets of three and rotated on magnetic rails. A complex magnetic elevator system was needed to go from one set of decks to the other.

Thierry was sharing his room with a Comac engineer. The Chinese engineer had spent a few years of his childhood in Burkina Faso when his father had been working as a security guard there. Thierry did not tell him that his father had been killed by just such private security guards in an anti-Chinese riot.

The following day, they did their first space sortie. For Thierry, it was both exciting and scary. When the airlock opened, he realized it was for real. His pressurized white suit was the only barrier between life and the void of space. At first, he had difficulty breathing and this, together with the constant feeling of falling when in weightlessness made him dead scared.

He carefully set his wrist computer to increase the oxygen concentration to 60%, but it took him some time before he started to breathe more easily, and felt he could move his limbs more normally. He was no longer paralyzed by fear. He was floating, twenty meters away from the airlock, attached to a cable. Their instructors were babysitting them.

He would probably have marveled at the glowing Earth

beneath them, if he had not constantly been scared of having his suit depressurized, of being accidentally thrown off course and smashed against the orbital station. He was not paralyzed anymore, but he was still scared.

The day after, Thierry and a few other engineers were put at the disposal of the Chinese National Space Agency to help with the assembly of the ring. They boarded a White Parrot, which 'parked' in the vicinity of the rings.

They had to maneuverer some cranes, and Thierry was happy he could help and prove himself useful. When he was focusing on an actual task, at least, he stopped thinking about how scared he was. Now and then, though, he would realize that there was only his suit between his living body and the void of space and he would experience a sudden feeling of fear. He would then take a deep breath, exhale, and focus back on his task.

On the third day in the orbital station, there was a joint fire drill with the other national space agencies. After the fire drill, they also practiced putting their escape suit on quickly, without getting a pulmonary edema, and evacuating the orbital station through the closest emergency door.

That was the scariest. They would just clip themselves with a rope to a section of the station and wait for a White Parrot to pick them up. What if, in the event of a real major catastrophe, there were no White Parrot to rescue them? Thierry tried not to think about it.

The next day was Friday, and Glover had chartered an Albaspace from Finnair. Private airline companies had been using Albaspace shuttles to ferry passengers between different locations on Earth, often taking advantage of its suborbital capability. However, there would be no regular lines to the orbital station before it opened to the public.

The trainees boarded the Albaspace while most of the instructors remained onboard the orbital station. As the Finnair Albaspace undocked, Thierry was happy he was heading back to Earth. He was happy he was not a safety specialist, too.

Thierry Diakité had just completed Basic Space Safety 1.

Meanwhile, the safety specialists, including Glover Johnson, were now completing their Advanced Space Safety 1 qualification. They were to parachute jump from the orbital station and land in Vaasa. As far as Thierry was concerned, Glover was a bit too ambitious. What was the purpose of this exercise? If there were a major incident in the orbit of the Earth, there would always be other astronauts and spaceships to pick up the astronauts.

The Albaspace shook when it entered the atmosphere. There was nothing to see in the windowless cabin as the TV screens were only showing the position on the map. He thought of his former employer, V-Space, trying to achieve the impossible with their V-liner. He was happy he was working at WARSEC, though he wondered if he would ever enjoy working in space.

For him, space equaled fear. He would have to do something about it. The Albaspace finally landed in Helsinki, and the trainees boarded three different connecting flights to Vaasa. Glover did not want them all to be on the same flight.

When Thierry finally arrived in Vaasa, Glover Johnson was already there. He and some of the other space safety specialists had successfully landed with their parachutes on the rally point. He was not happy, though: he was missing two of his safety specialists. One had landed in Oslo, and the other one in Saint-Petersburg. They had done it on purpose: they wanted to surprise their families. Glover gave them a warning.

Later that evening, the trainees were given their course certificate.

The following week, Thierry was back in Vienna. So was Glover. He was preparing for his wedding with Laura, whose parents had traveled to the Austrian capital for the occasion. Thierry was told that both Glover's parents had perished in San Francisco in the Big Two in 2081, while he had been lucky to be at the naval academy in Annapolis.

Thierry was one of the few invited to Glover and Laura's wedding, together with her parents, a few of her friends and his best colleagues from WARSEC. The formalities at the US embassy were expedited in 5 minutes, and they spent the afternoon and evening in a restaurant Glover had hired privately for the occasion.

Laura surprised everybody by wearing a wedding dress, while they had agreed to keep it simple. She was lovely though, and a pregnant belly made her even more ravishing. The restaurant owner, who had not been informed that it was a wedding, decided to charge more.

20: THE BRITISH REPUBLIC (MAY-JUN 2097)

Samir's second year of Civil Service went faster than the first year. In October, he had been moved to the endocrinology unit of Addenbrooke's hospital and found himself working with new *slavants* in the nutrition department. Carsten had instead been moved to the palliative care unit. While Carsten was taking care of dying patients, Samir had to take care of mostly seriously fat people.

He hated it. All these patients reminded him of his fat father, though they were in far worse shape. When he saw how these poor devils were condemned to eat steamed vegetables for the rest of their lives, he promised himself never to grow fat. In the nutrition department, there were also very skinny and underweight patients, and they were scary as well.

When the head of the clinic got to know that Samir was a trained cook, she asked him to work in the kitchen with the dieticians. In a way, she was a much better leader than cynical Dr. Green at the elderly home.

While life had been following its routine at work, it had not at the containers. A chain of break-ups had occurred, and Magnus was back in Samir's room, which meant that Emily had to move out. He spent more time at Emily's father's apartment, but cohabitation with his 'father-in-law' turned out to be uneasy.

Finally, both Emily and Samir crashed most of the time in Amina and Sanne's student flat. The two students shared a cozy little three-room apartment close to the geological institution, and Samir and Emily spent many nights on their couch. This was also convenient, since Sanne was helping Samir with evening classes in mathematics.

It paid off; he was accepted to start at the community college in September 2097.

At the end of May, Carsten informed Samir and Sanne that the old Gareth Fraser had been moved to his palliative care unit. He had had a bad pulmonary infection. Samir was allowed to work temporarily as an orderly in the palliative care unit. Gareth Fraser had been the only resident Samir had ever had true respect and affection for.

Sanne, who was now done with her exams, also spent a lot of time with Gareth Fraser.

"Remember," he told Sanne, "social integration is the only viable option... assimilation can't work, and societies collapse under the weight of congregationism."

"I know," Sanne said. "But be reassured, integration policies have come a good way down the road. There are integrating Civil Services, not only the EU, but in the South Asian Union, in the Western Asian Union, and in China. President Fang in the US has just passed the Federal Service Act."

"It's not enough…" Gareth Fraser objected, "What about interstellar colonization? Integration policy must be part of any new colony… Integration must progressively be extended worldwide… There should be a Civil Service for all the souls living on this Earth."

Sanne started to think that Gareth heard voices.

"When mankind goes interstellar…" The old man concluded, "the Civil Service must go interstellar… otherwise, human civilization will eventually fall apart."

Sanne felt sad for Gareth. Not many relatives visited him. The previous year, he had had quite a few visitors coming to see him to discuss sociology and politics. Not anymore. She and Samir were the only ones who were spending time with him.

She was thinking about what Gareth had told her. *Racial desegregation in the US in the 1960s had not led to racial integration. Sexual desegregation in Northern Africa in the 1960s had not led to sexual integration. Social desegregation in Europe in the 1960s had not led to social integration.* Mankind was a congregating species, not an integrating one. If she were ever to work at WARSEC and with interstellar colonization, as she hoped, she would have to keep that in mind.

On Sunday 2 June, they received an unexpected visit. Men in black suits, wearing headsets and guns under their arms entered Gareth's room. They were bodyguards. King Eamon was here. He greeted Samir, Sanne, and Gareth.

"Hi, king," Gareth answered smiling.

"Hopefully not king for long," Eamon replied, "The referendum is today. I'm not even allowed to vote."

"I'm not voting either..." Gareth said, "I had completely forgotten."

Sanne and Samir went out of the room to give Eamon and Gareth some privacy.

"They are making a big deal about this referendum," Samir said to Sanne when they were in the hospital corridor. "There were even nude pictures of Eamon broadcasted by *Tox News*."

Tox news was the nickname given to Fox News, for its biased covering of events which was often perceived as toxic.

"What would you vote for, if you were an English or Welsh subject?" Sanne asked.

"Emily is voting for the Republic", Samir replied. "But I would not vote at all."

"Why not?" Sanne asked.

"Republic, constitutional monarchy, that's the just the same. In both cases, you have a head of state paid to do nothing. A king is a king because his mother was queen. A president is a president because his or her parents were rich."

"You are so cynical," Sanne objected. "Monarchs deserve their position less than presidents."

"Whatever the outcome tonight, I will sleep like a baby."

"I won't, it's my turn to stay with Gareth."

At 23:00 the same evening, the results of the referendum were known. The subjects of the king of the United Kingdom of South Britain had decided to upgrade themselves to the rank of citizens: they voted for the establishing of a republic.

All in all, there were very few changes. The flag would remain the same. It would still be called the UK, but it would stand for United Commonwealth of South Britain. The Royal Guards would become Presidential Guards and keep the same uniforms. The British Republic would almost be like a presidential monarchy.

Of those they knew, only Carsten was sad: Denmark was now the sole remaining monarchy in Europe, and it was only a question of time before it would collapse.

It was announced that King Eamon would remain on the throne until Thursday 19 September, when the new president, meant to be elected on Sunday 15 September, would be sworn in.

When asked what he would do afterward, King Eamon surprised everybody by saying he would apply for a position as a medical officer at WARSEC, and he dreamt of being part of the first interstellar journey.

It was one night when Samir was staying in his room that Gareth started having serious difficulty breathing. He grabbed Samir's hand and held it.

It was twenty past four in the morning, and dawn started to show itself on the horizon. The room's window was oriented to the east.

Gareth removed his oxygen mask.

"Help me up… to the window…" he said.

"You need to have the mask on…" Samir said.

"I want to see the sunrise one last time…" Gareth said, "I'm dying… help me…"

Samir pushed the button to call for a doctor and carried Gareth to the window, holding him under his arms. Gareth gripped one of Samir's hands, as he watched the dawn lighting up the sky.

He felt Gareth breathe more heavily and quickly, until there was a last gasp of air and Gareth's head dropped.

Samir tried to feel his pulse. He felt none. Tears were dropping from his eyes.

"What are you doing?"

It was Carsten

"He wanted to see the sunrise one last time," Samir explained. "He is dead."

Carsten also started to cry as he looked for a doctor to pronounce Gareth Fraser dead.

The following week, life in Cambridge felt really empty. Gareth Fraser was buried on Thursday in Mill Road Cemetery, in the Atheist section. To Samir's surprise, there were hundreds of people at his funeral, though only a very few of them had visited him in his last weeks. Among those attending the funerals were Dr. Green, Ralf Åhman, the director of WARSEC, King Eamon but also the EU ministers of youth and education.

The Civil Service ended on June 30th, and there was a giant party. Cleaning the rooms with a hangover was difficult the following morning. Half of the slavants were leaving the containers to go back to their hometowns.

Returning to Denmark, Carsten Nielsen was unsure he was still willing to take over his parents' pig farm. Magnus Li would start some studies in Luleå, northern Sweden, far away from the irritating English rain. Johan Staël von Trollstein would spend the summer in his native Bavaria and then start a bachelor's in business at the London School of Economics.

Samir also used his train ticket to go to Paris, even though he would later remain in Cambridge. With him were Emily, Amina and Sanne. They did not stay in Paris. Instead, they took a train to Geneva, and from there to Randa, in the Valais, in the Swiss Alps. They planned to attack some interesting 4,000 m peaks, to practice their snow and ice techniques. Amina's friend Daniela Penzenstadler joined them.

Both Swiss girls had once again designed a hard-core program. After a few acclimation routes on the Alphubel and the Täschhorn, Amina led them on a so-called spaghetti tour:

Starting from Zermatt, they took the cable car to the Kleine Matterhorn and traversed the Breithorn summits on the icy ridge, continuing down to the Rifugio Guide D'Ayas, where they were served pasta. The next day, they summited the Castor and the Pollux and reached the Rifugio Quintino Sella, where they were served pasta. They attacked the Liskamm the following morning.

The ridge was only blue ice, and the cramponing was not pleasant. They somehow made it to the eastern summit, but the slope down to the glacier was fragile black ice.

As the two rope teams were struggling to come down the ice, they heard a rope team behind who complained in French they were so slow. Samir turned around. The rope leader was Aisha.

Aisha's mood toward them changed when she recognized Samir and Sanne. The three rope teams took a short break when they were safe on the glacier.

Samir introduced his girlfriend, Emily, Sanne introduced Amina and Daniela, and Aisha introduced her boyfriend, Éric

Legrand, a sergeant in the Alpine rangers. She explained to him she had met Samir and Sanne in Cambridge, two years earlier. Sanne was also the last survivor of the Martian colony.

Aisha gave them some news about herself. She was now a sergeant in the Legion, but in the mountain engineers.

"Are you going to the Refugio Margherita?" Samir asked.

"We are going down to Staffal," Aisha replied. "Our holidays are nearly at an end."

"You just told me you are taking an advanced course in mountaineering with the army," Samir said. "I still call that holiday."

"Not when you have to carry anti-tank mines in your backpack," Éric objected.

"Ah? You also do that in the European Army?" Daniela asked. "I thought it was only in the Swiss one."

"Our armies are equally intelligent," Aisha laughed.

The rope teams parted, and the Cambridge Four eventually reached the Rifugio Margherita, hanging on the top of the Punta Gnifetti. Once again, they were served pasta.

"The name spaghetti tour is well deserved," Sanne said. "At least fresh Italian pasta is really lovely."

"What I find lovely," Emily said, "are the buttocks of this Alpine ranger sergeant Aisha is dating. Samir, you have to work out more."

"Fuck you, Emil," Samir retorted.

"When we are back at the tent, Samir, tomorrow evening."

"You like Alpine rangers?" a man asked.

They were sharing their table with three other men, in their late twenties. They had had quite a lot of wine.

"What about air force pilots? That's the three of us. I see here four women and a man. I think you need three men."

"No thanks," Sanne replied.

"You are sure?" The man insisted. "We are in top shape!"

"We have been training to bomb Morocco for a year now," the second man said. "It's quite demanding to fly our AF5 Dachshunds at Mach 25 and then brake to offer close air support."

"Morocco is gonna surrender in three days if there is conflict," the third man said.

"No, you mean *when* there is conflict," the first man corrected.

The Cambridge Four and Daniela cast glances at one another, wondering what these three European Air Force pilots were talking about.

21: Shipyards On The Moon (Jun-Sept 2097)

Thierry Diakité had arrived in Kourou, European Guyana, on Sunday 9 June 2019. It was a welcome change of air after the last weeks spent in Finland. Space production director Tatjana Aydemir was with him. They first drove over to Brazil, to the subcontracting company on the other side of the border, to inspect the newly manufactured robots. In total, there were forty-eight of them. It was more than enough for the lunar manufacturing of the two test Space Bears and three test Space Hounds, as was intended.

The inspection proved satisfactory, and WARSEC confirmed the purchase of the robots. They were to be put into orbit through the Guyana Space Elevator jointly operated by NASA and the European Space Agency.

There were two space elevators Earth, the other one being located in the Pacific, on Tarawa Island, and operated by the Chinese and Japanese space agencies. Both anchored at the

Equator, the Space Elevators were in fact 50,000 km (31,000 miles) long cables made of nano-carbon fibers and attached to captured asteroids orbiting far beyond the geostationary altitude. Since their gravity centers were located slightly above the geostationary altitude of 36,000 km (22,400 miles), the elevators were orbiting synchronously with the rotation of the Earth, giving the observer on Earth the impression that they were immobile cables shooting vertically through the atmosphere.

For each elevator, there were two sets of cables leading to the off-loading station, located about 400 km (250 miles) above the sea level. Space containers ascended their way to orbit on one of them. Empty containers and passenger lifts descended to Earth on the second cable.

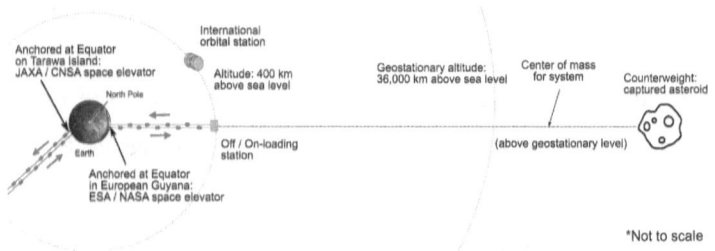

*Not to scale

Figure 5: The space elevator used to bring payload into orbit. Based on the work by Wikipedia users Skyway and Booyabazookan, but adapted to the story of this book.

The lift date was set for June 21st. A few safety specialists were to accompany them, among whom would be their director,

Glover Johnson. The robots were loaded into three space containers. Thierry, Tatjana, Glover, and the other astronauts followed in a passenger lift. The climb to the off-loading station was seven hours long and they had to wear white space suits, as the lifts were not as safe as Albaspace aerospace shuttles.

"You don't have a pregnant wife to attend to?" Tatjana asked Glover, as the space elevator started its pinion-pulled climb on the first section of the cable at the exasperating speed of 25 km per hour (15.5 mph).

"She is on a cargo cruise in the Indian ocean. She will be back in Vaasa at the end of July, so I have the time to check on the shipyard with you lot."

"When is the baby coming?" Thierry asked.

"She is supposed to come on October 12th," Glover replied.

"So, it's a she?"

"Yes."

Time went by in the elevator, and most passengers were bored as they were forced to keep their space suits on for the entire ride up. Thierry just hoped he would not need to use his diaper. Come on! He was not an old-timer yet! Glover broke the silence.

"When you think that, a hundred and fifty years ago, there were operators in skyscraper elevators. That's crazy."

"Why did you think of that?" Tatjana exclaimed.

"I was thinking of Eugene Bullard. I guess he would have preferred spending the end of his life operating space elevators to operating a skyscraper elevator."

"Who was Eugene Bullard?" Thierry asked.

"The first Afro-American fighter pilot," Glover replied.

"World War Two?" Tatjana asked.

"No, World War One," Glover corrected. "He was flying in the French Army Air Corps. He had previously served in the French Foreign Legion. When the US declared war on Germany later, he was denied the right to serve under the American flag because he was black."

"Yeah, that's the French paradox of the early twentieth century," Thierry commented, aware of the history of Burkina Faso. "They would treat an Afro-American as their equal, but not a true African from their colonies."

After five hours of slow climb on the pinion section of the cables, the lift had left the atmosphere and the passengers felt they were in weightlessness. The lift took only two hours to cover the remaining 350 km as it now was on the magnetic section of the cable.

The space lift reached the unloading station at 400 km (250 miles) of altitude, and they realized that the NASA astronauts of the *Orion* had already attached the robot containers to their spaceship. The WARSEC astronauts were invited to board the US spaceship.

The *Orion* was an American spaceship, and in that context, American meant roomy. A Chinese vessel of the same dimensions would probably take two hundred passengers. The starships of the Forward class being designed by WARSEC would have a similar size but take 120 astronauts on board. The *Orion*, however, only had a crew of four, and would accept no more than forty passengers.

The *Orion* had only one gravitational ring in the middle. The rest of the ship was in weightlessness. Tatjana recommended all the WARSEC astronauts enjoy the artificial gravity before being dropped on the Moon. She had been there twice, and she thought that the lunar gravity was very irritating, as it was harder to control one's movements.

The *Orion* had been the first spaceship ever equipped with an EM-drive. Using electromagnetic impulse powered by a compact fusion reactor, it could propel itself in space faster than spaceships equipped with chemical propulsion.

As a result, the *Orion* took only five hours to reach the unloading station of the Moon elevator, located 200 km above the lunar surface. The lunar elevator was slightly different than the space elevator, as Earth's gravitational pull had to be considered. Since the Moon's rotation speed was synchronized with its orbit time around the Earth, this had been solved by considering the whole Earth-Moon system. This meant that the captured asteroid holding the Moon elevator had to orbit around the Earth beyond what was known as the L1 Lagrange point of that Earth-Moon system in order to keep the cable vertically immobile above the lunar surface. In practice, it just meant the cable attached to the lunar equator was much longer than that of the Earth space elevator.

1,000 kilometers (620 miles) away, Thierry could catch a glimpse of the blinking lights of the lunar refill station. It was also hanging on a cable attached to the captured asteroid but anchored to the Moon's south pole instead. There, ice was mined in the Shackleton crater and hydrolyzed into liquid oxygen and hydrogen, before being sent through a pipeline to the refill station. Conventional chemical spaceships and aerospace shuttles could refill their tanks at this refill station.

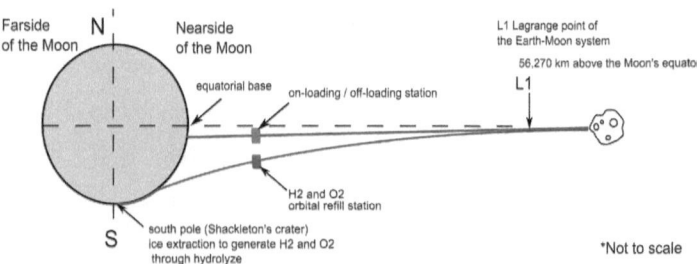

Figure 6: the lunar installation with the lunar elevator and the refill station. Based on the work by Wikipedia user Bryan Derksen, but adapted to the story of this book.

After the *Orion* had docked unto the lunar elevator's off-loading station, the WARSEC astronauts had to put their white space suits on again to carry out the on-loading operations.

Tatjana and four safety specialists took the first lift down to the lunar surface, while the other astronauts helped load the following cargo lift to send down the robot containers.

They themselves followed in the last lift.

When Thierry stepped out of the Moon elevator, he bounced off as he made his first step, and suddenly he realized he was on the Moon! Not bad for an orphan from Kodala! He started leaping around like a little boy, but Tatjana reminded everybody that, first, they had some work to do. They loaded the robot containers on some caterpillar vehicles and drove to the manufacturing base that was five kilometers (3 miles 188 yards) away.

Tatjana showed them around. A large landing pad had been levelled on the ground to enable White Parrots and aerospace shuttles to land. Along what could be called a lunar port were twelve large and high grey lunar dunes, with broad hangar doors in their hilly sides. These dunes were in fact manufacturing hangars, each six-stories high. They had been covered with alternate layers of water tanks and lunar gravel to offer a kind of protection against solar radiation. Parts of them were covered with solar panels. Though power supply was also provided from the compact fusion reactors needed to operate the Moon Elevator.

As they unloaded the robots from the containers and led them to their respective hangars, Tatjana explained that the three hangars to the left were assembly lines for the large Airbus-designed Space Bear. The next three hangars would be used to manufacture the smaller Boeing-conceived Space

Hound, while the other hangars would be used to manufacture more double-decker White Parrots.

The hangars were not pressurized and they had to keep their spacesuits on. However, each hangar was equipped with a pressurized room if anybody needed a break.

Below the hangars had been dug a gallery of tunnels, through which one could go from one hangar to another. The tunnels also led to the nearby lunar habitation complex that had been dug under the surface, to offer protection against solar radiation to its temporary residents. The lunar tunnels had been dug with modified electrically powered versions of the tunnel boring machines once developed by a company founded by Elon Musk, whom Michael Vahlroos, Thierry's former boss, worshipped so much.

The tunnels were not pressurized but made it possible to go from one lunar module to the next without exposing oneself to the deadly sun.

Tatjana also informed the new astronauts that the mining facilities were located a few kilometers away. Helium 3 was mined for the compact fusion reactors operated worldwide, but also all kind of metals that were processed into powder to be used in the 3D-printing arms of the robots.

The aerospace shuttles would also have carbon-based components and the carbon was brought by regular cargo shipments from Earth. This was the only reason why coal and graphite were still extracted on Earth, despite all the efforts to limit carbon emissions. Carbon was still needed to produce graphene and other carbon nanofibers vital to the space industry.

The operating team was small, and production was not meant to go fast the first year. Eight engineers would operate the robots to manufacture the Space Bears, ten would work with the Space Hounds, and six with the White Parrots. Another twelve engineers worked with the mining facilities and the reception of carbon cargo at the Moon tether.

These thirty-six workers were supervised by six team leaders, including Tatjana and Thierry, and babysat by twelve safety specialists. They would work twelve hours a day, ten days a fortnight and rest four days every second week in the orbital space station.

Currently, commuting between the Moon and the station was still inconvenient, as they had to rely on NASA's *Orion*, the only spaceship equipped with an EM-drive. However, NASA had developed some smaller EM-drive modules powered by a single compact fusion reactor.

The new version of the White Parrot would soon be able to dock into these EM-drive modules and use them to commute between the Moon and the orbital station in less than six hours, instead of three days as it was currently. That meant that the lunar workers would not be dependent on the *Orion* anymore.

In the last week of June, Thierry and Tatjana still had to

check all the robots and all the procedures were working. Working in the assembly hangars was strenuous, as they had to wear their lunar suits for twelve hours in a row. In their suits, they had access to water, carbohydrate and protein drinks, but they could not eat, and had to use their diapers if they had to, the prospect of which was so embarrassing that all the workers adapted their bladder and bowel movements so as not to have to go to the bathroom under working hours.

They spent their first four-day weekend at the orbital station, after which they resumed their activities on the Moon. Progressively, the two Space Bear and three Space Hound prototypes were taking shape convincingly.

The Space Bear had originally been a cancelled Airbus project. When WARSEC had partnered with private aerospace corporations in its WARSEC Ventures to start manufacturing cheap aerospace shuttles on the Moon, the abandoned Airbus project had been given new life and rebranded "Space Bear" because of its gigantic size. It was a massive eighty-meter-long (262 ft) aerospace shuttle with delta wings on the roof, two extra-large CUBIC-R engines and a rear cargo door. It was meant to transport up to 700 passengers in its charter version.

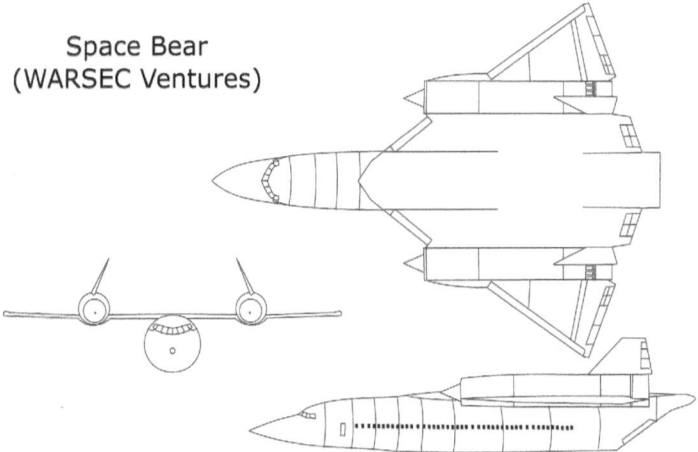

Space Bear
(WARSEC Ventures)

Figure 7:   The Space Bear (originally an Airbus Project) manufactured by WARSEC Ventures.

The Space Hound was a resuscitated Boeing project which had been rebranded so because of its smaller size and higher speed and its thin variable-sweep wings, making it look like a running greyhound. Its two smaller CUBIC-R engines could propel up to sixty passengers at Mach 25 in rocket mode. Under the impulsion of WARSEC, both the Space Bear and the Space Hound had been developed with vertical take-off capability in order to be able to negotiate a lunar landing.

Space Hound
(WARSEC Ventures)

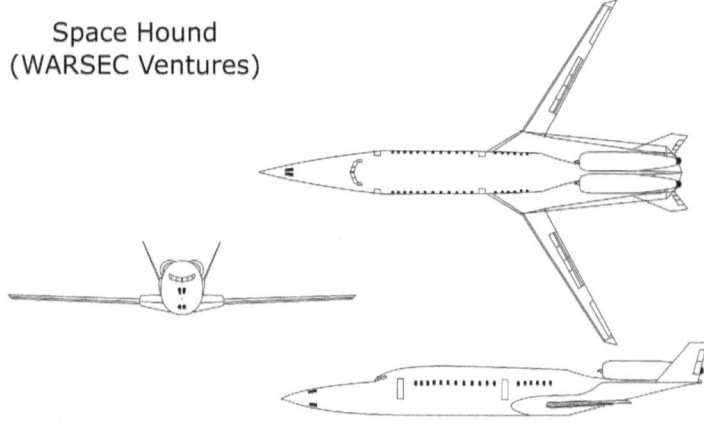

Figure 8: The Space Hound (originally a Boeing project) manufactured by WARSEC Ventures.

By July 15th, Glover was satisfied with the progress and left for Earth to attend to his pregnant wife. For Thierry, the mission continued. While he spent part of his time manufacturing the aerospace shuttles, the main purpose of his stay on the Moon was to investigate how to most efficiently manufacture the first starship of the new interstellar Forward class.

He had seen how V-Space was planning to integrate the V-liner vertically to save time and cost and wanted WARSEC Ventures to be as efficient as V-Space. One evening, he presented his suggestions to Tatjana over a lyophilized dinner. He had prepared a few slides he showed her on his laptop.

"I checked," Thierry said, "and the optimal plan would be the following. All the external cylindrical structure of the ship could be built vertically with 3D printers. You assemble it on top of the rear panel with the cargo door."

"What about the gravity rings?"

"They can also be built vertically with 3D printers, but in another location. Then, with a crane, you insert them into the hull of the ship. Then you add the placeholders for the nuclear reactors and the chemical tanks, and you close the lid with the front panel. Overall it would be much faster than the current plans."

"How much faster?"

"It would take only six weeks to complete the structure. Then you need another eight weeks to add all the components, drag the cables, etc. Then, you put the ship in orbit, using rocket boosters. When it orbits the Earth, it takes another six weeks to add the fusion reactors, and other fixtures and fittings not built on the Moon."

"So, only five months instead of ten to manufacture a single ship?" Tatjana said.

"Yes, but it requires an intelligent crane system to handle the 3D printers. The best thing would be to dig a deep hole, and build an assembly structure in it."

"I need first to check your work."

"We have just received a new batch of robots," Thierry said. "If I could spare twelve of them, and borrow five miners and two engineers, I could start looking into it. If my plan is flawed, it will not have cost us too much in terms of production output, since we are only building a prototype. If I am right, we will be saving four weeks."

Tatjana looked at Thierry.

"Do it", she said. "We have a bored geologist with us, and the miners work only half time at the moment. Use them."

Thierry was positively astonished at Tatjana's quick endorsement. Compared with his one and a half years spent at V-Space, this was a completely different approach to leadership.

Thierry spent the whole summer on the Moon, and he even stopped spending his regulatory weekends at the orbital station. Tatjana had come back to Earth for a summer holiday with her family, and no one could forbid him to work fourteen days a fortnight.

By the end of July, a giant hole, 100 m (330 ft) deep, 100 m (330 ft) long and 60 m (200 ft) wide had been dug. They covered it with a very large tent. Around the hole, they built metal rails to put a crane system on it.

He spent most of August managing the building of two advanced metal arm structures within the hole, to handle the 3D-printing of the cylindrical hull and of the gravity decks.

He hated when he was disturbed by fire drills or some other exercise, but it had to be done. He suddenly realized that he was so obsessed with his enterprise, he was not scared of being in space anymore. The Moon had become his new home.

By the beginning of September, the hardware was ready, but

Thierry was not satisfied with the movement and response of the robot arms. He spent hours and hours going through the code without finding the issue.

When Tatjana was back on the Moon, at the beginning of September, she was both impressed and shocked. When they met in one of the lunar habitation modules, she said:

"You were not supposed to be done! Nobody has checked your code yet. It was the summer holiday. You look as if you have not worked out properly for two months!"

It was true.

In the lunar module, Thierry realized that he had not washed regularly either.

"I'm going to send you back to Earth, now," Tatjana added. "One, you need to rest. Two, the debugging of the code does not have to be done from here, and three, from a regulatory perspective, the manufacturing of the Forward will not start before December or January anyway."

"No problem, I understand," Thierry said sheepishly.

"How has the manufacturing of the test Space Bear and Space Hounds gone?"

"The prototypes are done," Thierry replied. "The robots worked fine. The Airbus and Boeing pilots have tested the engines and the structure. They did some vertical take-offs and landings. However, the real maiden flight of the Space Bear is scheduled for a few days from now."

"I can let you stay until the first flight. Ralf Åhman will

come for the occasion. He has found potential customers for our aerospace shuttles and would like to show them the lunar assembly line."

22: Vahlroos Travel (Aug 2097)

In the first week of August 2097, Sophie Couillard had been called by CEO Michael Vahlroos to his private yacht off the coast of Florida. From her office in Burkina Faso, it had taken only four hours. Except that if things had worked out properly, it would have taken less than an hour.

She had first boarded an Albaspace operated by Vahlroos Travel and put at her disposal by Michael. The flight from Bobo-Dioulasso to Miami Executive Airport had taken just half an hour. There, she had been led to the drone departure area and boarded a unipersonal transportation drone developed by Vahlroos Corporation's V-lab. Equipped with electrically powered ducted fans, the unipersonal drone was to fly her to Michael's yacht anchored thirty kilometers (11 nautical miles) away, a seven-minute flight. Except that it did not.

As she had flown past the Biscayne Bay and been over the sunny Atlantic Ocean, the electric engine had stopped and the drone had suddenly plummeted toward the sea. Luckily, the drone's safety parachute had opened and the emergency buoyancy raft had inflated itself underneath the aircraft as the drone had ditched into the water. She had had her safety belt on and had not been injured.

She had, however, had to wait for two hours before a US Coast Guard helicopter picked up her floating drone and brought it back to Miami Executive Airport. There, against her will, she was put in another unipersonal drone which eventually made it to the landing deck of Michael's yacht.

Michael Vahlroos welcomed her with a glass of champagne. He was wearing cream long shorts, a red Hawaii shirt, sun glasses, and a straw hat.

"You have very uncomfortable clothes on," he said. "Please feel free to change in your cabin."

She was wearing a light brown suit with a pale pink shirt. She declined his suggestion and followed him to the yacht's large living room.

There was Jim Pattisson, the chairman of the board of Betalpha Inc., the holding company that owned the whole Vahlroos Corporation. He was a tall, potbellied old man with a white trucker moustache. He was also wearing cream long shorts but had a light grey polo shirt with the Vahlroos Corporation logo. Looking at his red, sunburnt bare arms, Sophie understood why they were meeting inside, rather than on the sunny rear deck.

Jim invited Michael and Sophie to sit on the roomy sofa in the corner, by the large window door giving onto the rear deck.

"Sorry for your trouble with the drone, Sophie," the chairman of the board said. "But the fact that the parachute deployed and the safety raft inflated properly is the proof that it is a very safe vehicle."

He laughed heartily, while Sophie, sipping her glass of champagne, silently peered over the top of it at his face. Michael smiled and added:

"We will soon commercialize this unipersonal drone on a large scale," Michael added. "Most previous similar projects have turned out to be commercial failures, but our drone will be a success."

They changed the subject as the chairman of the board asked Sophie to give a high-level summary of V-Space's new growth strategy.

"In short," Sophie said, "Cash is king."

Jim laughed again. "That's always a good strategy. But please, expand."

Sophie went on: "As you know, we are experiencing difficulty with the development of our V-liner, mostly with the warp-back-into-the-atmosphere protocol. We don't know how to subsequently stabilize the spaceship and have it land vertically the Elon Musk way. And there is doubt that it will ever be possible."

Jim Pattisson looked gravely at both Michael and Sophie: "I

have heard about it. How bad it is for us?"

Sophie finished her glass of champagne and said: "Not too bad, actually. We will turn it into an opportunity."

"How so?" the chairman asked.

"First of all, as it looks from the current trend, there is a high probability extraterrestrial mining within our star system will not be licensed to private corporations before ten or twenty years, so there is no need to rush."

Sophie saw how Michael was about to interrupt to contradict her vision. She quickly raised her finger in a firm signal for him to listen, and went on:

"Second of all, if we wait another five to six years, the newly developed purple matter will enable us to build a V-liner that warps at 40 times the speed of light. Our spaceship will be four times faster than the Forward class ships currently developed by WARSEC."

"I have heard of purple matter," Jim said. "Go on."

"Finally," Sophie added, "We have to brace ourselves for the risk of never being able to negotiate a warp-atmosphere entry with the V-liner and—"

"I will have to go ahead and disagree," Michael interrupted her. "If we use—"

"Silence, Michael," the chairman interrupted. "Let her talk."

"What I was saying," Sophie resumed, "is that even if the V-liner cannot warp back into the atmosphere and land, we could still design a V-liner able to conventionally negotiate an atmosphere entry, like the Elon Musk's rockets seventy years ago."

"Except under current legislation, operating compact fusion reactors are not allowed to enter the atmosphere," the chairman objected.

Sophie smiled and said. "Thank you, Mr. Chairman, you brought me exactly where I wanted to be, and this is what will be defining our current strategy. Regulations are never unchangeable. Tremendous progress has been done in the safety of compact fusion reactors. As a result, V-Space's new strategy is to develop an Albaspace Neo, equipped with compact fusion reactors, which we will make so safe that it will be certified for atmosphere entry, thus setting a precedent in our favor."

The Chairman of the board looked perplexed. "What's the purpose of having an aerospace shuttle equipped with some compact fusion reactors? They are mainly propelled through the combustion of liquid hydrogen and oxygen."

"So far, yes," Sophie admitted. "But if you equip them with fusion reactors, you can power an electromagnetic drive as soon as you have left the atmosphere."

Michael thought he had to explain what it was:

"An EM-drive uses electromagnetic waves to propel itself in space. It is much more efficient in space than chemical propulsion."

"As a result," Sophie added, "With the Albaspace Neo, you would reach the orbital station in six hours instead of eight, and you would be able to reach the Moon from the Earth in maximum twelve hours, when it used to take three days five years ago. Since the landing on the Moon will demand vertical landing capability, the Albaspace Neo will be designed to be given the possibility to take off and land vertically on Earth as well."

Michael seemed to be thinking quickly before saying:

"But in case of vertical take-off, the Albaspace will take more time to reach a suborbital trajectory."

"Ten minutes extra at most," Sophie admitted. "I expect pilots to still favor conventional take-off over vertical take-off, but if needed, they will have the possibility to land on a large ship. If she chooses our Albaspace Neo as the new Air Force One, the US president will be able to take off directly from the White House and land on an aircraft carrier if needed."

Jim Pattisson laughed and said: "That's fab, Sof. Though, I don't know if Washington DC regulations would allow an aerospace shuttle to fly low over their city, but I would definitely want an Albaspace Neo to bring me directly to my ranch in Texas. The Albaspace Neo is a great idea. Not only will its development help us certify the V-liner, but it will also generate some cash."

"That's the idea," Sophie concluded "WARSEC is currently manufacturing their new Space Bear and Space Hound shuttles. They are far from being as good as the Albaspace, but they will make the overall aerospace shuttle market grow significantly.

We have to surf on the wave and keep aiming for the premium segment."

When she was done, Jim Pattisson stared at Sophie in admiration. She had not told the entire truth. But by having a more conciliatory strategy toward WARSEC and just showing they were contributing to the booming aerospace shuttle market through healthy competition, she hoped to attract new talents to replace Tintin and Thierry and put them on the V-liner.

The chairman of the board showed his empty glass of champagne to Michael Vahlroos, who waved for the yacht's butler, who was standing outside the large window door, on the rear deck in sailor's uniform. The man entered the room and re-filled the three glasses with champagne before exiting.

They raised a toast to Sophie, and after taking a few sips of champagne, Jim said:

"Sophie, I have to admit you are brilliant. You have the vision. You manage to turn a setback into success, a liability into an asset. You are one of our greatest talents, here. I like it."

"Thank you, Jim," Sophie said, blushing. She did not like compliments.

"I have discussed it with Michael," the chairman added. "Currently, Vahlroos Travel and V-Space are two distinct entities. However, in what will soon be a booming market in the near orbit, it will make sense to tighten the links between these two. V-Fusion, which develops our compact fusion reactors, should also cooperate more with both V-Space and Vahlroos Travel."

Sophie was perplexed. What were they going to offer her? Michael gave the answer:

"As a result, it makes sense to appoint you a member of the board of both Vahlroos Travel and V-Space, while you will retain your position as the general manager of V-Space."

Sophie bit her tongue. She was promoted! In practice, it meant that her salary would be doubled, as members of the board were usually paid an excessively large remuneration to meet just five times a year. She was appointed members of the board of two large high-tech corporation at just thirty-nine. Not bad for a blond Canadian who had only studied space engineering to master's level.

She accepted the offer and they again raised a toast to her.

"The Vahlroos Travel office at the orbital station will open within two weeks," Michael said. "Even though the orbital station will open to the public in the spring next year, we will already have some activity up there, as we have to prepare our space attraction center."

"I understand," Sophie said.

Michael went on: "Because of your new promotion, I think it would make sense to take one of the basic space safety courses offered by NASA. I don't want to pay for those dispensed by WARSEC. I have registered both of us to the course starting next week in Houston. In the meantime, you can just stay on the yacht and relax."

Sophie could not believe it. Not only had she had her growth strategy validated by the chairman of the board, but she had also been promoted and would go to the orbital station for the first time in her life. It was well worth some bad sex with Michael while she remained on the yacht.

23: SPACE PROFIT
(SEPT 2097)

The first prototypes of both the Space Hound and the Space Bear had been completed and were being tested. Even though neither aerospace shuttle would be certified by the respective national regulatory agencies on Earth before April or May the following year, WARSEC Ventures was already trying to find their first customers.

The WARSEC director himself was leading the public relations work with business prospects, and therefore expected on the Moon for the first real test flight of the Space Bear.

Ralf Åhman and his two potential customers landed on the Moon on Wednesday 11 September 2097. They had come directly from the orbital station onboard a White Parrot docked into an EM-drive module. They had all passed their *Basic Safety Course 1* but were still escorted by some space safety specialists. For all three, it was their first time on the Moon, and they were jumping like children. One of the guests was the vice president for procurement of Ryanair, a European low-cost airline company. The other was a general from the European Union Air Force.

Thierry Diakité and Tatjana Aydemir were invited to join them over a lyophilized dinner in hut 3.

"It reminds me of my time in the air commandos," the European general said. "In the EU Air Force, the dry food tasted better, though."

"What plane are you interested in? The Space Bear or the Space Hound?" Thierry tried.

"The Space Bear," the Ryanair VP said. "With it, I could transport 670 passengers to anywhere in the world in less than 2 hours. We could also open some low-cost lines to the orbital station. With the vertical landing and take-off ability, we could take off from any minor airport in Europe and get more subsidies from local municipalities."

Ralf seemed to be in heaven as he heard the intent of the Ryanair vice president of procurement and he just replied: "We would welcome that. The more tourists to the orbital station, the better."

"What about you, general?" Tatjana asked. "Are you gonna buy the Space Hound? Are we gonna be able to compete with the Albaspace for EU Flight One?"

The general let a quirky smile appear on his face and said: "Not a chance! The president loves the Albaspace so much. The Space Hound might be good enough for the agricultural minister, though. On the other hand, the Space Bear is more interesting. When the president flies somewhere with the Albaspace, we could use the Space Bear to transport the limos and support helicopters. That would simplify the logistics a lot!"

Ralf was rather puzzled, as he had firmly believed the Space Hound would have proven more attractive for Earth activities. He pointed this out and said: "Honestly, I had never thought the Space Bear would interest anyone for another purpose than space exploration."

"You have no idea," the general said. "The Space Bear is any general's dream. Imagine being able to drop a battalion of paratroopers anywhere in the world within maximum two hours! The Space Bear has vertical landing capabilities. Imagine being able to deploy an armored brigade anywhere in the world within two hours! After that, you can scrap the navy, and only keep the air force."

"Cheers to that," the Ryanair VP said raising his baby bottle of water.

Thierry saw that Ralf and Tatjana both looked embarrassed. WARSEC Director and veteran UN diplomat Ralf Åhman certainly had not had that in mind when he decided to manufacture aerospace shuttles on the Moon.

"By the way, general," the Ryanair VP said, "Have you seen on the news—it was three, four days ago, in Casablanca. There was a very violent anti-Chinese riot over there."

"Yes," the general said. "Over thirty dead and more than a hundred wounded. China has threatened Morocco with reprisals. But I can assure you that the EU will invade Morocco before China does."

The general burst into hearty laughter, followed by the Ryanair VP.

"Are you serious, general?" Ralf asked, half-worried.

"Of course not," he laughed, "of course not. Forget what I said."

That night, Thierry did not sleep well. He had not liked the attitude of any of the VIP guests. What bothered him most was that while he was on the Moon, he had not followed anything of what had been happening on Earth, and it seemed he had a lot to catch up on. Was there gonna be a war? For what reason?

The following morning, the Airbus test pilots proceeded with the first flight of the Space Bear. The gigantic aerospace shuttle took off vertically from the landing pad and disappeared majestically into the starry sky. It orbited several times around the Moon before landing again. It repeated the operation again and also successfully docked onto both the Lunar Elevator's off-loading station and the refill station. The Space Bear landed back on the Moon after its long testing procedure.

"That's very good kit you have," the general said over the radio as they stood on the landing pad in their pale pink lunar suits.

"We also need to see its performance in the atmosphere. But I can already tell you that the EU Air Force is ready to purchase 200 exemplars if it meets our requirements."

"200?" Ralf said.

"Sure," the General said. "At least. We will want most of our transport fleet to be made of aerospace shuttles."

"You know, General, that space is demilitarized?" Ralf tried.

"Yes, I know, and yet we are allowed to launch intercontinental nuclear strikes. International law is funny," the general laughed.

"Tomorrow, we will show you the first flight of the Space Hound," Tatjana said. "We are waiting for the Boeing test pilots."

"Unfortunately, I need to go back to Earth ASAP," the general said.

"Why, general?" The Ryanair VP asked.

"A Moroccan diplomat has been caught in Orly Airport, Paris, with one ton of cannabis. He was flying a private jet belonging to the crown prince of Morocco. President Bonavita has called this a provocation. They have increased the alert level."

"Do you think there will be war," the vice president of procurement asked, "over some smuggled cannabis?"

In his thick lunar suit, the general turned slowly to the Ryanair senior executive and said:

"We have trained so much for this war. It would be a pity if it did not break out."

On 14 September 2097, two days after the EU Air Force general had left the Moon, the two successfully tested Space Bear prototypes were to depart for the orbital station. One would stay in orbit to test the orbital flight computers, while the other would test an atmosphere entry procedure and land in Toulouse, the Airbus headquarters, for a long series of atmosphere flight tests. It was the necessary procedure to be certified.

As one of WARSEC Ventures' stakeholders, Airbus had naturally taken the responsibility for testing the aircraft, the original concept of which had come from their R&D department. Likewise, the Space Hound being a former Boeing project, it was test pilots and engineers from the Seattle-based aerospace corporation who were currently flying the prototypes over the Moon.

The Airbus pilots who were to fly the Space Bear prototypes to the orbital station asked if they could give a ride to any of the Moon workers. Thierry volunteered. He had been sent back to the station, and he had previously dreamed of working at Airbus Space. Of course, he was thrilled to be one of the first passengers to fly in the Space Bear. To his surprise, Ralf Åhman and the Ryanair vice president also showed interest.

Was it safe? The Ryanair VP wondered. Sure, since even Airbus engineers were onboard. Inside the mighty shuttle, no space suit was needed. The compartment they were in could turn into a space escape pod in case of emergency. Thierry could just relax and go through the code of the crane modules on his laptop.

Half an hour later, the Space Bear was taking off vertically, raising its nose and soaring into the sky. Thierry liked this plane already. After reaching lunar orbit, the Space Bear docked into an EM-drive module. A moment later, they were bound for Earth and the orbital station. In the cabin, Thierry was seated not far from the Ryanair executive.

"Thierry," The Ryanair VP said, "You are a rocket scientist. There will be a war in Morocco within one week, I am sure of it. "

"If you say so," Thierry replied politely. He himself had absolutely no opinion on the matter.

The Ryanair senior executive went on: "What stock should I sell, and what stock should I buy?"

"Sorry?"

"With the war coming," the vice president of procurement went on, "I may want to buy some phosphate, as the price may go up even more. But imagine if the EU win the war in one week and decide to decrease the price? The phosphate index will go down. Of course, there is no guarantee that the price will go down, even in the event of an EU victory. Ah, damn it! Hard choices."

"Sorry, sir," Thierry said politely, "The Airbus engineer is waiving at me, I think I'm needed."

Thierry got up from his seat and sat beside the engineer, who was monitoring his instruments.

The Airbus engineer smiled at Thierry and told him in French: "*Tout va bien. Je voulais juste te sauver de ce connard.*" ('Everything is fine. Just wanted to rescue you from this asshole.')

For the first time in his life, Thierry was happy to be French-speaking. The engineer showed him around.

"The Space Bear is amazing," the Airbus engineer said. "If you deactivate the flight laws meant to assist stupid pilots, there is no limitation. You can do looping and barrels with it. As engineers, though, it is our role to limit the ability of the pilots, or they might crash the plane."

As the Space Bear was pursuing its six-hour long flight to the orbital station, Thierry tried to resume the debugging of the code of his 3D-printing system for the manufacturing of the Forward class ships. He could not find any errors. Finally, when the shuttle arrived in the vicinity of the orbital station, he received a message on his smartphone. It was from Tatjana Aydemir:

- » *Your 3D-printing system is working perfectly fine. Nice work!* ☺
- » *Next time, don't forget to rest and check the sensors are clean* ☺
- » *I will ask Glover and his team to certify it. Alice et al are reviewing the manufacturing procedures. Have a nice trip back to Earth. Tat*
- » *PS: with all the fire drills you did on the Moon, if you just could take a certification in MMU flying at the station, it will be counted as if you passed Basic Safety course 2. Please do it.*

He answered:

» *Copy that, boss. Will take a course in MMU. CU in Vaasa.*

MMU stood for 'Manned Maneuvering Unit' and was a single seater with chemical propulsion used by astronauts to fly around in space. He had now been three months in space; he could stay an extra week.

The Space Bear seemed to be a good aerospace shuttle. It was the only positive thing, as far as Ralf knew. He hated himself. He had been so naïve. He was manufacturing cheap aerospace shuttles on the Moon to boost private travels to space. But who was the most interested customer? The EU Air Force. They would certainly be followed by all the air forces in the world.

How ironic that a UN-backed consortium was to make their profit on army acquisitions! How could he have missed it? The Space Bear project had originated in a requirement by the EU armed forces, after the success of the AF5 Dachshund. It had been cancelled because it was too expensive. Now WARSEC Ventures would make it possible for armies around the world to acquire it at an affordable price.

At the same time, things seemed to be getting out of control in the world. Because of the Moroccan diplomat caught smuggling cannabis into Europe, the EU now demanded the crown prince of Morocco be extradited to France by September 19th 5:00, or they would invade Morocco to capture him.

Russia, Brazil, China, and South Asia were all supporting the

European demand. Of course they were! In truth, it was for the phosphate. Morocco had a monopoly on phosphate extraction and had recently jacked up the price, to the dismay of all other nations. Phosphate was a key component for fertilizers and, when its price went up, it indirectly caused food to become more expensive. No nation on Earth was really unhappy with the firm line now followed by the European president. The United Nations seemed to be the sole remaining institution that might be able to bring about a peaceful outcome. The UN secretary-general had now flown to Brussels for talks with the EU president.

Ralf was certain that Hira Dorjee-Sherpa would successfully negotiate a compromise. She was an outstanding diplomat. But he was outraged at the Europeans. An ultimatum! World War 1 had started because of an ultimatum.

After the Space Bear docked on the orbital station, Ralf floated his way behind Thierry and the Ryanair senior executive into the corridor pipes, while the Airbus crew remained in the shuttle to go through their debriefing.

Once in in the 0-G core of the station, both the WARSEC director and the Burkinabe engineer headed for the WARSEC gravity ring. Ralf was floating behind Thierry on their way to the WARSEC elevator when he heard clapping behind him. It was Michael Vahlroos.

"Ralf Åhman and his lackey from Burkina," he said. "I hope you are proud of yourself."

Ralf remembered Vahlroos Travel had just opened their office in the orbital station. While Thierry swiftly disappeared into the elevator, Ralf felt he had to act as a diplomat.

"Good evening, Michael. May I ask you what you are referring to?"

Michael was floating against the curved wall of the 0-G core and busy astronauts from NASA and ESA were floating between them, paying no attention to the two men. Michael went on:

"You created the World's Agency for the Regulation of Space Exploration and Colonization to, allegedly, bring peace to the galaxy, and now I hear from an EU general, who happens to also be a customer of mine, that you plan to sell 200 Space Bears to the EU armed forces."

"You are speculating," Ralf said firmly.

"How ironic that a UN agency is financing itself by selling aerospace shuttles to the armies of this world."

"It would be, at most, transportation aircraft," Ralf objected.

"And selling to the country that is about to invade another country."

"We don't know that," Ralf said.

"You are being so naïve that it is sweet," Michael Vahlroos said. "I hope at least you have a good conscience."

"What do you mean?"

"First, you limit the freedom of entrepreneurship in space. Second you do social dumping by manufacturing aerospace shuttles on the Moon and thus avoiding tax on robot labor. And now, you sell transportation aircraft to a country that is about to invade another one. Frankly, if I were you, I would quit the UN and join the current EU administration instead. You seem to have the right profile."

Ralf did not answer. He spotted Sophie Couillard floating out of one of the pipe corridors and looking insistently at Michael.

Michael saw her too.

"Now, if you will excuse me," he said, "an Albaspace shuttle is waiting for me. By the way, Vahlroos Travel is looking forward to the commercial opening of the station next spring. Bye."

That night, Ralf thought about what Michael had said. He could barely sleep. Was he really doing everything wrong? Had he really been that naïve? Would there really be a war between the EU and Morocco? Why did everybody seem to believe it? On the other hand, none of these people was a diplomat or a political scientist. Michael Vahlroos was only a businessman. The air force general was only an officer. Of course he wished for war. He was a career officer. The EU had not been in real conflict since it had become a federation, and all officers dreamed of an actual war.

He needed to talk to another diplomat, and he remembered his friend Esko Punainen, who was still the EU ambassador in Bishkek.

The next morning (Coordinated Universal Time), he checked the time zones on Earth. It was lunchtime in Kirghizstan. He called him from his new office in the orbital station.

"Hi Esko, how are things going for you?"

"Ralf, is that you? You know the situation has improved dramatically here, in Kirghizstan. The prime minister has started a reconciliatory policy. She plans to launch a Civil Service in the country to force citizens, be they Kirghiz, or Uzbek, or anything else, to live and work with each other. The UN has decreased its presence, and I would not be surprised to see them pull out completely within a year. Thanks for asking, by the way."

"What about Morocco?" Ralf asked.

"I knew you were not calling about Kirghizstan," Esko said. "Nobody gives a crap about where I live or what I do."

"No, I mean, you work for the EU diplomacy. Do you know what will happen?"

"Ralf, I already told you last year. The European president does not talk to me anymore. I have only talked twice with her over the phone since she was sworn in office. If you want more insider information, ask somebody else."

"I know nobody in her inner circle."

"That's a good sign! That means we can still be friends."

Ralf laughed.

"Seriously," he said, "Do you think she will really invade Morocco?"

"The only thing I know for sure is that she is not bluffing, Ralf."

After he hung up, Ralf Åhman pondered over what Esko had just said. Deep inside him, he was certain Esko was wrong. There had not been any conflict between states in decades. Within two to three years, they would launch the first interstellar mission. As far as the conquest of spacef was concerned, international cooperation had reached unprecedented levels.

In that context, how could one seriously expect the European Union to invade Morocco? It had to be avoidable. And he knew that UN secretary-general Hira Dorjee-Sherpa would work out a peaceful solution, even if the odds were a hundred to one.

Published books in the WARSEC series

Available now for paperback and Kindle on Amazon!

ABOUT THE AUTHOR

Ash Gawain is an EU citizen living in Northern Europe. When not working, writing, nor drinking, Ash is being kept in adequate physical shape by an ex-Swedish military, in order not to die of heart failure before the WARSEC series is complete.

About the WARSEC series:

When I went to the cinema and watched Christopher Nolan's INTERSTELLAR, in January 2015, I first thought I had got into the wrong theatre room. The film opened like a kind of documentary about farmers. After overcoming the first moment of surprise, I admitted the concept was brilliant, though I was willing to challenge everything else about the film.

At that time, I was studying political science, while spending a lot of my time with earth and ice scientists. This, added to a good dose of Finnish Vodka, led to the WARSEC interstellar series.

More on: **www.ashgawain.com**

ACKNOWLEDGEMENTS

The first four books of the WARSEC Interstellar Series could not have reached their final stage without the help of Deborah Murrell, whose thorough edits and comments in the margin have been critical. Any error or mistake is my sole responsibility. I am also forever grateful for Lisa Robbins's valuable feedback and advice, and most of all for her patience with a non-native English-speaker.

Of course, the book could never have been without a book cover. I would like to thank Mark Thomas, not only for his wonderful cover design but also the beautiful paperback edition.

Finally, I would like to thank my family and friends for their support and encouragement, especially Eliah, for reading so many of drafts, and Lumi for forcing me to spend less time in front of my screen and more time exercising.